# Lost in a
# MASQUERADE

## PALMETTO
### PUBLISHING
Charleston, SC
www.PalmettoPublishing.com

Hardcover ISBN: 979-8-8229-4380-3
Paperback ISBN: 979-8-8229-4381-0
eBook ISBN: 979-8-8229-4382-7

# *Lost in a*
# MASQUERADE

JILL SHTULMAN

To my husband, Leigh Page, who was lovingly there from the conception of this book and through all the labor.

And to my parents, Lee and Al Shtulman, who would have been so proud to be "book grandparents."

# LOST IN A MASQUERADE

Are we really happy here
With this lonely game we play?
Looking for words to say
Searching but not finding understanding anywhere
We're lost in a masquerade

Singer-songwriter Leon Russell

# PREAMBLE

## DANNY

"You can ask me whatever you want, but I'm not going to sit here and spill my feelings. That's what you guys do, don't you? Always trying to uncover those deep, hidden emotions?"

Walt regarded me with a benign smile, his fingers steepled before him.

I stared back defiantly. "I told you earlier on the phone. I don't want to be here. But what choice do I have? I'm being forced to prove I'm fit to spend time with my own kid. And Joanna, the one I'm sort of living with, thinks I need to be here, too. It sounded like an ultimatum: Do this, or we won't make it. Am I happy about it? Hell, no. The court system is an absolute joke. But here I am."

As I waited for him to respond, my eyes drifted around the office. Nothing about it surprised me: the beige couch with a few colorful throw pillows, the lamp with muted lighting, the bookshelf with pop psychology titles, and the picture of a leafy green forest hanging on the wall. And, oh yeah, a prominently displayed Kleenex box, something I wouldn't need.

The office was just as I anticipated, but Walt took me aback. He didn't look like any shrink I ever imagined.

The wheelchair. That was something different. Sitting in it, he looked like a slimmed-down version of Raymond Burr in the TV show "Ironsides." Maybe he thought his patients wouldn't see a wheelchair-bound shrink as threatening – the perfect ploy for them to let their guard down. I wasn't going to succumb to it, though.

He waited for me to meet his gaze again. Then he leaned forward and said, "I'm glad you're here. I realize this isn't something you want to do." He sure had that right!

"I understand your feelings. I read the court papers you faxed over. The charges could make just about anyone angry. Adultery. Abuse. Divorces can become ugly. It must seem unfair. So let me assure you before we go one step further. You're in a judgment-free zone here. I'm here to listen, not to make assumptions. Certainly not to judge."

I folded my arms and leaned back, massaging my neck to ease a sudden cramping. Yeah, he was trying to be reassuring, like all shrinks do. They must learn how to do that in shrink school. But they're not the only ones who have mastered that trick. It also comes in handy in the advertising business, where I come from. Your audience has to relax a little for you to do your magic.

Walt continued, his expression relaxed and friendly. "One more thing. In my practice, I focus exclusively on men. Many have been in the same place you find yourself in right now. It's an uncomfortable place to be. And no one wants to linger there longer than necessary. So why don't we start?

What would you like to get out of these sessions? Tell me a little about what brings you here today."

So now he has given me his little speech, and it's time for me to give mine. Spilling out my story so he can say a few nice words and absolve me of all my troubles. As if that has a chance of working.

I cleared my throat and sat up straight, just like I do in client presentations. "You probably mean well, but this process you have here isn't going to work on me. I don't do 'vulnerable' easily. But alright. I'm here, so I may as well give it a shot. Things began falling apart when I told my wife Sally that I wanted out. That was over two years ago. We met in college, during sophomore year at CCNY, back in 1969, which was – let me see – over 16 years from the time we split. Quite the record. It started well enough. The fancy wedding, the house in Westchester, and then the baby, our son Charlie. Are you following?"

"Oh, yes, please go ahead." Walt leaned forward so far in his wheelchair that he seemed ready to flip forward and fall onto the rug. I had his attention.

"I thought it would last forever. Well, it didn't. You know the song, "You Can't Always Get What You Want"? That was me, but I couldn't accept the next part: "You get what you need." I needed more than what Sally could ever give me. When everything began to fall apart, I was senior director of accounts at Cooper, Masters & Young. Heard of it?"

"Yes, it's one of the top agencies on Madison Avenue."

"That's right. Anyway, I was responsible for our largest client, Proctor & Gamble. Everything was going along fine. My boss liked me, and my colleagues did, too. I was only in my mid-30s and already making a ton of money. They called me Danny Boy because I was their golden boy. Quite a step up for a kid from nowhere who had nothing to look forward to."

Walt was lapping up every word. Now, it was time to shift to my sad and dreary childhood. Everybody loves a good sob story. Even when I talk to clients, I'd throw in a line or two if I sensed it would earn me some trust. It helps me control the narrative.

"My family wasn't exactly the Waltons. No 'goodnight, Danny, goodnight, Daddy' in our house. It was more like, "Get your ass into bed right now, and I don't want to say it again.

"I'd get into bed, huddle under the covers, and wait for the fun to begin. I never had to wait too long. First, the pop of an opened beer can, then the raised voices. And finally, the slaps, the screams, and the whimpers. Then, it all turned eerily quiet, and I finally went to sleep. The next morning, over breakfast, we'd pretend nothing ever happened, and I'd go off to school, just another kid in the playground."

"So, life was far from perfect when you were growing up," Walt said.

"Yeah, you could say that," I said. "But my old man never really laid a hand on me."

Walt appeared skeptical but eager, ready to impart uplifting words for his sad, broken patient. "You're a bright man, Danny," he said. "A successful one, too. So, you know, abuse takes many forms. I could say more, but not now. There's plenty of time to work it through. That is, if you want to share. You're the one in control of this process and how it unfolds. Not me."

Whew, I won't get a long sermon! Might as well give Walt a B+. And since he's so accommodating, I might throw him a few extra morsels to chew on.

"Yeah, my life started miserably, but there was a twist. I got into college, and I could leave my family behind. A little later, I met Sally. Maybe you've heard of Sally's father. Dr. Francis McAllister?"

"Yes, I know of him," Walt said. "He's chief of neurosurgery at Columbia Presbyterian. I've heard him give lectures about how the brain works several times. A very impressive intellect."

"That's right," I said. For some guy who talks to crazy people all day, Walt gets around. "From the moment I met my father-in-law, I could tell he truly was a big shot. I couldn't believe my luck. Me, dropping into the middle of this prominent family from the Upper West Side."

"Sounds like a stroke of fortune," Walt said, probably setting me up to bring things back to reality.

"I really respected the guy. For his sake alone, I wanted the marriage to work. When my son Charlie was born, I wanted to be there like my father-in-law was for Sally. I was determined to be a better father than mine was for me. If you believe anything I'm saying, you need to believe that. But I just couldn't make it work."

"Even with the best intentions, that can happen."

"Yes, lots of things can happen, alright. Joanna happened, and then...well, I won't get into more right now. It's not like I was doing something others haven't done before. You're supposed to work through the mistakes and move on or change course. You'd think Sally would understand. But not her. She was hellbent on making me pay – financially and in every other way."

"That must have felt very unfair," Walt said mildly. "Tell me, what do you think it might have felt like from Sally's perspective? Do you think she had any rationale for her anger?"

Here it comes. The judgment. "Okay, I didn't do everything right. Maybe she has a few points to make against me. More than a few. Maybe the stuff I did ended up hurting her. When I married her, I was young and misguided. I didn't have a clue what I wanted. Then, years later, I woke up and found I was a whole new person. Staying with Sally meant giving up any real chance to be happy."

"What does it mean to be happy?" Will asked. "What would that feel like to you?"

Whoa, Walt was getting all philosophical. I slowly shook my head. "How would I know? I've never been truly happy in my life. Who knows if I'm even capable? I don't want to be unhappy. Always dealing with people trying to change, analyze, or judge me. I've had enough of that. All I want is..."

I felt I was about to say more than I wanted to. I turned around and glanced at the clock. The time was almost up. "Remind me again," I asked Walt, How much do I owe you?"

# PART I

# CHAPTER 1

**SALLY**

When people ask me who I am, I tell them I'm Dr. McAllister's middle child and Danny Monahan's one and only. Wait, scratch that. I'm still Dr. McAllister's third child – the middle one out of five – but now I'm Danny Monahan's "done and lonely." In the eyes of others, I've become a sad cliché in the last two years: the bitter ex-wife.

I wouldn't have called Danny a ladies' man when I met him at CCNY. That came later. But there was something about him.

He had an angelic-looking face, crystal-clear blue eyes, a high forehead, and startling reddish-blond, short-trimmed hair. He struck me as very young, shy, and out of place. But then again, so was I. Although it was the late '60s – a time of sex, drugs, and rock and roll everywhere – we both were strangely removed from it all.

2

I was easier to figure out than Danny. From as far back as I remember, I marched to the beat of my father, Dr. Francis McAllister – a traditional thinker and a highly respected man. He was always Francis to his friends, never Frank. As the chief of neurosurgery at Columbia Presbyterian Hospital, he specialized in aneurysms, arteriovenous malformations, and carotid artery stenosis.

My father most certainly influenced my life. Growing up Catholic in a massive 1890s brownstone on the Upper West Side, I learned that if I followed the rules, modeled my values after my parents, and trusted in God, all would go according to plan.

We were a family of seven: my dad, my mom Maud – his former nurse who called herself "fertile Myrtle" – my older brothers Mark and Matthew, then me (Sarah, but everyone called me Sally), my slightly younger sister Kathy, and our little "caboose, Joey. We all gathered around the table for dinner every night before going off to play. With five lively children vying for attention, you can bet there'd always be a stimulating and provocative conversation.

"Who's heard of Yuri Gagarin?" My father would say.

"I know! I know!" Mark answered. "He traveled in space! Dad, will President Kennedy send one of our astronauts up there soon?"

"Don't know, son," my father said. "If I were a betting man – and I'm glad to say I'm not – I'd say yes. Let's remember all John Fitzgerald Kennedy has accomplished so far. He's our first Catholic president; we should all be proud."

Then he'd tackle a new subject. "Boys, tell me what you know about the Salk vaccine."

"It's going to end polio all around the world," Matthew said. "When I grow up, I want to be a doctor like you or maybe a scientist like Jonas Salk. So I can cure illness, too!"

I'd sit there pouting, hating to see my older brothers outshine me. My father would notice and turn to me.

"Don't you worry, Sally, there are plenty of ways girls can change the world. Why, you could grow up and be a nurse like your mother. Or a teacher – now that's a worthy vocation. Tell me, what did you learn in school today?"

"I learned about Saint Therese of Lis...Lis...Lisieux," I said, looking at him for approval. "She loved God and flowers, too, and she'd give them to people. That's why she was called "The Little Flower of Jesus."

My father beamed. "Always keep this in mind, kids, Great men come up with ideas, but God is the force behind them. God is always there for us when we lean on Him.

Religion was the foundation of what held my family together. A warm home life was the glue. Right from the start, I knew there was something special about our home. My father chose it because it was within walking distance from Columbia Presbyterian, where my father worked daily to save lives.

The house always got compliments from our guests. The living room had a plush velour sofa with matching armchairs, a Noguchi coffee table, an imposing fireplace, a grand piano for Kathy and me to take lessons, and a mahogany

China cabinet filled with crystal and elegant dishware. Each of us kids had a separate bedroom upstairs, with a wooden sleigh bed, a dresser and nightstand, a desk, and a comfortable chair for studying.

But for us kids, the basement was what we loved most. Early on, Dad redesigned it to function as a playroom. We became the first family in the neighborhood to get an RCA color TV with a 15-inch screen. It cost $1,000 – an absolute fortune. Kathy and I had all the best dolls – Barbie Dolls, Chatty Cathy, Suzy Homemaker. My friends would constantly clamor to come over. They'd say stuff like:

"Sally, can I play with your Easy-Bake Oven? Please? I'll be your best friend!"

"Mommy, can I get an Etch A Sketch like Mrs. McAllister bought for Sally?"

"Is it okay if I come over and play Twister or Broadside after school?"

We were also the first to own a ping pong table with those spherical and hollow ping pong balls nested in a container. My older brothers quickly mastered the game. While Kathy and I played with dolls or games, we'd hear the "tick tock tick tick" vigorous volley of Mark and Matthew and their friends. Punctuating the higher-pitched "ping" and the lower-pitched "pong" were the occasional "aww" and "got it" and "darn, so close." Little Joey wanted to join in, but they shooed him away when the boys were in a competitive game.

Thursday nights were particularly special for us and any friend lucky enough to sleep over after Dr. Kildare began airing on NBC. Sometimes, the boys joined in to watch it. Dr. Kildare reminded me of my dad, who wore a white coat and saved many lives. Except he was younger and so dreamy!

We knew duty and responsibility went hand-in-hand with the fun times. None of us questioned what my parents expected of us. On Sunday, before our midday meal, our family went to church. Woe to any of us who hadn't bathed and dressed by the time Dad was ready to leave. It was drilled into us: Jesus would weep if we disrespected him, sassed our teachers, lied to our parents, slacked off at school, or – for Kathy and me – harbored impure thoughts.

We also knew we better never talk back to our mother, who put her nursing career on hold to raise us. She took her role seriously – pillaging *Good Housekeeping* for new recipes, making sure the house always looked spic and span, and sending us to our rooms when necessary. However, she had a few indulgences, such as inviting friends over for cards every Wednesday afternoon.

I tried to make sense of their gossip. Some of them complained about their husbands – Uncles Joe, Luke, or John to me. "Want to hear what mine wanted to do? He gets those ideas from those off-color TV shows!" Another would add: "Yeah, that comedian on ABC started funny last night. Then, suddenly, he started going blue. I turned him right off." There were rules for everything in my little world, even TV shows!

Certainly, we followed the rules at school. When it was time to go, my parents vetted our school options carefully. Ultimately, they chose Holy Family, a Catholic school run by priests and nuns in an old brick building. The rooms had blackboards on one side, maps of the world on the other, and in the front, a glowering nun named Sister Mary Gertrude with a ruler in her hand.

I was awed by her and a little afraid. She seemed like a whole separate species of human. In my mind, Sister Mary Gertrude had emerged around the age of the dinosaurs, fully formed, already dressed in her black-and-white habit with her cross flapping and a wooden clacker with metal edges held tightly in her hand.

No doubt about it, she was tough, ready to rap knuckles. If we talked back, asked stupid questions, or chewed gum, our names would be put on the blackboard. It went on our permanent record if it happened more than three times.

I only felt the sting of the ruler one time when I asked a foolish question.

"Sister Mary Gertrude, are dinosaurs mightier than Jesus?"

We happened to be reading about dinosaurs in our science and religious education textbooks. One chapter discussed dinosaurs in the context of the six days of creation. I was obsessed with how gigantic and powerful they were. A snap of the ruler convinced me never to ask a question of that sort again.

At school, all of the girls wore a maroon jumper with a white, short-sleeved blouse, sensible flat shoes, a maroon cap, and ridiculous white nylon gloves. We called it The Uniform.

Statues of the saints surrounded us. We recited daily prayer each morning and the Angelus at noon. We marched to the church for confession on the first Friday of each month. Later, a stern-looking nun gathered us all together at assembly to recite what we girls facetiously called The Rules.

"Do not hold hands with a boy until you date him for six months."

"Do not sit on a boy's knees before inserting a thick newspaper between his knee and your...rear ends. Boys easily become aroused."

"And always remember this, girls: heavy petting and sex are reserved for after marriage when you are ready to have children. You do not want to get a bad reputation."

On weekends, my Jewish neighbor, Rachel, filled me in on the juicy stuff I hadn't learned at school. She whipped out a brochure called "The Wonderful Story of How You Were Born." It was filled with illustrations of that stuff down there. All this made me cringe. Imagining my parents doing the deed boggled my mind. They couldn't have done it just once. It had to be five times at least.

Armed with this new knowledge, I asked my sister, Kathy, only a year and a half younger than me, how she thought babies came into being. Her answer made me smile: "A dad wants a baby, and the mom wants a baby, so they decide to go to the hospital. Then they come home with a baby."

I told her to listen up and hear the real story of how it worked, as told by me. She rolled her eyes and made barfing noises. I did, too. All this stuff about penises and vaginas was too much for either of us.

Of course, it was bound to happen – hormones kicked in. We became teens, and Rachel and other friends started strutting their bodies in short miniskirts with their thick mascara and white lipstick. They seemed so much older and grown-up. Then, they started hanging out with guys and having make-out sessions at Brighton Beach. Some of them allowed their boyfriends to feel them up.

Me, I never had so much as a peck on the cheek, and I felt like a little kid in comparison. But impure thoughts ran through my head. How would my parents react if they knew what I was thinking? If I did something to displease God, I would go to hell.

"Preserving your virginity is well worth the wait for your future husband," Mom said. "He will love you more for it. Girls who succumb to temptation go to the baby home. Every time that happens, Jesus cries."

I managed to graduate my senior year with my purity intact but with pitiful knowledge of boys and dating. What would come next? When Mark and Matthew graduated, they went to Harvard and Princeton. Vassar and Smith wouldn't be the path for Kathy and me.

It certainly wasn't because my father didn't have the money to send us there. He just saw no need to waste it on girls who would, after all, be supported by their husbands. When college drew near, he encouraged us to apply to the New York City Colleges.

We both got accepted into CCNY. I decided to major in elementary education, and Kathy chose to pursue nursing. Meanwhile, Mark opted to be a neurosurgeon, like our father, and Matthew chose cardiology. They also followed my father's values.

"I can't imagine you and Kathy getting involved with the hippies, marijuana, and free love out there," Mark told me. "Why expose yourself to all that? You'll be protected from that craziness by commuting to school. And it's a good school, too. "

Ironically, CCNY was more radical than my brothers' Ivy League schools. I commuted daily, and it felt like straddling two worlds. My home life and my college life couldn't be more distinct.

At home, we watched Ed Sullivan and played canasta. On campus, practically every female student except me protested the war in Vietnam and went to the Student Health Center to get fitted for diaphragms. Pat Boone, Al Martino, and Perry Como crooned from our record player in my house. But they played Jimi Hendrix, the Doors, and Janis Joplin on campus.

That was me back then – the girl Danny met in a required history class during our sophomore year at CCNY. Danny stood out in a sea of students with long, unkempt hair, moccasins and Jesus sandals, love beads, tie-dyed shirts, frayed bell-bottomed jeans, and headbands.

You didn't mess with him. One day, a classmate sat beside him and said, "Hey, Danny Boy. The '50s are calling. They want you back, man!" Danny turned and looked at him with eyes turned ice-cold. He didn't say a word, just stared. "Whoa, sorry, man," the kid said, "it's all groovy," and moved to another seat.

Danny paid attention in class, took lots of notes, and disappeared when the class ended. Danny and I should have immediately connected as dual misfits in this hippie era, but that didn't happen. I thought he was cute. Despite his uncool look, he didn't seem goofy, just mysterious. I thought he was downright appealing, but he never glanced my way.

I tried hard to think of a way to start a conversation but came up with nothing. One day, I got a break. Classmates were paired up through a random process for a term project, and I drew his name as my work-study partner. He and I shyly introduced ourselves and devised a plan for carrying out the project.

We met in the Nielson Library, a modern place with an open, airy interior and large windows letting in natural light. Danny was all business. We outlined the paper without much interaction. I couldn't figure out quite what to make of him.

Gradually, he lightened up. He began imitating our dour professors and turned out to be a skilled mimic. That broke the ice. We discovered early on that we had a Catholic school background in common. Danny's spot-on imitations of the nuns made me laugh so hard that the librarian shot me a disapproving look.

I took the next step and shared some funny stories with him about my family. My father had always been insistent about attending early Mass every Sunday and being on time. All of us children complied except my brother Matthew, who always wanted to sleep in.

One Sunday morning, Matthew announced he was sick. Tell that to a doctor! My father touched his forehead and said, "You're fine. Let's go." By the time we reached the church, it was clear Matthew wasn't fine. He got up to receive Communion, with the priest bending down to give Matthew the Body of Christ. Matthew upchucked the wafer mixed in with a lot of bile. My parents were mortified.

Danny laughed so hard that tears appeared in his eyes. I said to him, "Now tell me one of your stories. What was your family like?" He tensed up immediately. "I'm an only child," he said. "Not many stories to tell."

We fell awkwardly silent for a minute or two.

"I wish I could give you an exciting story about my life, but I'm afraid it's boring," he said, "I grew up in Queens. My father was a union guy with the International Brotherhood of Electrical Workers. My mother was a housewife. And I served as an altar boy on Sundays. You know the drill: prepare the altar, distribute Communion."

I figured Danny wasn't revealing much because he felt intimidated. I lived on the Upper West Side, the daughter of a neurosurgeon. He grew up in a working-class family in Queens. I figured his parents were probably respectable

Irish folk who worked hard and did the best they could. That shows how naïve I was!

Things gradually grew more comfortable between us. I wanted Danny to meet Mom and Dad. After a few more study sessions, I screwed up my courage and invited him to join my family for dinner. I told him we'd go to the house from school some weeknight and spend some time on our project before we ate. He said yes.

I gave my mother a heads-up: a classmate from school named Danny Monahan would be visiting us. I had never brought a boy home before. My mother raised her eyebrows in approval upon hearing his name – a nice Irish Catholic boy. Yes, he could stay for dinner. My father said he would be happy to drive him back home afterward.

But when I told Danny, he politely turned down the offer of a ride. He said he was perfectly capable of getting home by himself, and he left no room for arguing.

Danny would be receiving a heaping helping of the McAllister family's hospitality. My mother began planning a dinner menu. It was one of my favorites – lamb with mint sauce, broccoli, and an apple cobbler for dinner. My brother Mark would be in town, and my youngest brother, Joey, would join us.

For once, my father arrived home on time, greeting Danny warmly and affectionately. I told Dad in advance Danny had declared business administration as his major. "I'm pleased to hear he has a head on his shoulders," Dad said.

Danny was nervous and eager for my family to like him. It was October 1969, not long before the Mets made the World Series. The conversation at the table centered on their phenomenal success. Mark said the Mets were a shoo-in for the pennant, thanks to a young and talented team led by Tom Seaver, Jerry Koosman, and Nolan Ryan and spearheaded by their incredible manager, Gil Hodges.

"It's unbelievable the Mets are doing this well," said Joey, wearing a Mets T-shirt. "They finished last place last year and won 100 games this year. The most in the National League!" Joey spun off all kinds of statistics: 100 wins, 62 losses, and a home record of 52-30. Tom Seaver pitched 25-5 with 268 strikeouts.

Dad, Mark, and Joey were talking non-stop about the Mets, with Danny joining in here and there. But gradually, he became quieter, listening attentively and nodding when one of them scored a good point. Every so often, he remarked on the delicious meal.

My mom turned to the McAlister men and said: "I think there are other topics of conversation more – interesting – to Sally and Danny and, frankly, to me, too!"

With that, she asked Danny, "What kinds of courses have you signed up for at college?"

"Accounting, finance, and marketing," Danny said.

"Now, that's just great. Very practical. Do you know yet what you want to do once you graduate?"

"I haven't made up my mind quite yet. I'm pretty sure I want to enter the business world. I like the marketing classes in particular."

My father asked Danny if his parents were proud of his performance. Danny blushed and nodded noncommittedly.

Dad couldn't let the evening go by without bringing up the Moratorium to End the War in Vietnam. CCNY had become one of the most active campuses in the nation in the anti-war movement with frequent protests and demonstrations. It had become a hot topic for him – especially since he served proudly in World War II as a lieutenant in Europe.

"I have to tell you, Danny – now, don't give me that look, Sally, I won't get carried away – I grew up with three firm guideposts. Love your God, your country, and your wife and family. No blaspheming, no anti-government slogans, and no womanizing.

"Your generation confuses me. All the protesting and welling up of anger. I almost didn't allow Sally to go to CCNY. But her mother and I knew we raised her right and taught her to stand up for what she believed in. You seem like a sensible young man. What are your thoughts on this lunacy going on these days?"

I held my breath. Danny and I only talked a little about the war or politics. But Danny aced his response. He told my father he was too busy getting through his classes, making it to work afterward, and completing his required homework to become involved. He would leave the war to others who were better informed.

My father beamed at him proudly and said, "Good lad." At the end of the evening, my father insisted on driving him back. Danny was equally insistent, saying he imposed enough on them and would be fine.

They shook hands at the door. "You have an open invitation to return any time you want," my father told Danny.

After Danny left, my father turned to me. "You've got a nice boy there," he said. "A little on the quiet side. But once he's been around us enough, he'll come out of his shell."

My father was reading too much into the visit. I didn't have a boy. Danny and I had never so much as exchanged a kiss. But all that was about to change – at least sort of. The next time we met at the Nielsen Library, Danny seemed more relaxed than usual. He told me how much he liked my family and suggested we head to the coffee shop in the student union building after we finished our research.

Danny wanted to talk. When we sat down in the coffee shop, his leg started jiggling. He wouldn't look me in the face, and I noticed a pulsing tic near his right eye. I felt sure he was about to give me The Speech: "Sally, I like you, but I don't want you to think there's anything but friendship between us." I was utterly wrong.

"Sally, I want to tell you why I became so quiet when the guys talked about baseball." He was talking in a monotone, gazing down at the table. "My parents, they're nothing like yours. Before I meet up with your family again, I want you to hear how I grew up."

16

"My father," he said, "wasn't what you'd call the warm and fuzzy type. He was abusive, and my childhood was anything but calm and ordinary. The police were always showing up at our door. He'd beat my mother, and some neighbor would call to complain."

I reached for his hand, and he continued.

"About the baseball thing – the only time my father and I hit it off was during a game. He was a huge baseball fan. I joined the Little League, and the old man loved that. Stopped acting angry and distant, blowing up over some stupid thing. He would come to see me play. Before the game, he got very calm and even seemed proud of me.

"Then, when I was 10, something bad happened that made it all fall apart again. We went into the end of the season facing a particularly tough rival. My team was leading by one game. Then, the other team pulled ahead. It was the bottom of the ninth, bases loaded, and there were two strikes against us; I was called up to bat. I searched for my father and couldn't spot him.

"The first pitch came in wide and low. I heard the sound I wanted to hear – the snap of my bat connecting. I hit a grand slam! Three team members made it to home base. My teammates broke into cheers and lifted me on their shoulders. They kept chanting 'DAN-neee,' 'DAN-neee!' I felt like the happiest boy in the world.

"I walked home afterward with the chants ringing in my ears. By now, my father would have already heard from a neighbor that I won the game. Surely everyone knew! But when I got there, the door was slightly open, and I instantly knew something was wrong. My old man was nowhere to be found, and my mother lay there, curled up on the floor.

"Her face – I'll never forget it. Drool slid down her chin, and her jaw protruded forward unnaturally. I wanted to call someone. But Mom made these frantic grunting sounds and shook her head. She didn't want the police to come. She had too much pride. I sat down for hours alongside her.

"Right then and there, I decided I would do anything to become the master of my own life. I wanted to find something to excel in. Not baseball. Great players are a dime a dozen. Something else."

I liked knowing Danny believed in himself. I believed in him. We left the coffee shop holding hands. But what he said put me off balance. In my life, parents were our role models, counted upon to protect us. I needed to talk to my father to find a way to digest what Danny shared. Deep down, everything would work out fine.

That evening, I told my father about the conversation. He listened intently, wincing when I told him the baseball story.

"I feel bad for him, Sally," he said. "What he told you speaks well for Danny. He was forced through this trial so early and emerged a fine young man. You've read your Gospel of James: "Blessed is the man who remains steadfast under trial, for when he has stood the test, he will receive the crown of life, which God has promised to those who love Him.""

"Danny might have turned his back on God and gone wrong. He didn't. Look at him! A business administration major at CCNY, holding down a couple of jobs, not giving into this rabble-rousing. Although, Lord knows, I could understand if he did after what he went through. He needs a woman who believes in him and a family who stands by him.

"Sally, it's still early in your process of learning about him. But from what I witnessed the other night, nothing he told you has changed my mind about the quality of the man he is today. If you're worried about what your mother and I think, don't be. Danny is a fine lad."

I suddenly understood that God had placed me in this relationship for a reason. If I kept strong, I would be his firm grounding, his boots on the ground, the first person he would confide in. I expected Danny to reveal more about his childhood in the months ahead, but I heard no more about it. I was pleased he opened up with me after the first dinner, letting me know what I was getting myself into. But now that he had unburdened part of his story to me? His childhood had once again become a closed book.

I tried to show him I cared, but I got mixed messages. He seemed to love the times we shared with my family. Yet when he and I were alone, he acted shy again. He showed little physical affection. I pushed things a little bit.

One night, when he kissed me goodbye, I asked him if he wanted to go further. He raised his eyebrows and glanced at me without meeting my eyes.

"Seriously?" he asked.

I whispered, "Yes."

Neither of us had a clue about what to do. All we knew was based on vague and unbelievable stories from classmates. A sexual revolution was raging across the country and in our school. The problem was that Danny and I had no idea how to partake in it.

We went back to Danny's apartment after class the next day. I tried hard to act blasé, though I felt secretly repulsed. I took in the linoleum floors, the caked-over hotplate, and the peeling olive-green wall paint. A yellow poster of two cyclists competing in the Track Cycling World Championship BRNO 1969 seemed out of place. Maybe it offered some insight into Danny? Surely nothing else in the apartment did! When he turned on a 40-watt lamp by the bed, I thought I saw a roach scurrying across the floor.

His bed consisted of a stained, sagging mattress creaking when we sat on it. Danny delivered a wet and open-mouthed kiss. It was so clumsy that I could barely breathe, very different from the few gentle kisses we had shared.

I heard his breathing becoming frantic and ragged. Hurriedly, we took off our clothes and regarded each other with awe. It felt like a monumental moment. Should we stop here? But we forged ahead, continuing to kiss and lick. Danny searched his pockets and brought forth a condom. His hands fumbled as he struggled to get it on. Abruptly, he slid inside me.

So this was sex? It hurt! Danny thrust one time, two times, three times, and that was it. The already filthy mattress appeared even more stained. I felt sticky and uncomfortable.

We smiled self-consciously at each other. Okay, we would get the hang of it. My life path had become apparent. I would be Mrs. Daniel Monahan, and we would raise a family. I'd be at his side for the rest of our lives. Except it didn't turn out that way.

# CHAPTER 2

**DANNY**

I fell head over heels in love during my sophomore year in college.

It took me years to fully understand that the proper object of my love was not my wife, Sally, but the entire McAllister family.

I needed a family, and they needed a cause to rally around. For many years, it was a match made in heaven.

I met Sally in a sophomore history class. She didn't bowl me over. She looked okay – long, thick black hair, pale, slightly freckled skin, deep-set inquiring eyes behind a pair of old-fashioned, black-framed glasses, angular features, a strong-looking jaw, and a thickset waist. She wasn't beautiful – not then, not now – but pleasantly familiar looking, like the Irish women I met in church and around the neighborhood. I didn't need a glamor queen.

When I met Sally, things were bleak financially. I had made a break from my past and only had myself to rely on. Though tuition was free, I still needed to deal with other expenses, such as finding a living place. I arranged a work-for-lodging exchange, doing odd chores for an elderly couple near campus. They had allowed their house to fall into total disrepair. My basement room was barely habitable but didn't cost me a cent.

I worked as a busboy at a local Italian restaurant two nights a week. In addition to bussing tables, I mopped the floors at the end of the shift. It was backbreaking work. But I needed the money. With 30 hours a week of classes, homework, and physical labor, I came home each night and fell into bed. I was running on empty.

I didn't trust anyone, especially at that point in my life. I had few friends and had hardly dated at all. At CCNY, students were pairing off like crazy, and I was maybe the only virgin left. My older former next-door neighbor, Maureen, tried fixing me up a few times, but I needed to be more of a conversationalist. I didn't have much time for dating.

Then came Sally. After we were randomly chosen to work together on a class project, I began to sense she was interested in me. I had yet to learn why. During our work sessions, it came up that her family lived in a big brownstone on the Upper West Side. It sounded like a dream to me. I got the picture: Dr. McAllister could be the father right out of "Father Knows Best," who guided the family with wisdom and patience. His wife was a loving and supportive mom. Then, there were three fun-loving brothers and a sister.

I liked hearing her family's stories. But I didn't want to talk about mine. What could I say? My moody, explosive father and my terrified rabbit of a mother would repulse Sally. I couldn't imagine what she would think about my former tiny bungalow and postage-stamp backyard in Queens, where planes flew 100 feet overhead to land at La Guardia Airport.

Eventually, Sally invited me to dinner at the McAllisters. She scheduled it for one of my nights off from the Italian restaurant job. No money for cabs – I took the subway. I walked three blocks up to a massive brownstone building on a wide, tree-lined street.

Sally opened the door, and her smile helped put me at ease.

She introduced me to her mom. "Welcome, Danny," Mrs. McAllister said, wiping her hands on her apron. "Please come in and excuse the mess. I'm still baking the apple cobbler for dessert. Have a seat and relax. Dr. McAllister is already back from the office. That's a treat! He's usually not here so early."

Dr. McAllister appeared in the foyer, holding a copy of *The Wall Street Journal.* I could see the resemblance between him and Sally. He was a tall, slender man with a long Roman nose and angular features, bushy dark eyebrows, thin lips, and intelligent brown eyes behind his glasses. He hugged Sally and turned to me.

"Nice to meet you, Danny Monahan!" He paused over my name and repeated it as if savoring a tasty steak dinner. "Sally doesn't often bring male friends over. You must be an extraordinary young man."

"Thank you, sir, but ..."

"Oh, don't say 'sir' to me, Danny! Call me Dr. McAllister. That's what all the young interns and residents call me at the hospital."

He paused, and his eyes twinkled. "I'm relieved you're not one of those CCNY hippies. Well, I'll be honest, I don't like them, don't like them at all. I would never allow my Sally to have anything to do with them!"

"Oh, Dad, really!" Sally blushed and shook her head at me.

"No, Sally, it's the truth." He laughed to let me know this was pro forma banter at the McAllister household.

She gave me a sideways look and rolled her eyes. But Sally needn't have worried. I already felt hooked. I didn't expect to be enfolded so quickly into the infectious humor and good-will of the McAllisters. In my constrained life, I had never met anyone quite like them. Dr. McAllister was kind and learned if a little (okay, a lot) opinionated. He openly showed warmth and affection to Mrs. McAllister and the kids.

Sally's older brothers and her sister, Kathy, loved to kid and tease each other and were friendly and welcoming. And Mrs. McAllister? She was everyone's idea of a perfect mother. Think Barbara Billingsley from "Leave it to Beaver." She had short dark blonde hair and a classically attractive face, and she wore a short-sleeved, light-blue shirt-waist dress with pearls. She struck me at once as capable – juggling parenting with what I had learned earlier was an active schedule of charitable events.

Most of all, I took readily to Sally's spindly little brother. Like me, Joey was a tech wonk and loved reading about the latest computers: the IBM System/360, the CDC 6600, and the UNIVAC 1108. As I later discovered, he often holed himself up in his room, building amplifiers and synthesizers. The youngest McAllister always became one of the top contenders in his middle school science fair. I loved Joey as if he were my own little brother. Deep down, I believed he would be the most successful of the whole batch.

At first, the dinners occurred twice a month or so. It took me a while to get the hang of things: there were two forks, one for the salad and one for the main course. There was a difference between a soup spoon and a dessert spoon. I never realized eating dinner could be so complicated!

I wanted to reciprocate, but I didn't have a dime to take Sally out properly, let alone her family. Back at school, I'd suggest one of the coffee shops or some free film showing on campus. Several weeks passed before I got up the nerve to kiss her goodnight. Not being much of a Romeo, I collided with her face, and her glasses fell off. We bumped our heads as we both bent down to retrieve them. As the saying goes, groovy.

Things took a step forward at the end of the year. After finishing my midterms, I got hit with the Hong Kong flu. It was spreading rapidly across the campus. I woke up one day feeling like shit – sore throat, muscle aches, cough, watery eyes, you name it. I didn't need a thermometer to tell I was burning up. I was supposed to meet Sally later. I called her and said I needed some downtime. I must have sounded like unadulterated crap.

I spent the next few days drifting in and out of sleep in this feverish fog, worried about missing shifts on my job. Sally called me a couple of times, increasingly concerned. I felt too crappy to croak out more than a couple of words before another coughing fit took over. She wanted me to go to the student health center or see a doctor, but I told her I'd tough it out. The truth is, I didn't have the money.

About four days into it, I heard a loud knock on the door. When I opened it, Dr. McAllister shifted around, looking awkward. I felt too miserable to be embarrassed about my cramped living space. I felt uncomfortable for him to see how I lived: an old stained sofa, a faded pair of blackout curtains, dirty laundry in the corner, and a rusty kitchen sink full of dishes. Through my stuffed nose, I smelled the stale air and body odor. I fought the urge to crawl into a corner.

Dr. McAllister scanned the scenario – his nose wrinkled in disgust – and assessed me with his professional eye. I averted my head and let out a phlegmy cough. He brushed past me and entered the basement door. "Sit on the bed, my boy. Let's see what's going on." Dr. McAllister pulled out his stethoscope, and I coughed again.

"I don't like the sound of that cough, Danny," he said. "It sounds like pneumonia may be setting in." He touched my forehead and peered at me with real worry.

He paused to think. "I'd like you to pack a bag and come with me now," he said. He took out a handkerchief, placed it over the mouthpiece of my wall phone, and dialed his home number. "I'm bringing Danny back to the house," he told Maude. "Can you prepare the au pair room and tell Sally he'll stay for a few days? Best if the kids stayed away from him until he's back on his feet."

I spent five days at the McAllister's. I could barely lift my head most of the time. But I loved every minute of feeling warm and cared for. Each morning, I'd wake up in a sunlit room, wrapped in clean, lightly scented bedsheets. I would hear cheerful voices and smell bacon sizzling on the stove. Later, they'd send trays of homemade meatloaf with sweet potatoes or Irish stew for dinner. This was the life I wanted to lead!

Dr. McAllister forbade all his kids – including Sally – from entering the room. His ban didn't stop her from opening the door, smiling at me, and asking how I was doing and if she could get me anything. As I drifted in and out of sleep, the thought began to take shape. I would marry Sally, and this whole life could be mine. What a lucky man I would be if she said yes!

As I built back my strength, Dr. McAllister came to me with an offer. "Danny, I spoke to a hospital billing department friend. They can use a part-time finance guy to help get the books in order. It pays about $2 an hour, and you can start the first of the month."

I couldn't believe my luck. I was hoping I could quit the busboy job. Here was my opportunity.

"I assume that is more than you are making now," Dr McAllister said. "It will allow you to focus more on your studies and stay healthy. When you don't get enough sleep, your immunity declines. That's why the flu hit you so hard. Can't have it happen again, can we?"

I gratefully accepted the offer. A promising future was starting to unfold in front of my eyes. I felt saved, whether through Dr. McAllister or Jesus Christ himself.

# CHAPTER 3

**SALLY**

Danny and I settled into coupledom – not in the same way as our classmates who were shacking up and thumbing their noses at traditional relationships – but instead, with a real sense of commitment.

We'd meet for lunch between classes at the student union and spend time with my family on Sundays. One afternoon, the subject of high school came around.

My father asked Danny what school he went to. Danny responded he attended Holy Trinity. My parents nodded approvingly: the school dedicated itself to providing a rigorous, faith-based college preparatory education. Danny was living proof it had fulfilled its mission.

Soon after, my brother Mark said he needed to talk to me about something important. A few years older, he always assumed the protective big brother role to a tee. Although he was a little more freewheeling than me, he modeled himself as a man of faith after my dad. He appeared troubled. I couldn't imagine why.

Turns out, Mark had a friend at college whose brother had also attended Holy Trinity High School. The three of them met up for dinner. Mark mentioned his sister's boyfriend, who would probably soon be his brother-in-law, had also been a student at the school. Perhaps he knew him? Danny Monahan.

The friend's brother got skittish but later owned up. He was familiar with Danny – not well, but he knew him. He recalled the boy in question had been expelled during his first year. There was some scandal – something about his father going to jail and Danny breaking some kid's arm. The last he heard, Danny had been banned to "the publics," and most of the kids he hung out with were cautioned to keep their distance.

My first reaction was disbelief, followed by fear. Was it true? What else was Danny keeping from me?

The next time we met, Danny could tell I was acting uncharacteristically remote. He asked me if I was angry at him for some reason. I blurted out what I found out from Mark.

Danny appeared somber, and tears filled his eyes for the first time since I met him. "Yes, it's true," he said. "I didn't want to tell you the whole story. I thought…well, I thought you wouldn't want anything to do with me. Most people don't.

"When my old man went to jail, I was – what? – 14 or so? Not long after the Kennedy assassination. The time in life when kids are their nastiest. I tried not to talk about it, but everyone knew. I can't tell you how exposed it made me. As if I had shown up in class without my pants or something.

"Most of the kids left me alone. They avoided me or didn't bring it up. But this one kid, an asshole if you ever saw one, wouldn't let it go.

"He'd crack jokes all the time about how my father was now someone's bitch. How he bet he was already eating cock. How I was probably like my old man. One day, this kid took it a step too far. He asked me who was fucking my old lady since my dad had gone to the slammer. Questioned whether perhaps I was doing the deed. Said I must be some deviant who would get off ramming it into my mother.

"I'm being crude, and I'm sorry. But you need to understand what I was dealing with then. Anyway, I lost it and twisted his arm behind his back. I yelled at the kid to take it back. He spat in my face. I was bigger and taller and just learning my own strength. I wrestled him to the ground and heard this popping sound, and the kid screamed his bloody head off. His arm hung at some unnatural angle, and I thought, 'Wow, I'm in for it now.'

"Turns out I was. The nuns came running out, and someone called the headmaster. He grabbed me and tossed me against the wall. Other kids rushed to help the kid whose arm I broke, and he whined away like a little girl. I felt all these eyes on me, judging me, thinking I belonged in jail with my father.

"Well, the wheels of justice move fast. Within days, I got expelled from the Catholic school my parents paid $350 a year for – they had to skimp and save to do it – and threatened with juvenile detention.

"Eventually, the case made its way into court. A social worker got involved. Told the judge I was a straight-A student and had witnessed violence at home since early childhood. The prosecutor and judge decided to let it go. No one wanted to ruin my life, even though my life was already a mess.

"I transferred to a public school – I had to take a long bus ride to arrive – where the good kids mostly ignored me. My reputation preceded me. My old friends? Their fathers told them to stay away. They said, 'Aye, aye, captain, yes, sir.'

"That's when I learned friendship is conditional. Couldn't trust myself, let alone anyone else. I had little left to do but study. There were no baseball teams and activities like in my first school. And there you have it.

"So now you've heard the whole sordid tale. I promise it's the only thing I've kept from you. I graduated from public school with high grades. You know what happened next. I went to CCNY and met you. You've heard the worst of it. What do you want to do, Sally? I love you, but I understand if this is a non-starter."

For the first time, Danny used the word "love." I knew what I wanted to do.

# CHAPTER 4

**DANNY**

Telling Sally about my past was among the hardest things I ever did.

I wondered if she would choose to stay with me. I had nothing to offer her. I didn't even know who I really was. As far as I remember, I spent every day in survival mode.

But she did. Without question, she did. There was nothing we couldn't face together. Right down to my core, I believed that I loved her and would continue to do so for the rest of my life.

# CHAPTER 5

**SALLY**

I told Mark what Danny had said. We decided to go to my father with the news. It would have been unthinkable not to let him know. Dad was reading *The Wall Street Journal* in his den when we arrived. The sun was shining through the bay window.

"Yes, please interrupt me," he said. "You kids look very serious. What's up?"

His face darkened when we told him the story. "I'm not so much upset he did those things. It happened years ago, and he was a kid then. But I am troubled he hasn't told you until now. He kept it from you, Sally."

"Yes, Dad. I don't know what to do."

"Of course you're confused." His expression softened. "However, I must tell you, I do like Danny. I only want the best for him. It would have been painful for him to tell you about this. From now on, he must be truthful to you about everything. There cannot be any secrets. Certainly, that can't be allowed in a marriage."

"Dad! He hasn't asked me to marry him! But you're right. He's got to learn to share. I promise I'll work to make it easier for him."

I did not tell Dad that Danny had just told me he loved me. Our relationship was more vital than ever despite the sobering news. Or maybe because of it. Danny slowly came out of his shell. He was not only funny but kind and self-effacing. I suspected it was because he felt safe with me.

He asked me to marry him in our senior year at CCNY. My parents were giddy with excitement. With all the arrangements needing to be made, the date was set for about a year after graduation. My mother went into high gear planning the wedding.

Mom and I went shopping every weekend. In Bloomingdale's, we found an elaborate satin dress with a veil and tiara. The outfit made me feel like a princess. My father convinced the Archbishop of New York to officiate at St. Patrick's Cathedral. Three hundred people were expected to attend the reception. There would be a three-tiered chocolate cake with raspberry filler and white frosting. Dad took Danny to purchase a tuxedo and a boutonniere. He began addressing him as "son."

Danny prepared for our Pre-Cana interview, which is required to be married in the Roman Catholic Church. This involved six marriage counseling sessions with our parish priest, whom I had known for years. We needed to discuss what we expected from our marriage honestly. We had to be open about finances, our marital roles, our desire for children, and any other expectations or apprehensions we might have.

I believed I knew Danny's heart. We were in lockstep. We both recognized marriage as a sacrament. I wanted three or four kids. ("Let's get through the first and see how it goes," Danny would say). We each knew how important it was to save money and not spend frivolously. Our children would be baptized and educated in the Catholic Church.

We brought up and rehearsed everything in preparation for our canonical interview. But we still needed to talk about Danny's parents. I knew I was broaching a painful topic, but I had to ask. "I know it's hurtful to talk about your parents. But I need to know. What happened to your father after he got out of jail? And your mother? How come you never mention her?"

Danny crossed his arms protectively around himself and wouldn't look me in the eye. When he did that, I would usually back off. But not this time. I sat there silently. He took a deep breath.

"Okay, my father. He came here from County Cork when he was a young child. Right around the Great Depression. He didn't have it easy. But he had dreams. None of them came to pass. He always had a volatile temper and got fired a lot. He wanted a big family, but my mother had a hard time carrying a baby, and he ended up with just one. Me. My mother got disgusted with him and put him down – not that he didn't deserve it.

"More and more, he began acting out because life didn't go his way. He became abusive. You already know he spent a few months in prison. He wasn't allowed to come back to the house right away. But he had nowhere to go."

"He had no other family to take him in?"

"No one. My grandparents had died, and his brothers wanted nothing to do with him. My father ended up rooming with this friend of his from his union days. Gene. He was stinking drunk half the time, but my dad thought he was a helluva guy. The loser and the abuser."

"Where did they live?"

"In a grimy one-bedroom near the expressway. It had a convertible couch. My father picked up some pocket money while working in a warehouse somewhere. He spotted Gene some drinks in exchange for the couch."

"Sounds like a perfect match. What happened to your father?"

"He drank himself to death. He came out of jail about 20 pounds lighter. No surprise, he had cirrhosis of the liver. The vomiting, the itchy skin, and the yellowed eyes. I never saw any of this personally. I heard about it later, after the funeral. Which I did not attend."

"And you and your mom? What happened to the two of you?"

38

"The same old, same old. In the past, my mom's cousin Elsie might have taken us in. But Elsie didn't want to help her until she gave up on my father. My mother wasn't prepared to take that step. She was always ready to take him back. After he died, she became bitter and broken. We stayed in the same rundown place.

"She took on some cleaning-woman jobs to make ends meet. She'd come home and drink herself stupid. After high school, I left home and never spoke to her again. She might have tried to reach me, but I'm guessing not. How hard could it have been to find me?"

"What are you going to tell the priest about all this?"

"I'll tell the priest I learned not to be a father like him. In my book, a father has two jobs. To love. And to protect. My father was a dismal failure on both counts. Your father and mother will be mine, too. They're the only ones I want our kids to call grandma and grandpa. I've put the past behind me, and you should, too."

As it turned out, the topic did come up in our Pre-Cana interview. Danny knew what to say. After all, he had been through a dress rehearsal. The priest looked kindly on his self-awareness and willingly granted us consent to marry in the church.

# CHAPTER 6

**DANNY**

I did all of the wedding hoopla for Sally. As far as I was concerned, the canonical preparation and the wedding itself were just extra hurdles the church was making us jump through.

In my mind, I'd be paraded out in a dog-and-pony show. Everyone would be in full appraisal mode, wondering what Sally and her family saw in me.

If it were up to me, we would have eloped. Or at least have a small wedding with just the McAllister family. Sally, however, wanted the whole fairy tale. The white gown, the bouquet of roses, the hair and make-up artists, the photographers, the caterers. All I wanted was to make her happy. To take my place in the McAllister family.

As we worked through the planning, the only snag was picking bridesmaids and groomsmen. Sally wanted six bridesmaids – her sister, one of her cousins, and a few close childhood friends. Me, I couldn't think of one person in the world who I could get to stand up for me.

Not having groomsmen wasn't an option for Sally. So, she came up with a solution. Her three brothers would do it. We could add one of her friends' husbands and two of her cousins. Just like that, we had a wedding party.

The date was getting closer. I couldn't wait to place the ring on her finger and get started with the rest of our lives. How could it not be anything but grand?

# CHAPTER 7

**SALLY**

Our wedding would be the first of any of the McAllister siblings.

Between my father's colleagues at Columbia-Presbyterian, cousins, other family members across the East Coast, and long-time friends, the wedding would be the event of the season. A writer from *The New York Times* contacted us, asking if we could provide a brief overview of our love story along with photos. It was going to run in their Sunday column.

Danny was excited but increasingly overwhelmed by the planning. I thought he'd be more comfortable adding someone he liked – perhaps a childhood or college friend – to the list. Surely, there must be someone!

He finally came up with his childhood next-door neighbor, Maureen, and one or two casual friends we knew from CCNY. No way was he inviting his mother or even his cousin Elsie. The vast majority of guests would be from my side of the family. Danny didn't object. My family was his family now, he said. They were the only people he wanted.

My father had two exciting surprises for Danny and me before our wedding day. He had spoken to his boyhood friend, Jared Morgenstern, the director of accounts at Cooper, Masters & Young. It was widely known as one of New York's top advertising agencies. Danny was going to be interviewed for a junior account executive position there. Dad felt sure Jared would offer him the job. The salary would be a whopping $14,000 a year with the potential to earn a lot more later.

The second bit of good news: Dad intended to co-sign a mortgage for us to buy a house in White Plains. "Just make sure I have lots of grandkids," he said. Dad winked at Danny, who smiled and blushed.

The wedding couldn't have been more wonderful. Six bridesmaids and six groomsmen. Walking down the aisle with my father, I basked in all the oohs and ahhs. At the altar stood my handsome husband-to-be in his rented tuxedo, with his mane of reddish-blonde hair. He beamed as I stepped up to join him.

We held hands as the archbishop welcomed our guests and gave a meaningful sermon about the significance of marriage. With everyone important to my life watching us, we exchanged vows and rings. The archbishop presented us to the congregation as husband and wife, and deafening cheers rang out.

We chose Roberta Flack's "The First Time Ever I Saw Your Face" for our first dance as husband and wife. We circled on the dance floor and couldn't take our eyes off each other. Then the dance floor filled with friends and relatives, swaying to songs like "Rockin' Robin," "I'll Take You There," and "Too Late to Turn Back Now." When my father awkwardly tried to dance to "Let's Twist Again," the house exploded with laughter.

Later, we cut the cake, holding the knife together. It was a tiered chocolate cake with raspberry filling and vanilla icing. On top were laid sprigs of greenery and sprawling chamomile blooms. Chuckling, we smashed the cake into each other's mouths. Our friends and family cheered.

Too soon, it ended. We said our goodnights and retired to our bridal suite. Danny loosened his tie and turned to me. "Hey, Mrs. Monahan," he said softly, removing my veil and embracing me.

"Hello, my dear husband," I whispered. It was the happiest day of my life. I thought it could only get better and better. But I was wrong.

# CHAPTER 8

## DANNY

Those first few years of married life seemed surreal for Sally and me. With growing excitement, we took our first tentative career steps. Sally passed the New York State Teaching Certification Exam and landed a job as an elementary school teacher in the White Plains public schools.

And I passed muster with Jared Morgenstern, my mentor at Cooper, Masters & Young. I was rewarded with a small office and started learning the ropes from one of the senior account executives.

Sally and I made nearly $25,000 a year, more than any of her married friends. We had taken our place as adults. But it seemed as though we were still kids. Two kids playing house, posing as grown-ups. Sally told me our faith in God would lead us the way. "He has a plan for us," she assured me.

She signed us up at St. Patrick's Church, the oldest and largest Catholic church in White Plains. It was a magnificent

Gothic Revival structure with a towering spire. And boasted over 2,000 worshippers. St. Patrick's offered an entire menu of activities, from education to social services to outreach for the poor. Sally eagerly volunteered us for a few committees.

The months went by fast. Each Sunday after Mass, we'd drive into the city and spend the whole day with the McAllisters, capped by a sumptuous brunch prepared by Sally's mom. Sally was also taking a cooking class and did a surprisingly worthy job, making fantastic meals for us on the weekdays, like veal chops with mushroom sauce or stuffed crown roast of pork. On Saturday nights, we'd get together with some of Sally's friends, also newlyweds.

Sally wanted at least three or four children. But we decided to wait a couple of years before starting – at least until we turned 25. I could feel her impatience gather. Other McAllister children by this time were engaged to be married. Dr. and Mrs. McAllister clearly wanted grandchildren. Who would give them the first?

Turned out Matthew and his new wife Katie won the competition. When Katie got pregnant, Sally became obsessed with being next. I had just gotten a raise. My wife worked out the numbers and decided she could quit work when the baby came, and we could manage on my salary alone.

We stopped using condoms and expected Sally would get pregnant just like that. Well, it didn't work that way. We tried for five months. Sally turned to her faith to keep herself positive. "God's timing may not always seem perfect to us. But He knows best," she said. "I will get pregnant."

Even so, it became increasingly emotionally difficult for her. She compared herself to her mother, the "fertile Myrtle." It didn't help that her sister-in-law, Katie, had managed to get pregnant right off the bat. Her sister soon did, too.

"Sometimes I feel as if I'll never have children," Sally said one day. Her eyes welled up with tears.

"Sally, don't say that," I told her. "Of course you will." Actually, I suspected the problem might have to do with me. I kept that to myself.

After six months of discouraging pregnancy tests, we finally got a positive result. When the doctor's office telephoned the news, Sally screeched with joy. I felt happy, too.

"Danny, we can't tell my parents yet," Sally said. "Their 30th anniversary is coming up in a month. That's when we'll tell them. You've got to promise not to say anything before then."

Two weeks before the anniversary celebration, I heard a wail from our bathroom. Sally sat on the toilet, doubled over, with visible blood on her underwear.

"Oh, Danny, how could this be happening?" she wept.

I called her doctor. He advised us to come right in. After performing a physical examination and a blood test to measure her levels of human chorionic gonadotropin (HCG) – a hormone produced by the placenta – he left the room briefly. When he came back, his face was glum.

"Sally, I'm sorry. You are having an ectopic pregnancy. It means your fetus is developing outside the uterus in your fallopian tube. It's a life-threatening medical condition. The pregnancy cannot go to term."

My wife was sobbing uncontrollably, and he let her absorb what he was saying before letting the other shoe drop.

"I'm going to prescribe some medication to terminate the pregnancy. You should experience some cramping. There is really no other way. I know it's a heartbreak. But you kids are young and healthy. Eventually, you will be parents. I suggest you wait three months to try again. I have little doubt the next time will bear better results."

We waited for her to heal. Sally did not want to tell her parents what we had been through. She thought it made her appear defective. In the meantime, life went on. Her sister Kathy was about to give birth, and Mark's new wife, Jennie, was also pregnant.

One Sunday, all the kids were visiting the McAllister home. Everyone else was boisterous at the dinner table, but my wife looked miserable. Sally's brother Mark poked me in the ribs. "When will it be your turn, Danny Boy?" he said. "Maybe you need some more practice?"

He was trying to add some humor to the situation. But Sally burst into tears and fled from the table. We finished the meal in silence. Afterward, Dr. McAllister invited me to walk with him around the block. It was a beautiful, crisp fall day. The leaves were changing color.

"Son, are there problems I might help with?" he asked.

"No, not really," I said. "The doctor is telling us everything is going to be fine. We just need to be patient."

Dr. McAllister nodded but looked troubled. "My wife never had any…" he said and then stopped.

Every month, we kept trying. Nothing. More trying. Still nothing.

Back home in White Plains, I tried to console Sally about the whole thing. My initial enthusiasm for bringing a child into our lives had waned. I wanted to let my wife know it would be okay if it were just us.

"Sure, not having a child is tough. Even if that were to happen, I think we could live with it," I said.

"What is that supposed to mean, Danny?" Sally shot back. "Are you saying you don't want to have kids?"

"Well, it's not the outcome either of us want, but we could survive if it didn't happen. We'll have each other. It's not a big deal."

"It's not a big deal, huh?" Her voice rose. "Are you kidding me, Danny?"

"I didn't mean it quite that way. But you know what I'm saying. I had a crappy dad. He was a terrible role model, and …"

"Are you telling me you think you'd be a lousy dad, too, Danny?"

"Not exactly. I think I could learn to be a good dad. Then again, we don't have to be parents. I could still be happy without kids."

"Well, I couldn't," Sally said. And that was that.

From then on, I kept my feelings about parenthood to myself. I also didn't discuss religion with Sally. She told me

God has a plan for everyone. How could He have created people like my mom and dad? What was the plan for me? I decided that sometimes there is no reason why certain things happen. There is no "God's Plan."

After a year of unsuccessful attempts, we returned to the doctor. Sally underwent a battery of tests, and the news turned out to be devastating. Her fallopian tube was damaged – possibly because of the ectopic pregnancy – and the treatments were limited.

We broke down and finally confided in Dr. McAllister, who was visibly shaken. He reached out to his most esteemed colleagues at Columbia Presbyterian. The head of obstetrics suggested Sally undergo a salpingostomy – a procedure to open up a blocked fallopian tube. The operation only attained success about half the time. But at least it gave some hope.

She opted to do it. The salpingostomy would be followed by tubal microsurgery to repair the damaged fallopian tubes. This delicate surgery was costly, and our insurance only covered so much. We decided to dip into our savings. But Dr. McAllister wouldn't hear of it. He freely offered to pay for the procedure despite its uncertain success rates.

We hoped the surgery would solve the problem, but it didn't. Sally turned to prayer. Despite my growing skepticism, I went with my wife to the prayer group at St. Patrick's. I did a reasonable job of being a supportive husband. She was clearly struggling.

Mark, Matthew, and Kathy were already parents and planning to bring more babies into the world. Sally didn't want to go to McAllister Sunday brunches anymore. She sometimes invented excuses to stay away. She had a stressful week at work, or she had to correct students' homework.

When we did show up, Dr. McAllister still invited me on walks with him, but he didn't have encouraging things to say anymore. He'd glance at me worriedly as if he were assessing a prize racing horse with a game leg – even though it wasn't my fault.

Sally began putting on weight. She was never a slim woman, and by our fifth year of marriage, she had gained 40 pounds. I wish the extra weight didn't bother me, but it did. Nothing I said or did would make her feel better about herself or our situation.

Tentatively, I brought up adoption. Sally went crazy. For her, it was all or nothing. Her brothers and sister had their own children, and by God, she intended to have them as well. She wouldn't listen to reason: an adopted child would still be our child and loved every bit as much as if she had birthed the baby herself. I gave up trying to be rational.

"What if...," I said. "Adopting a baby is God's plan for us?"

She glared at me. Quickly, I dropped the topic. There was no winning with her.

# CHAPTER 9

## SALLY

As a little kid, I was sure I would be a mother someday. And a fertile one at that. I didn't want to play with Barbie dolls all the time the way my friends did. I didn't have their love for some glamorous cutie-pie with her eyes on a career. No, I related far more to my Suzy Homemaker doll, who I could imagine producing babies, one after the other, as my mom did.

When I was in the right mood, sex with Danny was good. Great, even. But it was never sex for its own sake. For me, it had a deeper meaning. The most important thing was knowing we were creating a new life. Maybe not that very time, but shortly. I knew with certainty that soon I was going to become pregnant, and then I would slowly switch into mother mode.

From the get-go, my mom had filled me in on how it would go. My belly and breasts would get bigger. I would feel the little guy – or gal – kicking inside me. Everyone would see and comment on how big the baby was growing. Strangers would stop and congratulate me. I'd feel this special glow. Danny and I would pick out all the merchandise. The cribs, onesies, pacifiers, car seats, carriages. And we'd take on the most vital role – Mommy and Daddy.

Months passed, and I didn't get pregnant. At first, I thought it was because we didn't have sex often enough. So I'd surprise Danny on weekends in the middle of the afternoon or when he walked in the door from work, just dressed in my bathrobe. I'd open it up for him, and he would dive in.

Those were fun times. Yet, after a while, I realized it was all to no avail. Every month, just as I was getting my hopes up, I'd get my period again. My mom told me I needed to have faith in God. Friends would wink and tell me to enjoy the waiting. "Trying is the fun part," they said.

Well, it was no longer fun for me. I gradually became less interested in sex, and Danny noticed.

"What's the matter, Sally? I miss those afternoon and after-work surprises," he said.

"I don't know," I said. "Every time we make love, I gear up for another disappointment two weeks later."

"Come on, Sally. We're not in a hurry."

"Sometimes I think you're happy I'm not getting pregnant."

"This again? Why wouldn't I be happy?"

"Because maybe you don't want to become a parent."

"For the millionth time, Sally, that's not true."

"Okay, we may have to wait longer. But I wish sometimes you would take care of me. Ask me every so often how I'm feeling. Tell me how you're feeling. But you don't. You spend more and more time at the office."

"What do you think I'm doing there? Do you think I'm coming on to the secretaries? Is that what you think?"

"Oh, of course not. It's just that I miss you. You come home at 8 o'clock, and it's almost time to get ready for bed."

"Sally, I have more responsibilities. That's good for both of us, isn't it?"

"Yeah, but will you be coming home at eight every night for the rest of our lives?"

"Oh, come on, Sally. There are plenty of nights I get home on time. It's not that bad."

Worse yet, Dad agreed with Danny.

"Sally, that's what a responsible husband does," he said. "He provides for his family. That's what I did for all of you. I understand this hasn't been the easiest time for the two of you. Maybe you should see the priest together. You could talk it over."

"Well, I guess we could do that," I said. "But Dad, I never see Danny anymore."

My father turned to me seriously. "Sally, you have a good man there. I wouldn't want to see you burden Danny at a time when he is taking on so much to build his career. Your mother never did that to me, and that's one reason why we've had such a wonderful marriage. I bet he's as unhappy as you are that the two of you aren't parents yet."

I nodded glumly. My father didn't know Danny as well as I did. I had begun to suspect that Danny's focus was now almost solely centered on his work, a subject he rarely delved into at home. I knew little about how he was regarded at the agency. But I caught a rare glimpse when we invited Bob Bolsen, Danny's creative director, and his wife, Bunny, to dinner.

That night, I witnessed a side of Danny I didn't know – supremely confident, animated, even charismatic. He held court at our table, mesmerizing Bob and Bunny with hilarious stories about his immediate boss Evan's gaffes at client meetings. Every story ended with Danny diplomatically saving the day. Bob, who apparently believed Danny could walk on water, sat rapt as Danny tossed out ideas for the creative team to consider for the next presentation. Bunny said little, but her worshipful gaze said it all.

Bob shifted in his seat and winked at me. "Evan's not a fan of smart women. Now Danny here, he's got the girls on our team eating out of his hand. He listens to them, respects their input, and gives credit when credit's due. He's not the same guy who walked in the door a few years ago. People are taking notice. He's not flashy or anything, but I'm telling you, he's a rising star."

Danny blushed a little and shot Bob an aw-shucks look.

Bob was just winding up. "You know, my associate creative director, Frieda, almost quit when Evan acted like a beast at her last concept presentation. Danny saved me a lot of heartache by convincing her to stay, promising he'd run interference when Evan's in the room. She adores Danny."

Then he teasingly added, "Your husband's broken many hearts by making it clear he's a devoted family man. You should be proud of him. He's going far, and he's not compromising his integrity, like a lot of the assholes we work with. He's *the man*."

I watched Danny straighten up and glow. It was then that I knew Danny would be fine no matter whether we had children or not. He had found his calling in life. Me? I couldn't even imagine that sad possibility.

# CHAPTER 10

## DANNY

I indeed had increasing responsibilities at Cooper, Masters & Young. Recently, I had been promoted to account executive. That meant I was in charge of ad campaigns and managed a creative and production staff team. I reported to Evan Wells.

Evan had great connections. He went to prep school at Choate and then to Yale, where he joined the secret society Skull and Bones. Bonesmen help each other with their careers. When Trans World Airlines fell into financial problems in 1985 and severed ties with Ogilvy & Mather, a fellow Bonesman helped Evan snag the TWA account.

Evan's background made him golden at Cooper, Masters & Young. But he had one huge flaw. No one – not even the TWA folks – liked him much. When a new executive took over ad agency relationships at TWA, he asked for another account director. Evan went to the Proctor & Gamble account, and I followed him.

Evan's personal life was a mess. Though barely 40, he had already been divorced once, paying a ton of alimony. Then, his second divorce battle flared up. Never much of a ladies' man, except in his own mind, he became a flaming misogynist.

At team conferences, Evan offered play-by-plays of his divorce. "You know, women can be absolute witches sometimes," he would say. "They know all your weak spots, and they hammer away."

No one would say anything. We'd all groan silently. The agency was starting to recruit more women at the time, and several of them were on Evan's team. They would glumly stare at the tabletop as he carried on.

"I fix one problem her attorney brings up, and wouldn't you know it, she's got another one. These things are a real bitch, and so is she. Hear me when I say this – a man would act more sensibly and get the damn thing done and over. He'd handle the problem and move on without all the damn drama."

Evan reported directly to Jared Morgenstern. He did not want Evan to muck up relations with such an important client. After all, one of the new top execs at P&G, Reba Knauss, was a woman. Also, Evan wasn't much of an innovator. It took a lot of work even for Jared to get him to accept new ideas. That's where I came in.

Jared summoned me to his office one day. "Danny, I've been hearing good things about you. First and foremost, from Francis McAllister. He's your biggest fan. By the way, how's that goddaughter of mine?"

"Sally's doing fine."

"That's good." Jared paused. "Look, I've got an unusual favor to ask. Francis told me you've got a strong background in market research, and I want to put it to use. P&G is determined to maintain its lead in customer research. They're particularly interested in barcode scanning."

"What could P&G be doing with barcodes?" I asked. "They've been around since the early 1970s."

"Yes, barcodes themselves have been used for years. But P&G wants to take them a step further and use them to better understand their customer base. For example, they've been testing a new shampoo to reduce frizz called Pantene Anti-Frizz. By scanning the barcodes on the coupons customers redeem, they want to learn more about what products they're buying and what offers are working."

"I get it. That would help P&G develop smarter marketing campaigns."

"Precisely. So here's the thing. We've got a presentation scheduled for next month. Evan will be in charge. He's got a solid media plan: TV buys, radio buys, the works. That's fine. But I want to add in point-of-sale, and he's been resisting."

"So you'd like me to whisper something in his ear?"

"Well, not exactly. I'd like you to base your suggestions on some good research. It's better if it comes from you. As I already brought the matter up, Evan might think I'm reprimanding him If I push him more. And you – you have a non-confrontational style that goes down well."

"Well, thank you, Jared."

"Yes, I mean it." He stood up. "Do this for me; your efforts won't go unnoticed."

I immediately went to work on a strategy to win Evan over. The women on my team agreed to set aside their distaste for him and follow my plan. They liked me. They viewed me as safe because I was a married man. We had a load of fun cheerfully teasing each other.

When Evan started pontificating about his divorce at our next team meeting, I changed the topic and headed it in the right direction. "I guess divorces can be pretty awful," I segued. "There are a lot of situations where a cool, even-tempered point of view can be helpful. This upcoming Pantene presentation, for example."

"What about it?"

"I took the liberty to do a little research. I'm not as good as you are with it. But you could take some of what I've come up with and weave your magic into it.

"Go on," he said, a little suspiciously.

"Right now, P&G has the largest share of the shampoo market in this country, with 32%. Unilever is in second place with 25%, and Johnson & Johnson has 15%. Now, the anti-frizz shampoo market is relatively small. I have a bar chart right here." I handed it over.

"That's old territory," Evan said brusquely.

"You're right." I smiled. "My only point is we need to differentiate P&G so it can maintain its leadership position."

"Sure." Evan was attentive now.

"It seems we've got quite an opportunity with in-store advertising. Of course, I'm sure that's already occurred to you. I feel a little foolish bringing it up."

"Oh, no, go ahead."

"We could use the in-store displays to inform women about the shampoo's unique formula, Pro-Vitamin B5 and silicone. Then we can suggest to P&G that they use bar scanners in a new way. To gather information on buying habits based on the coupons customers are redeeming. Here's a handout on some of the preliminary research. It's promising."

"Shelf displays and coupons." Evan seemed suspicious once again. "I always thought of them as low-hanging fruit. Nothing to bother with. But hey, I have an idea! The displays could feature a woman with smooth, frizz-free hair."

"Wow, Evan! Sounds great."

"Yes, we can do some A-B-C splits testing pricing and coupon offers. Measure the metrics. Try testing messaging and graphics on the coupons. Good thought-starter, Danny."

"Thanks." I shot him an aw-shucks grin.

"I know we started with your idea, but certainly you'd agree it needed a lot of work. The more I develop it, the more I like it. I'm really onto something now."

I slid him over a comparative analysis report, and he glanced at it and tucked it under his arm. Then he stood up.

"Okay, kids, get out of the playground and back to work."
He strode imperiously from the room.

I looked at the team. "You didn't like Evan's great idea?
After all the work he put into developing it?"

Everyone laughed. "Danny, you're the lion-tamer,"
Tamara, one of the women on the team, said. "You're incredible. Why are all the good ones married?"

I thought I may have a few things going for me after
all. But then I had to take the 6:33 train home. When I
opened the door, Sally, dressed in sweats, would wave hello, turn around to the kitchen, and serve dinner. Afterward,
we'd silently watch "Starsky and Hutch" or "Welcome Back,
Kotter." We'd exchange a few words and climb into bed with
our backs turned away from each other.

It went on like this, day after day. My home life was becoming unbearable. I began to feel I had married a stranger
and a depressed one at that. I muddled through by spending
more time at work. Then, a miracle happened. Years after the
surgery, just as we were giving up hope, Sally got pregnant.

# CHAPTER 11

**SALLY**

We were ecstatic, and my parents? They were over the moon. Everyone acted so happy for us. We decided to name our baby Charles Francis. It was a solid name. We'd call him Charlie. I couldn't wait to meet him – and I was thrilled by Danny's growing excitement. It felt like the old days between us again.

The pregnancy had its obstacles. At the end of my fifth month, I developed preeclampsia. My blood pressure shot up, and my ankles began to swell. I felt increasingly nauseous and started experiencing throbbing headaches.

Danny couldn't take many days off from his demanding position to care for me. We agreed my parents would do a better job, anyway. So, I moved back into the big brownstone, reclaiming my old room.

With only Joey still living at home, my parents were glad to see their house a little less empty. My room was not much different than it was in high school, including the crinoline bedspread. I didn't change the decor except to add a picture of my husband on the night table.

Danny stayed at the brownstone whenever he could. My bed was too cramped for two people, and I wasn't feeling well. So he took Mark's room. He came to the house directly after work each day, looking exhausted and anxious. Both of us were aware of the risks I was facing: damage to the kidneys and liver, lung, or heart, and fetal growth restriction.

My father kept the conversation positive. He also brought in the best obstetricians. They recommended a C-section at 37 weeks.

When the day of birth finally arrived, we rushed to the hospital, terrified but excited to finally meet our little boy. The nurse gave me an epidural, and Danny accompanied me into the operating room. Talk about anxiety! I thought he would pass out. But after about an hour, we heard the lusty cry of a healthy newborn.

Miracle of miracles, Charlie arrived safely on a sunny June day in 1982. He weighed 5 pounds, 9 ounces. The doctor spoke to me afterward about family planning. "Owing to your difficulties, I think you should seriously consider not having any more babies," he said.

"You can't mean that, doctor," I said. But the grim expression on his face made it clear he did. I reluctantly put off thinking about what he had just told me. I trusted in God's plan; if more kids were part of it, it would happen. For now, I had a healthy baby, and that was enough.

"You are truly blessed," my mother said. "Charlie was worth waiting for." She now had the grandchild I had been trying so long to give to her and Dad.

After a few more days in the hospital, we returned to our White Plains home with Charlie. My father made sure I had a full-time nurse for six weeks while I recovered. But it soon became evident Charlie would not be an easy baby.

He woke up frequently, red-faced and crying at the top of his lungs. It took forever to calm him down and get him back to sleep again. Soon, he'd be awake and whimpering, then howling inconsolably.

Bleary-eyed, I'd pick him up. He would twist and writhe, screaming into my ear. It was a big deal for us if he slept half an hour. The nurse helped me set up a feeding schedule to calm him down. But the screaming would become so intense that I'd depart from the schedule and put him on my breast. Sometimes he'd suck greedily, and other times he would refuse to take anything.

It didn't get any better. He shrieked uncontrollably for his first bath. It took a lot of work to complete a face washing or efficiently change his diaper. When I started him on Pablum, he screeched, twisted, and spat it out. Sometimes, I felt he hated the mere sight of me! Even when he was relatively calm, I had to deal with all the repetition of caring for a baby. The burping, the pacing, the wiping.

I had little time for myself. Showering, brushing my teeth, or combing my hair took too much energy. None of my nieces and nephews were acting this way. Had I spawned some strange demon?

Danny wasn't much help. He'd reach over to the crib, pick Charlie up, and walk around a bit, speaking softly and patting his back. But the baby would return to the crib within a few minutes, screaming louder than ever.

"Do something!" I'd yell at Danny. He'd gaze at me with a blank expression. He would reach over and mechanically pet Charlie like you might pet a rabid dog. Then he would disappear. Later, I asked him where he went to. He said he needed to work on a presentation for the office.

A few months into motherhood, I realized I hated my son. I wasn't too fond of my husband either. I wanted my old life back.

# CHAPTER 12

## DANNY

Yes, it got better. It couldn't get much worse. Once Sally and I made it through the first few months, Charlie began sleeping longer, and he actually smiled at us from time to time.

He resembled the McAllisters – black hair, angular features – and I was glad. Deep down, I was afraid he would turn out to be like the Monahans – a tiny replica of my father with his constant temper tantrums. Yeah, I'll say it: I feared what I might have created.

Deep down inside, I loved Charlie. I loved his pudgy cheeks and his sudden sunny smiles. I loved how he rocked back and forth on his hands and knees to get himself into a crawling position. I loved his silly little giggles and how he reached out to grab my coffee cup and Sally's wristwatch. Part of me – the best part – wanted to keep him happy and safe for the rest of his life.

But there was also some restlessness growing inside me. Now that Charlie had started acting mostly human, Sally became totally absorbed in him. I never quite saw anything like it. A high-pitched, sing-song voice replaced her usual cadence. In the rare times we did go out with friends, she monopolized the conversation with photos of Charlie. Here he is with his blue elephant toy. Look, here he is, reaching for the butterfly collage Grandma got him.

She constantly fretted. Is Charlie bundled up tightly enough? Should he be near Kathy's little girl? I thought I heard her cough. What is that little red mark on his cheek? Do you think he might choke on that new toy?

Her siblings and her friends cast her a wide net. They knew how long it took for Charlie to come into the world and how much Sally had to endure to give birth to him.

Our life as husband and wife took a hit. Sally was never adventurous in bed, to begin with. Lately, I had to do almost all the initiating. Anything out of the ordinary made her squeamish. It was already heading in that direction before Charlie's birth, but now sex was indeed the last thing on her mind. Sometimes, it felt like we were roommates, coming together for one express purpose: to ensure Charlie was well-fed and cared for.

The boisterous family times at the McAllisters also waned. All of them – except for Joey – began spending more time with their newly created families. Six grandchildren with one more on the way. The talk around the brunch table centered on their milestones. Kaitlin is walking! Maura cut her first tooth! Seamus said a whole sentence! I liked watching my little munchkin playing with his cousins or mastering a skill and looking at me for approval. But I missed the days when we had some adult conversations.

Sally acted as if her one purpose in life had been fulfilled. Her weight never went down; it went up, and I constantly caught her reaching for homemade cupcakes, supposed to be for the little ones. Unlike her sisters-in-law, who spent time on their appearance, Sally rarely wore makeup anymore. She often reached for the nearest clothes available – usually a CCNY sweatshirt and sweatpants.

Once, I lingered in Dr. McAllister's den after an off-hour client call, jotting down some notes. Sally and her mother entered the adjoining room, unaware I was within hearing distance. They were deep in conversation.

"Honey, I know you're tired, but you must try a little," said my mother-in-law. "Remember what I used to tell you and Kathy? Every Wednesday afternoon, I had a standing appointment at the beauty parlor. I always freshened up before your father came home. Even the best men can give in to temptation. Dear, you need to take that baby weight off. Kathy's having a hard time, too, so she joined a gym. Maybe you can go with her?"

"Mom, would you stop throwing Kathy in my face? Her Cal's always been a flirt, and you know it. Not my Danny. He never even dated before he met me! He owes everything

– our home, his job, and now Charlie – to me. He's grateful for all that, and he's not going anywhere. I've never so much as seen him glance at another woman. Where would he go?"

Mrs. McAllister sighed. "You might think he won't stray, honey," she said. "But when we were at that church social after Mass on Sunday? You didn't notice it, but two pretty girls were staring right at him and whispering to each other. It's not the first time I caught girls looking at him. You have a good-looking husband. It's a matter of time before he re-alizes it. Getting married is easy. Staying married is what we women need to work on."

Sally must have rolled her eyes. Mrs. McAllister said, "Okay, I see your expression, and I've said my piece. Let's go get that table set up for brunch. Come along now."

I stood there frozen for a few seconds. So, my wife con-sidered me lucky to have her? She thought I wasn't worth the effort? During the daytime, I handled multi-million-dollar budgets, bantering with whip-smart women who wouldn't have given me the time of day a few years back. I was feeling like part of something much bigger than myself. It was fun and stimulating, and I was someone for the first time.

Back at home? All I heard was, "Danny, do this" or "Danny, do that." Wipe up Charlie's spit. Change the light-bulb. Figure out why the dishwasher isn't working. Go into Charlie's room and try to calm him down because I've been stuck with him all day. When she'd walk into the bedroom, I might have been another piece of furniture for all the atten-tion she paid me.

I only wanted Sally to stop treating me like a charity case she picked up a decade ago. Sure, I was grateful, but I had come into my own since then. Just once, I wanted her to say: Thanks for all the hard work you're putting in for our family. Or: I'm so proud of you for all you've achieved. You're doing great. Or even: You're so sexy, honey. I'm so glad you're all mine.

I probably sound like a whiny little kid. But I was changing while Sally was standing still. Was it too much to expect a wife to offer emotional support, treat me with kindness and compassion, and express her feelings inside and outside the bedroom?

Anyway, that was my state of mind when I first met Joanna.

# PART II

# CHAPTER 13

**DANNY**

My relationship with Joanna began innocently enough. She made a presentation at my agency. I was immediately struck by her. But it wasn't like I was on the prowl.

I was putting in a lot of hours to make a name for myself. My efforts were paying off. At home, Sally had her hands full with our son Charlie. She and I had fallen into a rut. That happens to a lot of married couples.

Charlie had what doctors are now calling ADD – attention deficit disorder. Back then, it was still referred to as hyperkinetic impulse disorder.

My son was constantly fidgeting and couldn't easily focus. It got to Sally. She grew up in a perfect family. When Dr. and Mrs. McAllister wanted their kids to do something, they all fell in line. No questions asked! That never happened with Charlie. He was always hard to deal with. It wore Sally down. She became tired and crabby.

Two years went by, then three, then four, and Sally never did get pregnant again. We didn't even bother with birth control anymore. We were fortunate to have Charlie, and it gradually dawned on Sally that another baby wouldn't happen. Creating a sister or brother for Charlie never came up between us now in conversation. This was, of course, occurring at a time when her siblings were procreating like rabbits, bringing one perfectly mannered child after another into the world – and to the McAllister dinner table.

I wasn't about to give up on her. I owed everything to Sally and her parents: my career, my beautiful suburban home, my fabulous lifestyle, and, of course, my family. For better or worse, I was in it for good. Or so I thought. Then Joanna walked in the door.

She was a video production sales rep, and she was presenting to my agency. I expected the usual dog-and-pony show: a perky girl in a Dress for Success power suit: the jacket with padded shoulders (extra points if it was pinstriped), a straight skirt, a floppy silk bowtie.

Instead, this dynamic woman waltzed in, full of confidence, with her long, auburn hair. She wore a pricey double-knit suit punctuated with brass buttons. It accentuated all her – umm – assets.

I was the new hotshot with my own team at the agency. But we were there only to listen and weigh in later. My immediate superior, Evan, was the man who would decide on Joanna's fate – a self-important little man with a bulldog face and a gravelly voice. Lately, he had taken to sporting a pompadour haircut that cost him $25, highway robbery at the time.

Joanna led us through her company's strong points. She had a great reel with tons of commercial and corporate videos. Carefully, we listened to her lay out her case, discussing creating video content through storytelling using the most advanced technological tools. She took her time walking us through each example. Painstakingly, she explained how layers of special effects could be created and keyed over a background. I am a tech wonk, so I ate it up.

The kids – the junior account execs on my team – were sitting with their mouths open. Her company already had some prestigious client names to their credit. But this was the mid-1980s, and there was no way a chauvinist like Evan would hire Joanna.

Evan was gearing up for the inevitable put-down, and it wouldn't be pretty. To soften the blow, I asked Joanna a few technical questions. She seemed pleased that at least someone in the room was paying attention. Then Evan harrumphed in that ridiculous way of his.

"You do realize, young lady," said Evan, who looked prematurely aged (he was just a little more than a decade older than her). "Our primary client is Proctor & Gamble. Packaged goods. We've got responsibility for Pantene, the hair care products line. Now, I don't see anything that even looks remotely like shampoo in this...umm... ambitious presentation."

I was surprised to see a flash of anger pass over Joanna's face. I expected her to try to flatter him. Instead, she laid out her points.

Her production company could program and record the moving path of the shampoo. They would come in with all the extra frills and fresh perspectives a company with the stature of Proctor & Gamble would like. This woman knew how to stand her ground.

"We've seen what we need," Evan concluded. "We'll let you know the outcome later this week." Then he left. The younger members of our team followed him out like a gaggle of geese. I stood by the door, and when she walked out, I whispered, "You did a great job, and he's an ass!"

Joanna shot me a grateful smile. But, of course, she wasn't awarded the job. Evan hated doing the dirty work, so I was appointed to deliver the news to her.

"You almost made the cut," I told Joanna over the phone. "But I'm sorry, we had to go with someone else. Although you had the edge in technology, they had tons of packaged goods experience. I wish you the best of luck."

For some reason, I added this: "I hope our paths will cross again someday."

Even with those words, having an affair with Joanna was the last thing on my mind. But I ended up bumping into a few weeks later on the train home to White Plains.

It had been a day of back-to-back meetings, and I was fried. I had promised to take Sally and Charlie to Bennigan's, a casual dining place close to home. I didn't look forward to the commotion Charlie would cause. I would rather stay home and watch "The Cosby Show" or "Family Ties" for some laughs.

I was near the door, and commuters were jostling by me. It was hard to concentrate on my newspaper. Seeking a diversion, I glanced across the aisle from me. There was Joanna. I almost didn't recognize her in her sleeveless pale yellow floral dress. Without makeup, her face was lightly freckled, and her auburn hair was pulled back in a ponytail.

Her face lit up when she saw me, and she waved. We started in on some small talk. The man beside me offered to change seats with her so we could catch up. We took him up on it. Joanna sat beside me, holding a package with wrapping decorated with baby monkeys and tiger cubs.

She was going to watch a friend's little daughter for the weekend. She made a point of letting me know she lived in the city, not up here in the suburbs. For some reason, I wanted her to like me, so I tried some humor.

The conductor was walking the aisle, punching tickets. "Remember to show him your passport," I murmured to her. "He will ask you to exit the train if you don't."

"What passport?" she asked.

"The one city people must show when they get to the suburbs. Remember, it's like a foreign country up here!"

I got a full throttle laugh from her.

We reminisced about our meeting at my agency. I imitated Evan's haughty demeanor. "That's fine, young lady. We've seen more than enough from you. Now, we'll be stepping back into our dusty cobwebs. We'll provide you with a full rejection a little later in the week."

She laughed so hard that tears ran down her face.

I pointed to the wrapped present on her lap. "It must be slow in the video business if you have to moonlight as a nanny in the suburbs."

"Yes," she said. "I'm hoping my trial period works out. If it doesn't, maybe you can hire me to care for your kids, which I assume you have. Unless, of course, someone with tons of experience applies for that job, too."

I recognized the jab. "You should have gotten the job."

"You bet," she replied.

"You're smart, clever, and so…" I stopped when I realized where I was heading. We lapsed into silence.

"Nice haircut," she said. "I like the new beard."

"Really?" I touched my chin. "I'm growing it out."

I locked eyes with her a little too long, and she blushed. I also caught her staring at my left hand. She seemed to be looking for a wedding ring. Which I had on.

"The next stop is mine," I said. " I'm taking my wife and son out to dinner."

"There are actually restaurants in the suburbs?"

"Sure, if you can call Bennigan's a restaurant."

I said goodbye when the train pulled into the station. When I got up, our legs brushed against each other inadvertently, and I thought I heard her breathing quicken.

As I walked from the station to my car, she remained on my mind. We had a pleasant little flirtation back there. I believe Joanna enjoyed it as much as I did. But she must have a few boyfriends on the line. And though my marriage was far from perfect, I had no plans to betray my wife.

I didn't expect to see Joanna anytime soon. It turned out I saw her the next day. Sally and I went to the local A&P for the weekly grocery run. We had to take Charlie along. Arriving at the store, he started playing "choo choo," steering an imaginary train through the aisles. We had just bought him a train set. He loved it so much that we began calling him Choo-Choo Charlie.

To speed things up, I searched for items on the next aisle. I picked up some snack packs, a bag of pretzels, and those nasty-looking yellow Hostess cupcakes. I was gathering the cupcakes when I heard a mighty crash and a child bursting into tears.

I heard a voice: "I told you not to touch. Why don't you ever listen?" It was Sally. Years later, I would hear the same shrill voice accusing me of anger management issues.

I raced to the scene. Charlie was wailing in front of a demolished display of canned sweet peas. Cans were rolling every which way.

"Danny!" Now I had become the object of Sally's anger. "Where in the heck were you? Didn't I tell you to watch him? Do I have to do everything all the time?"

I ignored her put-down and scooped up my son. He buried his face in my shirt, sobbing inconsolably. Every so often, he glanced up to see if his wailing had an effect on me.

The worst of this little drama was over. That's when I saw Joanna. She stood down the aisle, holding a packet of Jolly Jumbo popsicles. I thought she noticed me but wasn't sure.

I imagined this scene through Joanna's eyes. Me, wearing the same shirt she saw me in the evening before, looking disgusted. My wife in a worn sweatshirt from college – overweight, with messy hair and glasses perched halfway down her nose. And our son, acting like a single woman's worst nightmare of how her eventual offspring would turn out.

Joanna single-mindedly steered her cart away from the rolling cans and disappeared down the aisle. I figured she must be totally disillusioned with me after all those laughs on the train. Here I was, so damned ordinary. Or worse yet, maybe she wasn't thinking anything about me. She didn't acknowledge me.

Following the fiasco at the A&P, I was surprised to hear from her a week or so later. She called me at work and suggested we meet for a drink. I was glad she still wanted to see me. But I wondered if even a totally innocent meeting would be a good idea.

"Sure, I could meet you," I said with some hesitation, "But I'll have to make it fast. I have to catch the 6:33 train. Let's meet at a bar called My Place."

At the bar, we got to talking, and I missed the 6:33 train. Then I missed the one after that and the one after that. When I arrived home three hours later, Sally was livid.

I chose a convenient lie. "Sorry, honey, I had a last-minute emergency. Things are really hectic right now at work."

"You could have tried calling."

"You're right. I should have. It was so crazy." The sniveling I had to go through felt uncomfortable. But I didn't regret the time Joanna and I spent together. She was funny and easy to talk to. I needed that.

Our rendezvous became standard. We'd share a drink and some conversation at My Place every week- sometimes twice a week. She was enjoying herself as much as I was.

We'd talk about the news, like the nuclear reactor explosion in Chernobyl and the crash of the Space Shuttle Challenger. We also spoke about upbeat things, like the Oprah Winfrey Show, which was starting. Joanna was already hooked.

She lapped up my stories about work. I told her I was reading a book I suspected would become an advertising industry standard, "Rocking the Ages: The Yankelevich Report on Generational Marketing." She had a copy of it the next time we met.

Meeting up with Joanna was a rush for me. My life wasn't all that interesting. I was amazed Joanna thought it was. No other woman had ever pursued me except Sally.

I told myself we weren't doing anything wrong. We didn't even hug. I enjoyed having a little extra attention, and why not? I had a demanding job, and ditto on the home front.

Sharing stories about my family would be a natural thing to do. Yet I didn't want to go there. That should have been my clue these meetings weren't as innocent as we pretended.

I always tried to steer the conversation back to Joanna. She was living an exciting life. She'd tell me stories about visiting clubs with friends, participating in music and shows, and attending the latest restaurant openings. And, of course, she was busy establishing her own career.

One night, she opened up the door to her childhood. Her brother and his wife were coming in from Minnesota.

"My brother was always a picky eater," she recalled. "As a kid, he would only eat hamburgers. Except he called them "hamboogers.' Whenever we went out to eat, he would shout, 'I want my hamboogers!'"

"Hamboogers? Sounds disgusting."

"Yeah, I know," she said. "Anyway, I'm trying to figure out what greasy spoon to take my brother and his wife to. I hope my stomach survives!"

"There's always McDonald's," I said. "The hamboogers there won't set back your budget."

She laughed. "What about you? Do you have brothers or sisters?"

The familiar numbness set in for me. I wasn't meeting her eyes, but I could tell she was watching me.

"You're sure you want to hear the story of my life? Okay, here it goes. I grew up in an all-American family. You know, father who knocked the crap out of mother regularly. Particularly when he was drinking, which was about every night. Mother, who might as well have pinned a 'hit me' sign across her back."

I looked over at Joanna. She was listening intently.

"Yes. My family was quite a trip," I said. "Every now and then, my mom or some neighbor called the police. By the time they arrived, Mom had a change of heart. It happened so often that the police knew me by name. They'd call out to me, 'Hey, Danny Boy! How're you doing, sport?'

"After checking to ensure mom wasn't badly hurt, they'd roll their eyes and walk away. What else could they do? My parents were a joke to them. No one cared what they did to each other. I was an only child. I had to cope.

"No, I can say nothing good about my childhood," I told her. "Not one damn thing."

Joanna was still listening. When I tell the story of my childhood, I'm used to getting all kinds of reactions. Some people start fidgeting and want to change the subject. Others lavish me with praise: 'How courageous you were to survive all that.' And others, like Sally, give me the pep talk: 'God has a plan for you.' "

Joanna surprised me. She met my eyes calmly. "You were a child and didn't deserve that. I can't imagine how hard it must have been. Living as if something bad could happen at any moment. I'm sorry you had to go through those times. I'm here to listen if you want to talk more about it."

"Nah, I'm fine," I said. Then she did something unexpected. She told me about her childhood. It wasn't rosy, either, but she survived. I let her know I would never reveal what she said. To this day, I've kept my word.

After our conversation, something changed between us. I felt a rush of closeness to her in ways that scared the shit out of me.

I'm pretty sure Sally never knew anything about the secret meetings at My Place. I would spend a little time with Joanna, get a little adrenalin rush, and get on the train. Back home, Sally would drone on about how hard it was to deal with Charlie. Now, it was my turn to take over.

It never occurred to her I'd had a challenging day, too, that I needed to unwind. Yes, I felt resentful. After a while, I began to have this nagging feeling: There had to be a better way to live.

# CHAPTER 14

## JOANNA

Let me recount what really happened between Danny and me. It's going to sound a little different from the version he recalls. But it's closer to the truth.

The first time he and I crossed paths was at a presentation I gave to his agency, Cooper, Masters & Young. I had just landed a sales job in a pioneering production video company. They had skilled cinematographers and creative technicians. They needed someone to sell it.

That was my job. I had to reach out and convince almost all-male decision-makers at leading ad agencies that we were the best choice. I knew I had the resourcefulness to do it. I was the complete package – willowy and vivacious. At 28 years old, I considered myself intelligent, ambitious, and a go-getter, too, but that was just an extra plus for my male colleagues.

Danny's agency was one of several well-known Madison Avenue shops asking for a request for proposal. When my boss heard Evan Wells, who laughingly called himself a lady's man, would be the key decision-maker at Cooper, Masters & Young, he chuckled.

"Evan's going through yet another divorce. He has an eye for the ladies. Full of himself, but you can handle him," he told me. "You're the natural lead presenter."

My senior colleagues spent days coaching me, reviewing each step in the presentation. Then they set me loose to "work my magic," as they put it. It was my first time representing the company on my own.

When I arrived at their conference room, I noticed Danny right away. He was a grown man who still went by his childhood name, but that's the thing about him: he could get away with it. He was tall, with this cherubic face, high forehead, thick reddish-blond curls, and those eyes! Cornflower blue, and he had that innocent expression down pat – non-blinking, non-judging. He could have bottled and sold that look.

On the other hand, he was at least a week overdue for a haircut. He was carelessly dressed in a somewhat wrinkled, light-blue Oxford cloth shirt with long sleeves and a button-down collar. He had on a pair of beige chinos without a belt. His overall demeanor showed a man at ease in his body, smiling freely.

Of all the people in the room, I only knew of Evan. But I sensed Danny might be someone of consequence. The younger team members periodically glanced at him and avoided eye contact with Evan. I calculated he might very well be someone of influence whose input could sway Evan's ultimate choice.

Let me be clear: with every ounce of me focused on getting the agency account, Danny was nothing more than another important team member. At that point, my only interest in Danny was as someone who might help determine whether we won the business. I felt so focused on my presentation that it wouldn't have mattered to me if he had been Richard Gere.

I really thought my presentation had been a shoo-in. I did a great job highlighting my company's strengths and letting them know we were the right fit. But Evan? He turned out to be a classic women-hating asshole, not a lady's man at all except in his own puny mind.

I wasn't shocked when I didn't get the job. Danny called and told me himself. I was disappointed, but I had a full roster of client presentations to do after that. Cooper, Masters & Young was already in my rear-view mirror.

I didn't give Danny a second thought until I saw him again. Actually, I ran into him two times. Once on the train, I headed to my friend's house for the weekend. She was in a bind and asked me if I could babysit her toddler. Danny and I sat near each other and struck up a conversation. I found him to be easy to talk to and amusing, especially with his parody of Evan.

A day later, I went to the A&P near my friend's house. I wanted to gather some treats while my friend's daughter had a scheduled swim class with her little friend and her mother for an hour. I heard some screaming in the next aisle, so I walked over to see what was happening.

I was stunned to see Danny with a woman who had to be his wife. They were arguing heatedly. Their son had knocked over a food display and was making quite the scene.

Danny's wife was nothing like what I imagined. She looked so ordinary. Did he knock her up and have to marry her? She was actually sort of heavy, and those black-framed glasses! I could have slapped myself for being so uncharitable. With all this talk about sisterhood, it wasn't how I wanted to assess another woman.

A week later, Danny called and asked if I'd like to meet him before he caught his train home. He was stammering a bit. It was not how he acted at the presentation or on the train. I found it endearing.

I was more than a little curious about what this proposed "meeting" would be about. Danny suggested we get together at a bar near the station called My Place. He probably chose it so he would get his 6.33 train.

The day got away from me, and I was five minutes late. When I finally arrived, he was seated with a Coke on the far side of the room. (I found out later he never drank alcohol.) He twisted the straw into a bent shape, tapping his finger against his lip and glancing at the door.

His face broke into a smile when he spotted me. We talked shop a bit and went on to other topics – a movie we had both recently seen and a story about a mutual acquaintance.

Somewhere along the line, he mentioned his wife, Sally. She worked as a per diem teacher to spend more time with their young son, who knocked over the display. He didn't ask if I had a significant other, and I didn't volunteer.

I couldn't figure out why he had suggested the get-together. Until that night, I was pretty sure Danny and I would run into each other a couple of times a year. It seemed odd he wanted to keep in touch.

We began meeting regularly at My Place, once a week or so. I suspected we were heading toward a friendship. You know, people who meet every so often to catch up. It would be fun to do after work, before heading home. We traded jokes and talked about our work. It didn't hurt that he was so damn sexy, with a "look but don't touch" vibe. I knew a lot of men like him – the kind who have a hard time opening up because they think it makes them appear weak.

After a few get-togethers, we began to relax with each other. Once, I asked him if he had grown up in the city. He told me he originally came from Queens and winced. He clearly didn't want to talk about it. Okay, he doesn't want to go there, I thought. No biggie.

A few weeks later, everything changed. Danny arrived at My Place looking grim and stressed out. His son Charlie had bitten one of his nursery school playmates when his favorite toy wasn't returned. The child's mother had made a big fuss, and Danny was pissed.

"She even took her kid to the doctor as if Charlie had rabies or something," he told me. "And then Charlie was booted out of school. Now we're going to have to find another childcare situation."

Danny felt he had somehow failed Charlie. Of course, that was hardly true.

"It's not easy being a father," he told me. "I had a bad role model. My father died a few years back. He was never much of a dad. He spent a few months in the slammer for domestic abuse against my mother."

Danny remembered many nights with doors slamming, shouting and cursing, and cries of pain. During these times, he made himself scarce. Once, he opened his bedroom door a crack and saw his mother on the ground as his father delivered blow after blow with steel-tipped work boots. Danny felt helpless as he watched her writhe and try to edge away.

"My mother always took the bastard back," Danny said, "even after he broke a few of her ribs. The police were useless, but who could blame them? My mother wouldn't press charges."

Danny didn't harbor fond feelings toward his mother, either. "She couldn't get up the nerve to leave him. Yeah, my mom and dad were the all-American couple, straight out of *Reader's Digest*."

He laughed bitterly. When he saw I wasn't laughing with him, he became serious. "By the time I turned 18, I was out of there. It wasn't a moment too soon."

Despite all the chaos at home, Danny managed to get excellent grades and received his acceptance letter from CCNY. Back then, the school was free for New York residents. He took a nighttime job and moved into a basement apartment owned by an elderly couple. In exchange for the room, he took on house maintenance duties. He also took a night job as a busboy to pay the bills. He never looked back.

It was his mixture of strength and vulnerability that made me start to fall for him. "You were just a kid," I told him. "You shouldn't have had to endure all that." I paused. "I understand what you went through. Pulling away from something like that took a lot of courage."

Danny stiffened, drawing back. "You think you really understand?" he said. "How could you possibly understand a family like mine?"

I sensed my next words would be crucial. But I was every bit as self-protective as Danny, so I held back. But I did offer up one thing.

"My father was absent growing up," I said.

The truth was far darker. From the time I was young, my father spent weeks – sometimes months – away from home. I'd miss him terribly. I loved his scent of Old Spice aftershave and the cherrywood from his pipe. The house smelled differently when he wasn't there. It was an absent smell.

Just as I was getting used to living without my father, I'd come home from school, and he was unexpectedly there again, waiting for me. His feet would be up on our sofa table, and he would puff away at his pipe. My dad would raise me in the air to greet me as if he had only seen me that morning.

I was always a daddy's girl. My name combines the names of both grandmothers, Josephine and Anna. My dad would always get dreamy when talking about his mother, Josephine, whom I never met. "She was a rare beauty, and you're her spitting image," he used to say to me.

So I was beautiful, and he loved me unconditionally! Our bond was far tighter than what he had with my brothers. I'd hand him the homework the teacher returned, with the circled A at the top. He'd shake his head playfully and say, "You're my smart little kitten."

I'd try to be the best girl I could be, cuddling in his lap, giggling as he blew smoke rings through my fingers. But I never knew when he would leave again. I would walk home from school one day, and he would be gone.

My mother was left to pick up the pieces. After he departed, it was like he had never been there. I knew better than to ask where he had gone and when he'd be back. My parents didn't argue. He wasn't home long enough or often enough. A big secret sat at the core of our household, like a ticking bomb ready to explode.

When I was 12, my mother received a letter, postmarked in Atlanta, from an unknown woman. She claimed to be my father's common-law wife and sent photos of her pretty two young daughters. (I looked much more like my mother).

"I've known about you for the last two years," the woman wrote my mother. "I am tired of living a lie and covering up his dual life. It's time to come clean and put an end to this secret, one way or the other."

My mom took her own time to tell us kids. Finding out my father had other daughters shook me to my core. I imagined each of them bringing him their homework and him saying, "Wow, all these A's! You're my smart little kittens." These girls were probably cleverer, more beautiful, and more cherished than I ever was.

I decided to become the most successful, brilliant, and desirable person I could be. Or at least I would appear that way to others. I put on quite an act. I feared that anyone who got too close would uncover my unworthy part. Once they found it, they could never truly love me.

I didn't tell Danny this whole story or let him know he was one of a handful of people who knew my story. But what I did share with him seemed to touch him deeply. That night, we went from casual friends to confidantes. He missed his train, and we talked for nearly three hours.

Reluctantly, he said he had to go. When he got up, we spontaneously hugged. It was hard to break away. Then he disappeared into the labyrinth of suburban-bound commuters. I wondered how he would explain his late arrival to his wife.

# CHAPTER 15

**DANNY**

I vowed to stop this thing right then and there. But I couldn't get Joanna out of my mind. I had lived so long in survival mode. Now, I felt truly energized and alive.

Even though I forced myself to do the right thing, I couldn't control my thoughts. I dreamed about her at night and fantasized about her during the day. On the rare occasions Sally and I made love, it was Joanna's face I saw.

I fought my desire for Joanna as long as possible. But after a particularly rough night at home, with Charlie screaming and Sally adding to the commotion, I couldn't resist any longer. I called her.

"Hey, I'm sorry I've been out of touch. It's been a busy time."

"No problem, it's been busy for me, too," she said.

"Wondering if you have time to meet at My Place to-night?" Before she could answer, I blurted out: "Or – how about – maybe we could go to your place instead?"

I gave a nervous chuckle. What was I doing? Had I over-stepped?

I didn't expect her answer to be casual: "Hmmm...okay. Sure. Do you need my address?"

Quickly, I scribbled it down. This was going to happen! It was hard to focus on the endless meetings. I kept glancing at my watch. One of my co-workers caught me in the men's room for the second time that afternoon, running my comb through my hair and staring at my reflection. He laughed out loud and, in a falsetto voice, began singing, "I feel pret-ty...oh so pretty..."

By the time I showed up at Joanna's door, I was petrified. I didn't know what to expect. Sally was the only lover I ever had, and we weren't – shall we say – overly experimental. Certainly, someone like Joanna expected something more than to link up with a confused married man. But maybe she was between boyfriends and bored.

I knocked, she opened up, and our mouths immediately found each other's. Her hair was soft and silky and smelled like fresh berries and the autumn earthy tone of sandalwood. And her skin was so soft.

Silently, she led me into her bedroom. I barely took in the soft white-painted walls, large bay windows, abstract paint-ings, and queen-size bed. All of this was a mere backdrop to the vision laying before me.

I don't think I've ever seen such a beautiful woman. Her body was a wonderland: her flat stomach, slender waist, slender legs, and full breasts tipped with dark nipples. And she wanted me as desperately as I wanted her.

Our time together was like having every one of my fantasies come true. An eruption was building in my groin and up into my shaft. She gripped me tighter until every part of me quivered. It was a pent-up release, like putting a finger over the head of a hose and then letting go.

Afterward, I felt more exhausted – in a good way – than I'd ever been. It felt unbelievably fantastic. I didn't want it to end. But it had to end.

As far back as I can remember, I always believed the people I liked would eventually figure out who I was and walk away. Would this happen with Joanna? If I were going to end up stupid and vulnerable, it would be better to exit now. To get back to my wife and son.

But this thing with Joanna had a life of its own. It was crazy. I didn't want to be with Sally. I just wanted to be with Joanna.

An instinct for self-preservation told me: Danny Boy, bad idea! My inner voice has always served me well, but this time it was beaten. My willpower was now the size of a pea. That was definitely not a good thing.

# CHAPTER 16

## JOANNA

From the moment Danny and I left My Place, a new chapter in our relationship was in the making. Seeing him the next time was like being caught in a video freeze frame. All my energy was so focused on his face that the rest of the scene – the bar, the other chatting customers, the ring of the cash register – faded into the background.

"I have this personal issue I'm dealing with," I told Danny.

I was seeing an environmental consultant named Gregg. He had begun asking for a greater commitment. At the very least, living together. When I pushed back, he asked me why.

Taking on an analytical role, Gregg tried to understand me. He knew I emphatically rejected traditional suburban life. That wasn't his thing, either. He offered an exciting alternative – an urban life filled with cultural activities, art openings, and music. If that wasn't what I wanted, what did

I want? Why did I seem so unwilling to accept his genuine affection for me?

He finally spat out, "Be honest with me, Joanna. Are you one of those women who never wants to settle down? I really care about you, but I'm not going to waste my time if we're not coming from the same place."

I told Danny I wasn't exactly sure what I wanted to do with Gregg. We had been seeing each other for a little over a year.

Danny gazed at me with those mesmerizing blue eyes. "Okay, I'm not going to encourage or discourage you from staying with Gregg. I don't have the right. That's a decision you need to make. But I will ask you a few questions. Maybe it will help you come to a decision."

"Okay, shoot."

"First, how much are you attracted to Gregg?"

"Well, a bit, I think." I blushed and avoided eye contact with Danny. He smirked and made it clear he was enjoying my discomfort.

"Okay, let's say you move in with him. What will it be like three years from now when he's sitting there in his boxers and undershirt with a few days of beard growth?

"I sort of like beards," I said, my eyes lingering on Danny's.

Danny reflexively reached for his chin and blushed. "Okay, moving on. What would happen if you came to realize you made the wrong choice and you're already married to him?"

"Doesn't sound like you have such a great view of marriage."

"What? No, I'm not speaking about my own marriage," Danny said. "We're talking about Gregg here. Marriage can be a long slog. It's never exactly what you think. You have to be prepared."

"Okay, you're confirming what I need to do," I said. "I'm going to let Gregg go."

After I met with Gregg and gave him the news, I felt free to become more flirtatious with Danny. He turned out to be the master of sexual innuendos.

I knew where we were heading, but I wasn't going to take the first step. A few days later, he called.

"So, how about meeting tonight? Should we go to My Place again?" Then he paused.

"Or...," he said tentatively. I could almost hear the wheels turning. "Maybe this time, we should try your place?"

At that moment, everything changed.

Danny recalls we fell into each other's arms, but it wasn't like that. He was visibly nervous. He high tailed it straight from the door to my living room couch and sat down, running his hands through his hair and staring straight ahead. Every so often, he stole a sidelong glance at me.

I felt uneasy, too. If something was going to happen, I didn't want him to blame me for starting it. I wanted the first move to come from him.

I sat down next to him.

Still averting my eyes, he croaked: "What do you want to do?"

I couldn't stand it any longer. "This," I whispered. I gently pressed my lips onto his.

We fumbled a little bit, but his tongue was strong and probing. We were both gasping. The lovemaking that followed was electrifying. We undressed each other, and I loved seeing him unclothed. But he wasn't really naked until he took off his wedding ring and placed it inside his pocket. I never saw him wear it again.

We fit so well. He was all hardness, and I was all softness – his long, muscular fingers opening and exploring my yielding and wet opening. I explored each inch of his body, even the imperfections – the series of brown moles on his back, his appendix scar, and another nasty and uneven scar below his breastbone.

We met each other's eyes and smiled. And the sex, oh my, the sex, the easy way our two bodies recognized and claimed each other's. Feeling him throbbing deep inside me like a beating heart, tasting the saltiness on his heated skin. Some moments in life you never forget.

Once we had reached this point, there could be no going back. We were both silent as we dressed afterward.

"Just so you know, I'm never leaving Sally until Charlie is grown," he said.

"I'm not going to make you do that," I replied. "And just so you know, I'm not taking on the role of the other woman."

We believed each other. Still, what we had took on a life of its own. We'd meet every couple of weeks at my place. We never planned ahead, nor did we ever introduce the word "love" into the equation.

# CHAPTER 17

## DANNY

I felt euphoric when I left Joanna's place. Her high-pitched mewls of pleasure, the feeling of being surrounded by her warmth. I never knew anything could be so amazing.

That feeling lasted until the train pulled into the station. By then, one emotion overpowered all others: intense guilt.

I kept interrogating myself: what did I just do? What kind of man betrays his wife that easily? What's going to happen now? What if Joanna starts calling me at home? Or if Sally finds out? What have I set into motion?

When I arrived home, I decided to be extra kind to Sally. She and Charlie were sitting on the living room floor, working on a puzzle, a box of Dunkin' Donuts in front of them.

"Hey, little buddy! Hi, Sally. You look great!" I kissed her lightly on the top of her head.

Munching on a doughnut with her glasses halfway down her nose, Sally glanced down at the new turquoise sweats she had purchased at Target. "Oh, these things?" I was rewarded with a tentative smile.

I bent down to Charlie and picked him up. Swinging him around the room, I gave him a loud kiss and hoisted him down.

He yelped for joy. "Giddyap, Daddy!"

"Someone looks like he had a very good day," Sally observed, cleaning her glasses on her sweats. "Little on the late side, but I guess you've had to work long hours lately."

"Yes. I think there'll be less of that now. I had this major project. Pretty much wrapped up. Glad to be back home."

"Well, pardner, we're glad to see ya," Sally drawled.

We went to the living room. I let myself fall onto the couch, watching my wife and son, who were absorbed in locating a missing puzzle piece.

"Tell me, how was the playground today?" I asked.

"Since when were you interested in our time at the playground?" Sally said. "It was all right, the usual, I guess."

Later, I tucked Charlie into bed and read him a story. Then Sally and I went to bed.

"Come here," I said. "I'm sorry I've been so absent lately." I reached for her, but she pulled away.

"Good thought, but too tired. Can we take a raincheck?".

"Sure, honey, that's okay." I wouldn't have had anything left, anyway.

I couldn't get to sleep, so I went downstairs and turned on the TV, lowering the volume. Nothing to watch, just talk shows. I picked up the last Sunday's newspaper and brought it to the kitchen table. I absently read it all the way through, even the clip-out ads.

When Sally drove Charlie to a playdate the next morning, I called Joanna.

She answered on the first ring. "Oh, hey."

"We can't do this all the time," I said. "Not regularly, I mean."

"Okay, Danny." I heard her sigh.

"I'm not going to leave my wife," I said.

"Understood. Got it. Anything else?"

"No. Well, yes. I enjoyed our time together. Damn, that sounds lame! Look, I loved last night. I just can't make it a regular thing."

Joanna chuckled. "Relax, Danny," she said. "I won't clear out half of my closet just yet so you can move in. Now, why don't you enjoy your weekend, and we'll talk...whenever. Whenever you're up to it. Okay? I promise you won't find me camping out on your steps tonight."

I got off the phone, embarrassed but with a sense of relief. That, too, didn't last long. The thing is, I wanted it to happen again. I wanted it very much. But it was wrong, pure and simple. Certainly, it wasn't going to lead anywhere good.

# CHAPTER 18

## JOANNA

I predicted Danny would call the following day and say we should slow things down. I was right.

"I'm not going to leave Sally." These were the first words out of his mouth. "Maybe we should lay low for a while."

"Sure, Danny, whatever you want," I said. I put on my cool-and-calm act. I was pretty sure this wouldn't be the last time we would make love. That is if I didn't spook him out.

We didn't talk for a while after that. He didn't call, and I wasn't going to call him. I was aching to see him but knew the consequences of acting too needy.

His next call came after a couple of weeks. It ended with, "Can you meet me at My Place?"

I got to the bar early, wondering what state of mind he'd be in. I was watching the door and saw him enter. He took my breath away – so handsome and casual, with his reddish-blonde hair and ruddy complexion. He smiled shyly.

"Glad you called when you did," I deadpanned. "I was about to redesign my bedroom so you could move in. What side of the bed do you prefer?"

Danny shot a quizzical look at me, then laughed out loud.

"I know it's been a long time since we last saw each other," he said. "I've had a lot going on. I can't meet with you all the time, just to let you know."

"I hope you don't use that line on your new clients," I said. "You're a great fit, but I can't meet with you all the time. I'm really busy!'"

"Oh, I didn't want it to come off like that," he said. "I really enjoyed, um, the time we spent together. I'm just trying to understand what you're looking for. I'm a married man."

"Yes, I know, you're a married man. Really, Danny, can't you take it easy a little bit? As the song says." I sang a few lines of the Eagles melody: "Lighten up when you still can; don't even try to understand."

Danny perked up and sang another line from the song: "I've got to know if your sweet love is going to save me."

I laughed, but he didn't. "I think I do want to know," he said.

I reached out and took his hand. "Don't try to overthink it right now. I don't know what will happen, but I'll tell you this much: I'm not trying to own you or anything. I hate to think you're spending your time tossing and turning – at least when you're not with me!"

He chuckled. Then he said: "I just have to be careful. I'm not ready to...I don't want to mess up with her. Perhaps we could meet next Wednesday. Sally is taking Charlie to her sister's for dinner. I could come over to your place. That is if you're okay with it."

"Wednesday night is fine," I said, figuring out how I was going to get out of a dinner. "Make sure you get some rest between now and then." I shot him a wicked smile.

"Then I'll see you next Wednesday," he said, a little cheerier.

"I should be getting back," I told him. I needed to attend to a few things – such as rearranging my dinner plans.

Danny still had time before his train, so I was the first to leave the bar. When I glanced back from the door, I saw him assessing me. He looked a little puzzled and a little smitten at the same time. I liked that.

# CHAPTER 19

**DANNY**

So many times, I've asked myself:

What if Joanna had never walked into Cooper, Masters & Young that October day?

What if I hadn't acknowledged Joanna on the train a few weeks later? Or what if I simply nodded at her and went back to reading my paper?

What if, after the first time at My Place, I simply told her I was uncomfortable meeting this way and wished her well?

What if I hadn't blurted out, "Or maybe we could go to your place?" Or turned it into some punchline as soon as the words were out of my mouth?

And what if, when I reached for her and pulled her close to me, she hadn't said, "Yes. Yes. Oh please. Yes."

# CHAPTER 20

**JOANNA**

I left My Place feeling triumphant – there would be a next time with Danny after all – and strangely nonplussed.

I kept thinking of Danny's question: where did I want this to go?

I would be pushing 30 in a few months. It wasn't as if I didn't have many men wanting to go out with me. I was aware of my own star power. I had gone out with men who other women would kill to date: not only Gregg but also a distinguished Columbia professor of game sciences, an executive director of an art museum, and even an up-and-coming politician on the New York scene.

All had been crazy about me. Any would have shared the life I claimed to want – a life filled with adventure, travel, and the good things. I was on an upward trajectory myself. The media was taking notice of my production firm. I was primed to be made a partner. I lived in the most fantastic city in the world. And I was taking New York City by storm, bringing in one major account after the other.

Why did I want Danny? What was it about him I needed so badly?

The chemistry was undeniable. Did I want a passionate fling for a while? Maybe, but it seemed more than that. He had taken up permanent occupancy in my mind. I wanted him any way I could get him with a force that surprised me.

I wondered if it was a coincidence that I had begun to have increasingly intense thoughts of my father, who left me and my family some 15 years ago. Something about my relationship with Danny seemed to trigger memories of the past.

One of them kept haunting me: when my mother got the letter from my father's common-law wife. My mother sat me and my brothers down in the kitchen and explained the situation.

"Seems your father wants two different families," she said. "But that's not the way it works. You deserve more, and so do I. You will not be seeing any more of him. He will no longer be part of our lives."

I began to cry. "Can't he just come back? What if he's really sorry? You said we should always forgive someone who apologizes. I miss him, mom!"

"You can miss him all you want," my mother stated. "But you will not see him. Joanna, I forbid it."

What was a 12-year-old girl supposed to do? I had no idea how to contact him. I didn't know then that the letter was postmarked in Atlanta. I fantasized about saving my allowance and hiring a private detective to find out where he lived. Of course, I didn't have the means to do it.

I thought about my dad every day throughout my teenage years but had no contact with him. He didn't call or write, even on my birthday or Christmas. Finally, in my first year at Hunter College, my mother decided I was old enough to know where he was.

"He's living in Alpharetta, Georgia, not far from Atlanta," she said. "I thought you should know." She angrily added, "He's been married to that woman for all these years."

I visited the New York City Public Library and looked up the White Pages for Alpharetta. There he was. I had his address now. One of my college friends planned a trip to visit cousins in Atlanta that summer. I asked to go with her.

I had made some money selling Avon products on the side. It would be enough to rent a car in Georgia and stay a few nights at the Days Inn in downtown Alpharetta. Once I got there, I didn't waste a minute. I drove to his home, a ranch house located on a quiet, leafy street. It had a garage and a large fenced backyard. I parked the car across the road and waited.

Eventually, a black Chevy Camaro emerged from the garage. I saw two figures in the front and two in the back. I followed the car to a place called Stone Mountain Park. My father emerged in a red T-shirt and plaid shorts. He was whistling and carrying a picnic basket and blanket. Two girls in their mid-teens flew out of the car. A small, unassuming woman took a little more time to emerge.

"Josie!" my father called out to one of the girls. She stuck out her tongue at him. So, my father's new daughter was also named after his beloved mother, Josephine. My little replacement. Josie was beautiful, slim, and wiry, with my father's red-blonde hair flowing down her back in curls.

I walked behind them to their picnic site and watched them spread their blanket and table. Then I left and went back to my motel room. The next day, I drove to the house again. This time, I rang the front doorbell. Josie opened the door and peered at me inquisitively.

"I'm here to see your dad," I said in a quivering voice.

She stared at me for a minute, turned, and hollered, "Dad! Someone's here to see you."

My father came to the door and stopped in his tracks when he saw me. It was hard to decipher what he was thinking. Was he fearful, ashamed, or maybe a little pleased?

"Joanna," he said unsteadily. "Won't you come in?"

He led me to his den. The side table was filled with photos of family outings and close-ups of the girls. His second wife was nowhere in sight, but I could hear the girls whispering to each other in the living room.

He closed the door. "I don't know what to say." His voice trailed off. It had a different timbre than I remembered. He tried to smile. "You're so grown-up and beautiful. I've missed you a lot."

"How come you never tried contacting me, then?"

"Your mother – well, she thought it best that I keep my distance. I agreed with her."

"Not even a Christmas card."

"It must have been hard for you. But it had to be a clean break."

My voice shattered. "Why, Dad? Why did you want to leave us?"

He shifted in his chair. "Oh, honey, it's so complicated. I loved you to the moon and back."

"So how did this happen, this second family and all?"

"I never went into this thinking it would come to this. I met Brenda on a sales trip. Oh, you don't want to hear this. It was just a fling. I never expected it to last, but she got pregnant. I had the best intentions. I wanted to help Brenda through the first months. Somehow, I kept going down there again and again and..."

"And mom didn't know anything about it!"

"No, only when Brenda sent the letter years later. I was struggling because I gradually realized I loved Brenda, but I didn't want to lose your mother. I loved her, too. Then Heather came along. I had two families, and I was caught in the middle."

He produced that winning salesman smile and threw his hands up in a modest shrug. As if he expected me to have sympathy for his "dilemma."

"Do Josie and Heather know about me?" I asked. "And about Mom and the boys?"

"Brenda knows, of course. But Josie and Heather, no. Their mom and I thought it would be best if they didn't know about you guys. Yet."

Of course, I didn't know about them, either, until yesterday. "You didn't think we'd want to look you up?" I was shaking. "What the hell, Dad?"

"No need to raise your voice, Joanna. As I was trying to tell you, your mom, Brenda, and I agreed it would be best for all the kids if we made a clean break. That way, you and your brothers wouldn't have to be burdened with the mess I made of everything. And the girls would have some security. Then, when you were older, I could begin seeing you again. We were thinking of all of you and how best to salvage this."

"Meanwhile, you had Josie and Heather. You chose them over me. That's what it comes down to, right?"

"Oh, Joanna. Please don't think of it like that. Look how good you turned out."

I stood up and approached the den door.

My father sighed. "Here's the exciting thing. You're here now! Let's start where we left off," he said. "You and I can have dinner together tonight. We'll go to a nice restaurant. But I think I need to wait to tell Josie and Heather. They're still young, and ..."

I had heard enough. I went out the front door and didn't look back.

# CHAPTER 21

**DANNY**

We were consumed with lovemaking in those early days. It felt like Joanna and I had invented it.

I met Joanna at her place between the end of the work-day and the train ride home to Sally and Charlie. She was wildly imaginative about our arranged get-togethers. I loved her wicked imagination. The maid's costume. The handcuffs. Nothing was off limits with her.

Except talking about our pasts.

After our initial conversations, I didn't want to dwell more on my family, and Joanna was closed off about hers, too. We seemed to silently agree that the former part of our lives was off-limits. So I was surprised when she started to probe one evening.

We were lying next to each other, all spent and giddy. She raised herself up and peered earnestly at me. "Remember not long after we first met, and you told me how you grew up?

I've been thinking about that. I want to know more about you, Danny Monahan."

I tried to keep a neutral expression. "You really want to know?"

"Yes, I do! I want to hear more about what it was like with your parents. How did you break away from them?"

Okay, I thought. She wants to hear about the whole agonizing mess that was my childhood. Here goes.

"Alright, my old man was a real bastard, mostly to my mother. I don't think they belonged together, but maybe, in a way, they did."

"How did they meet?" Joanna asked.

"Believe it or not, in church. My dad was a toddler when my grandparents brought him here from County Cork. My mom was the second generation. Her name was Rosalie, and he called her his little Irish rose. But I don't think she ever really loved him. Her closest friends were marrying, and she didn't want to be left out."

"So they paired up, and along came Danny."

"No, it wasn't like that. It took a while before I came into the picture. He wanted to have lots of kids. She was good at getting pregnant but not so good at carrying the baby to term. My mom had four miscarriages before I came. It was a hard birth for her. They told her it would be dangerous to have any more."

"Wow. Didn't you once tell me that happened to Sally, too? The miscarriages?"

"Did I? Well, it's actually more complicated. But it did take us a while before Charlie. History has a way of repeating itself."

"Ouch. Sorry," Joanna said.

"Shit happens. I was an only child, and my father worked two jobs. He was an electrical contractor. He also took on some construction work. But he never brought in enough money to satisfy her. 'Why are we still stuck in Queens?' she'd ask. 'Why can't we move closer to my cousin Elsie on the Island? The schools are better, the houses are newer, and the neighborhood is much safer.'

"You see, Elsie was kind of a sister to her. She lived in Levittown. When my mother visited, her head would become filled with what a perfect life she'd have if only she would convince my father to move there. Whenever my parents fought, my mom would tell him she wanted to take me and move near Elsie. That drove him crazy. He'd grab a beer...then another...and soon the hard stuff. She would, too. Before long, they'd both be soused, and it all headed south fast."

"And then he'd hit her."

"Plenty of times, she'd get a bloody nose or a black eye or a dislocated shoulder or whatever. She'd stumble away to some other part of the house. He'd move over to his La-Z-Boy, staring into space. Shaking his head as if he were the one who needed sympathy."

"He really was a bastard."

"Yeah, but I can't say she was entirely blameless. I kept wondering, why didn't she ever shut up about Long Island? And why didn't she ever stand up for herself?"

"Well, no one deserves that kind of treatment. As a kid, you must have been confused. And frightened by it all. I can't even imagine."

Danny let out a harsh laugh. "Hell, yes! My dad was a huge guy, stocky and over six feet tall. I hadn't even started my growth spurt yet. He could easily have done to me what he did to her. But he didn't. I figured he loved me in his own crazy way. I was his boy. Whatever that meant to him."

I'm usually reticent about my childhood. But the sun was setting outside Joanna's window, and I knew I had to leave soon and catch the train. I felt sad. And reflective. I wanted her to know what she was getting into. So, I began sharing the story I had yet to reveal. Not even to my own wife.

"I couldn't invite friends over because things could blow up at my place. My friends and I played at a deserted construction site several blocks away. We were all about 12 or so. It's the time when kids begin to go a little wild. None of us drank before. We got it into our heads to try some beer. One of the kids said he'd try to get his older brother to buy us some.

"That's when I piped up with, 'Hey, I've got a better idea.'

"My father kept these six-packs in a shed behind our house. I told my friends I would sneak into the shed, grab a six-pack, and bring it to the construction site. He had so many stacked up he wouldn't know one was missing. Then we'd get nice and drunk. We would sober up before we were due back for dinner. What a plan!

"We were living right off Ditmars Avenue in an old bungalow with a forest green and white awning, a small backyard, and a padlocked shed. The same guy with the older brother said I should take my time. In an hour or so, he and his brother would drive over, pick me up – we wanted to avoid neighbors seeing us walking in broad daylight with the beer – and meet up with the other guys.

"My luck – that would be the day my father would come home early from his union job. He had just been laid off, but I had no way of knowing. He caught me red-handed. I knew I was in a shitload of trouble. If I had any doubt, I knew for sure when he reached behind me and locked the shed's door.

"'Stealing my beer, you little shit,' he muttered. He closed the door and began to undo his belt. Then he stopped. "Nah. Not this time. You're going to drink every one of these Buds you were going to snitch. And I will sit right here and make sure you do it."

"Inside, it was dark and cramped, with his work tools spread across the table and the smell of mold and turpentine in the air. He forced me down in a chair across from him. Then he slammed down the first bottle on the table between us. I had never had a beer before but didn't want to let on. I picked up the bottle and chugged it as best I could.

"He pushed the next one onto the table. It took me longer to finish, and I started to feel bloated. But I'd be damned if I let him know."

Joanna didn't say a word. She reached for my hand and tightened her fingers around it.

"My dad gazed at me stonily and handed me the third can. This was going to be more challenging than I thought. I burped and tried to hold back the urge to pee. My bladder ached something fierce. I stood up to go outdoors, but he slammed me back into the chair.

"'Gotta pee,'" I protested.

"'You got to finish first. All six of them. Now sit the fuck down.'

"I drank the third bottle and started on the fourth. I felt a stream of sticky urine flowing down my leg. My jeans turned dark and wet. Joanna, are you sure you want me to go on?"

Joanna gave a barely perceptible nod. She lay next to me, frozen, barely moving a muscle.

"So I started whimpering, but he wasn't about to relent. 'Take the next one,' he barked.

"Halfway through the fifth bottle, I doubled over and barfed, my jeans now stinking with the smell of urine and vomit. When I stooped over, heaving, he demanded I keep going. When I wouldn't, he forced my head back, pushed open my mouth, and poured the contents down my throat. I gagged, cried, and heaved.

"Then the final bottle. When it was over, he got up, left me lying there, and padlocked the shed behind him. At midnight, he came back, pulled me to the house, made me take off all my clothes, and threw me under a cold shower. I sputtered and threw up what remained in my stomach.

"He tossed me a towel. 'Go to bed,' he said. 'Tomorrow morning will be here fast, and I don't care how bad you feel. You're going the fuck to school. Now quit crying like a girl and listen to me: I'm not going to watch my son turn into a bum like me.' That's one of the more heartwarming stories about him. It's the reason I don't drink."

Joanna had tears in her eyes. "Oh baby," she whispered.

I pulled away and looked at my watch. "Hardly a nighttime children's lullaby. But that was my childhood. Now I better get up and get dressed if I'm going to catch the next train."

I wondered what Joanna thought about everything I'd told her. She seemed about to say something for a moment and thought better of it. When I left her apartment, she kissed me gently on the mouth.

On the way to Grand Central, I began to have doubts again. "I told her too much," I thought. "No one can process all that. And no one can love a man who went through those kinds of things."

# CHAPTER 22

## JOANNA

After Danny shared that unsettling childhood story, I felt closer to him than ever. I suspected he was having second thoughts about revealing too much. He needn't have worried.

What did I see in Danny? He was handsome, witty, sweet, and tantalizingly private, like a gift package I wanted to open up. I could sense this hurt little boy side of him that made me want to scoop him up, cuddle him, and make everything alright. Gradually, a deeper answer took shape: I knew the clandestine plans and confidences I shared with Danny were risky for him. And that revealed he wanted me very much – the way I needed to be wanted. I believed Danny and I would end up together, even though he swore would never leave Sally.

Inevitably, he would leave her. But for that to happen, I would have to make myself so irresistible he wouldn't be able to live without me. I was good at that. I'd done that all my life. Deep down, I felt unworthy but would never let it show.

Danny and I had no past and no future. We focused all our energy on the now. We gorged ourselves with sex. But no matter how satiated we became, there remained an empty part deep down inside us that wanted more.

Increasingly, we took more chances. I'd go to the restroom in the bar, and he would follow me. He'd push me against the stall door and enter me while we were standing up. We'd emerge, scarlet-faced, to a line of people and some disapproving stares.

We became experts at deception. We'd duck into a Gap store, gather a few clothes for our ruse, and head for the fitting room. We only later realized a security camera had probably recorded our lovemaking. We would lie to our bosses about an urgent client matter or a doctor's appointment and dash over to my place for a quickie.

On the weekend, Danny would tell Sally he was going out jogging and meet up with me. One time, he woke up next to her around midnight and "remembered" he had left an essential document in the office for an early on-site client meeting. He raced down to the city and knocked on my door. We furtively made love before he headed back home. He was exhausted the next day, but he pulled it off.

We were familiar with every inch of each other and every thought in each other's head. But what did we really know about each other? I began to realize I was looking for an idealized relationship, just like I had done years ago with my father. Both gave me the love and attention I craved when I was with them. Both were also absent much of the time. Their loyalty was to others.

# CHAPTER 23

## JOANNA

Danny told me he had a meet-up date with his childhood friend and neighbor, Maureen. They planned to get together on Friday night at The Campbell Apartment – a restaurant in the former Campbell's Soup Company offices at Rockefeller Plaza.

"I've told you about her," he said. "She's the one who lived next door to me when I was growing up. I'd like you to meet her. Want to join us?"

"Does she know about…" I said, trailing off.

"Nothing gets past Maureen. Yeah, she knows. It's okay. Believe me, she's not the kind of person who will judge what we're up to. I think you two will like each other."

Danny was right. I liked Maureen from the get-go. She had one of those wide-open faces with a direct gaze and a warm smile. Her brown hair was short and curly, and she wore a no-frills suit. (Danny had told me she was a social worker at a non-profit providing child welfare services).

Danny and I sat facing each other, and Maureen slid in next to me. We ordered quickly: roasted chicken with mashed potatoes for Danny, salmon, and French fries for Maureen, and I decided on the shrimp scampi. Once the drinks were served – Danny ordered a Coke, and Maureen and I asked for a glass of Chardonnay – we relaxed and started hitting our stride.

Or Danny and Maureen did. I was still a bit nervous. They laughed at old childhood memories: the Entenmann truck showing up in their neighborhood, the time they got on their bikes and followed it until the driver shooed them away, and Maureen's family dog, who followed Danny around like she was in heat for him.

"Look at us now," Maureen said. "All grown up." She asked (overly politely, I thought) about Sally and Charlie. Danny's answer was non-committal, switching to some home improvement project he was working on.

Maureen countered with a story about the challenges of raising her pre-teen daughter. She mimicked her so well we all started laughing. With some gentle prodding, I added in a few memories of my own, and pretty soon, it felt like we were three old friends catching up.

Maureen talked me into splitting the Grand Marnier Soufflé or the Profiteroles with Chocolate Sauce. As we debated the merits of each choice, Danny glanced at his watch.

"Damn, I've gotta go," he said. "I promised Sally I'd be on the 8:16 train."

"But Danny…", Maureen said in an exaggerated parody. "There's a pay phone right outside. I'll even give you some change. Call her and tell her you're taking the next train." She rolled her eyes at me, and Danny grimaced.

"Sorry. I promised. Why don't the two of you order dessert and linger? I'll take care of the bill on my way out."

He stood up. Maureen got up and embraced Danny before he took off. I stayed seated. I felt uncomfortable showcasing our relationship in front of Maureen.

"Love you, Danny Boy," she said. "Don't let yourself get too PW-ed."

Once Danny was out the door, Maureen moved to the other side of the table, so we were facing each other.

"What is PW-ed?" I asked her.

"Pussy whipped." Maureen laughed. "She sure keeps him on a tight leash. I'm amazed the two of you are pulling it off."

I squirmed a little, but her eyes were kind. "Look, there's no particular love between me and Sally. I'm no great fan of the holier-than-thou McAllisters," she confided. "I met Sally a few times when they were dating and right after the wedding. It didn't take much for me to get the picture.

"She thought she owned Danny, hook, line, and sinker. She's never been too thrilled about me, even though I've never been more than a friend."

It was fascinating to hear Maureen's angle on Danny's life.

"I think Danny believed the McAllisters were a kind of salvation for him," she went on. "A way to escape the life he grew up in. He's been under their spell ever since. I never thought he had the balls to stand up to them, and now here you are."

I avoided her gaze and changed the topic a little. "Danny said you helped him out a lot when you were kids. He told me all about his childhood, with his dad and all. I'm impressed he's doing so well."

Maureen appraised me. "Do you think Danny escaped unscathed?"

"Oh, I'm sure he didn't. There must be a lot of emotional scars."

She was silent for a while. "Let me give you a fuller version. I know I'm talking out of turn, but I think you should know."

She certainly had my attention now.

"My backyard was right across from the Monahans. We always heard the rising voices and the crashes and, now and then, the police sirens. When it was going on, Danny would often sneak over to our place to get away. He was always welcome at our home.

"One night, it got particularly bad. We heard these slaps and thuds and loud screams. My mom was concerned. "Should we call the police?' she asked my dad. 'I don't think so,' he said. 'Unless Rosalie – that's Danny's mom – is willing to press charges, it won't do any good.'

"Danny came over the following day. He was 13 at the time. I was three years older, which can be a massive gap at that age, but we had a good understanding. I was watching Gilligan's Island on TV. Without a word, he sat down beside me. We ate some homemade brownies my mother had made the night before. The phone rang, and it was my boyfriend. I went into the kitchen and talked to him for 15 or 20 minutes, leaving Danny alone. When I got back, he was gone.

"That happened sometimes. He would suddenly take off. So I shrugged and went to use the bathroom. I found him in there. He was just finishing doing his business. His pants were down, and his butt was toward me. I saw all the welts on it. Some were oozing with blood, and some were healing.

"He quickly hitched himself up and brushed past me. He looked so shamefaced! He probably wished the floor would swallow him up. I eventually rejoined him at the TV. He wouldn't look at me.

"We never discussed that incident – not then, not now. We had an unspoken agreement. I would never bring up anything unless he did. That didn't happen. But Danny knew I knew. I figured out pretty early on that he, too, was a victim of the violence in that house.

"Sometime after, Danny's dad was particularly brutal. He broke Rosalie's collarbone and smashed her face. That time, she finally did press charges. His old man was arrested and went to prison.

"I love Danny like a younger brother. He went through hell. I became a social worker partly because of what I saw happening at the Monahans. What he needs is someone to love him unconditionally for who he is, not for what someone wants him to be. That's different from what the McAllisters are offering.

"Okay, I better shut up now. Danny says I need to stop talking constantly, and he's right. He can be guarded, but that doesn't mean he doesn't care for you. You must be very important to him if he's willing to risk his life with Sally."

There were tears in my eyes now. We finished our desserts and looked at each other. Maureen placed her hand over mine. "I think I upset you, but I care about Danny."

"Oh, no, really," I said, wiping my eyes. "I'm glad you told me."

"I always feel I have to advocate for someone who has been hurt. It's an occupational hazard. You may just be what Danny is looking for." She paused. "I hope so."

# CHAPTER 24

**DANNY**

I wished I could have lingered at the restaurant. I was concerned about what Maureen would tell Joanna after I was gone. She loved to talk – too much, in my opinion. But I was under a strict curfew. If I came home late again, Sally would have been furious. She was already suspicious about my comings and goings.

When I stepped inside our home, the first thing I heard was Sally's raised voice in the kitchen. She was staring Charlie down from across the table. Her glasses were propped up on her hair, and her bangs hung limply around her face. She had been wearing the same damn sweatpants and sweatshirt for three days running.

"Charles Francis Monahan, you're in for it now," she said. "Your daddy's home, and he won't tolerate this behavior." She turned to me as I entered the room. "Daddy, you won't believe what your son just did."

I turned to him. "What did you just do, little buddy?"

"Daddy, I hate that stupid meatloaf. Mommy puts tomatoes in it, and she knows I hate it! I'll throw up again if I eat it. I dumped it in the garbage, and Mommy's mad."

I chuckled at Charlie's melodramatics. That didn't sit well with Sally.

"You think it's hilarious? I spent all that time preparing dinner, and Charlie wouldn't eat it. Then he defied me and tossed it away. He knows that's wrong."

I couldn't completely wipe the grin off my face.

"That's funny for you?" she said. "Let me tell you what's not funny. Being stuck here with a brat who willfully disobeys me. Then you waltz in here, hours after your workday ends, and laugh with him at my expense!"

I didn't know who was acting more like a brat, but I dutifully defended my wife. "Charlie, I know you don't like tomatoes in your meatloaf. The time you threw up was because you ate three brownies before dinner without permission, not because of the tomatoes. You don't have the right to throw good food into the garbage. Apologize to your mother now. Then it's off to bed with you."

"You heard your father," Sally screamed.

Charlie burst into tears. "I'm not going to apologize to her. Never! She's MEAN!"

Sally's face darkened. "Charles Francis, go to your room now and think about what you've done!"

Charlie ran out of the room sobbing. I followed him out, and then came Sally.

133

"I want to talk with you," she said. "This is not working. I'm getting zero help from you."

"Sally, enough! Why do I not race back home as soon as the workday ends? It's this. Walking into a scene like this every night is not pleasant.

"Oh, I'm sorry if dealing with your son is unpleasant for you," Sally jeered.

"Sally, get a grip!"

Her voice turned cold. "Maybe these scenes wouldn't happen so often if you would step up and be a father once in a while. Maybe Charlie wouldn't act out all the time."

I went upstairs, took my time showering, and got ready for bed. I laid down with my back away from her. A while later, I heard her enter the room and stand over me for a moment. I pretended to be asleep. She took off her clothes and got into bed.

Soon, I could hear her snoring. I was wide awake, thinking of Joanna. How I wished she was beside me. I moved my hand down to my erect penis. With my wife lying next to me, I brought myself to climax.

With my passion spent on thoughts of Joanna, I drifted into sleep. But only after making a resolution: it was time I took the leap and explored whether Joanna and I could make it as a couple. I owed it to Joanna.

Yeah, right. I owed it to myself!

# CHAPTER 25

## JOANNA

My days fell into a pattern. I felt happy and energized when I was together with Danny or planning to see him soon. Otherwise, I was living in some limbo. I couldn't even pretend I had control over the situation. He had become my everything.

I lulled myself into thinking it could go on like this. Then things changed.

Evan got an offer too lucrative to resist, and Danny was promoted to take his place. He was now the senior vice president of accounts. In his new perch, he fell into the good graces of Reba Knauss, the recently appointed wunderkind of the P&G skin and personal care division.

Danny was awed he had her ear. When he spoke about her, his tone became almost worshipful.

I would have been jealous were it not that she was nearly a decade older than him and, I believed, part of a well-established power couple. Still, he spent a lot of time working with her, sometimes way into the night. Those meetings took away from the time he and I spent together. At the same time, I recognized the extra hours and work that came along with the promotion.

My worries took on a life of their own. It wasn't enough I had Sally to contend with; now there was Reba, too. One day, an acquaintance told me she ran into Danny and Reba talking animatingly over a glass of wine one night at a trendy restaurant. Then I read in the Society column that Reba's husband – some big deal in the cosmetics business – had just filed for divorce.

On one of our rare nights together, Danny retold a story he had heard from Reba. I got teary-eyed. I hated for him to see me like this, but it was time I knew where I stood.

"Tell me straight out," I said. "Are you attracted to Reba?"

Danny looked at me as if I had gone daft. "Joanna, where is this coming from? Reba is my client. She's nearly ten years older than me. She's officially still married! What's going on with you?"

I told Danny what I had heard. "Yeah, it was a late night of work. We were both getting bleary-eyed. She suggested we have a glass of wine rather than keep plugging away in the office. It's work, Joanna. That's all it is."

Then he changed course. "Look, I know it's been hard on you. It's been hard on me, too. Between my work and my marriage, you've been getting short shrift. I will need to change that, and I promise I will. I'll think of something."

# CHAPTER 26

**DANNY**

The jig was up. I was giving her less and less of my already scant time, and something had to be done. The last night together, Joanna cried. She is not the kind of woman who easily cries. It made me feel like shit.

Joanna had this floor-to-ceiling glass mirror in her bedroom, and when I got up to leave, the two of us stood there, staring at our reflection. Afraid to meet each other's eyes.

I had tears in my eyes. But all the time, I thought perhaps that's what she truly loved about me. My reflection. Who she wanted me to be and not the real person.

I was in a bind. Scared to move ahead with Joanna and positive I didn't want to stand still. I had to do something to keep her in my life. The opportunity presented itself in a way I never imagined.

# CHAPTER 27

## JOANNA

Danny's work efforts had the desired effect; P&G billings soared at Cooper, Masters & Young. The firm took note of his successes. Soon enough, along came the spoils. One of them was an invitation to attend the prestigious Innovations in Advertising Conference, which would be held in sunny Phoenix for a week in November.

Danny was happy to escape November in New York with its slate-gray days and windy streets. At the lavish Arizona Biltmore, he could take laps in the pool. More importantly, the conference would cover the latest tricks of the trade and help put him at the top of his game.

"Eat your hearts out," he joked to envious colleagues.

I was not thrilled about the trip. Danny had even less time for me because of his preparations. Even when we were together, he couldn't get the conference out of his mind. He had never traveled too far from New York – and never to the

West Coast – and he constantly talked about the upcoming trip.

To get his mind back on me, I teasingly asked him to name what he loved the most about me. I hoped that would grab his attention. Distractingly, he replied, "I love that you're so into me." It wasn't what I was hoping to hear.

Then, a few weeks before the flight, he called me late at night from home. He never did that. I expected bad news. Was he going to be staying in Phoenix a lot longer? Or was he taking Sally with him?

I was surprised to find out what he actually said. "I've been thinking. What if you came with me?" he asked. "Please say yes!"

"Seriously? Do you mean it? Of course!"

This was going to be interesting. We had never spent an entire week together. We'd be doing things other couples take for granted. I'd learn so much more about him! I did not know how Danny woke up in the morning. Would he be groggy or leap out of bed? Did he take his eggs over easy or scrambled? Did he chatter away or ease into the day?

I cleared the week at work, which was relatively easy since November was a slow time. Out of discretion, we agreed I should book my flight separately, using my credit card. He wanted to reimburse me, but I said no. I was making almost as much as he was.

We landed in the sunny desert and took a taxi eight miles to the Biltmore. Nothing quite prepared me for the majestic mountains, the infinite sky above, and the Art Deco architecture of the hotel. We were giggling like children. Right before us was a stained-glass window, "Saguaro Forms and Cactus Flowers," designed by Frank Lloyd Wright, reproductions of the geometric 'sprite' statues, and a solarium.

The bellboy deposited us in a room with a covered patio, a firepit, and direct access to the Paradise Pool. I stood at the window, reveling in the towering view of the mountains.

While he was unpacking, I checked out the hotel guide. "Let's go see the Garden Wing," I told Danny. "It just opened."

He smiled and held up his hand. "First things first. I promised Sally I'd call her when I arrived," he said. "Give me a few seconds." He sprawled across the king bed with the phone, asked for an outside line, and immediately connected with her.

To my happy surprise, his tone was remarkably transactional, without a hint of intimacy. "No problems with the flight," he told her. "Right on time. The room is quite nice. My first meeting is not until tomorrow at ten. I think I'll order room service to have time to sleep in."

Still, I couldn't help but feel dismissed. To stir things up, I unzipped his waistband and took his already-hardening cock into my mouth.

Danny kept breathing steadily as he talked to Sally. He ran his hand through my hair as I pleasured him. His voice never quivered. She must have told him she loved him. I heard him murmur, "Me, too."

He hung up the phone and finally gave me his full attention. Our lovemaking was fierce. He kissed my mouth, my breasts, my hips, my thighs, my private places. Every nerve in my body was on high alert, like a school of tiny minnows flickering under my surface. We came simultaneously.

Afterward, my insecurity took over again. I was like every other woman who ever prostrated herself on the altar of hope.

I teased Danny. "How do you function with two women keeping you busy all the time?" I hated my whiny tone but couldn't help myself.

Danny looked at me intently. "You think that's what's going on? It happens at home far less than you'd imagine."

"Why?" I asked. I didn't expect a serious answer.

Not breaking eye contact, he said, "You've never seen Sally with her clothes off."

The callousness of his remark took my breath away. His comment betrayed Sally far more harshly than our lovemaking ever had. Still, isn't this what I wanted? Affirmation that I was the only one he desired? Then, a darker thought: what if Danny and I had focused so much on our physical attraction that we hadn't nurtured the rest of our connection? Had I deceived myself there was something more?

I hesitated and plunged in.

"Is it...what we have...all about how good I look to you? If I were to put on some pounds, would that be the end for you?"

He was quiet for several seconds.

"The thing is you wouldn't do that. Let yourself go, I mean."

"But what if I did?"

Again, the hesitation. "I won't deny physical attraction is important. To you, too. Would you be here with me now if I had body odor and this big tummy?"

He thrust his stomach out and chuckled to lighten the mood. I wasn't having any of it.

Danny sighed. "Okay. The thing is, it's more than Sally's weight. She's...well, she's checked out. She simply doesn't care. Wears the same old thing day after day. Makes sex with me seem like a chore. Acts as if she did me a big favor by bringing me into her life after my dreary childhood. Like she saved me or something. Do you want an answer from me? I'd be worried if you gained weight because it's not you. I'd want to talk. See what was going on with you."

"So she's depressed?"

"Damned if I know. She puts on a big show about how God is in control, how fortunate we are, and on and on. She's a hypocrite. She's unhappy with me, Charlie, probably even with herself. Especially with herself."

I took it all in. It was the first time Danny had ever criticized Sally to me or hinted there was trouble in the marriage.

"Hmmm...guess there are things I didn't know. But I do know one thing."

I turned to him and met his eyes. "I've seen you without your clothes on. And, just in case you haven't realized it yet, that's impossible for me to resist."

He reached for me, kissing me tenderly, then passionately. I would have given up everything – my career, my lifestyle, at that moment, my very life – to have him with me all the time. What was I doing, bartering away my future for so little?

I've often wondered what I was thinking that night. I never had a problem attracting desirable men, so why did I go for Danny? Some people might believe it was simply lust – the unbelievable chemistry that few experience. They would be wrong. Others might postulate that a part of me felt unworthy of the men I was attracting. Men like Gregg. Perhaps that's a part of it, but it wasn't all.

It's taken me years to realize I was conditioned to want what was unattainable. I had been from the very start when my dad went away for good. Danny was very guarded and very handsome, like my father. This time, I wanted to keep him with me forever.

We made love and stretched out in the hot tub, holding hands. The desert air tingled on our faces. We dressed and went to dinner at the hotel restaurant, where Gracie Allen, Fred Astaire, Bob Hope, and Ava Gardner had dined. We ordered filet mignon, and I added a pricey glass of wine. I got a little tipsy on the wine and the love.

Back in the room, Danny asked me to close my eyes. His hands fluttered on my neck, and something cool lingered there afterward. He led me to the mirror, and I saw a delicate necklace of small crimson stones in a concentric pattern of two intertwined circles. I gasped.

"I wanted to get you something," Danny said. It was his first gift to me, and he looked pleased with himself.

The time we shared at the Biltmore was as perfect as life could be. The real world didn't exist. He did not say a word about Sally or Charlie. I avoided any subject that would puncture the perfect moments we were creating.

But our days in Phoenix were winding down. The next day, we would go back to our separate homes. I would go back to living without him. I dared not ask him more about his feelings – or lack of them – with Sally. What did he see in her? And where did I fit into the picture?

My thoughts were focused on this the morning of our last full day in Phoenix. Danny went downstairs and brought back some coffee and croissants. He caught me crying and shifted around uncomfortably. He didn't like dramatic scenes.

"Maybe taking you on this trip was unfair," he said. "I was only thinking of myself. How much I wanted you with me. I never stopped to think of the toll it was taking on you."

He was about to say more, but I motioned him to stop. "Look, I've never been good at pretending. Maybe you know what I'm about to say. I've been trying my best not to make you uneasy. But I can't hold back any longer. I love you, Danny. I love you so much. So now I have to ask: Where are you in all of this?"

I was afraid of what he'd say next. When I looked at him, his expression had darkened.

"You think I've never thought of you and me together? Of course, I have. But I can't just throw away the marriage. There are practical matters to consider. How do I tell Sally

– and Charlie? She'll feel betrayed, and Charlie – I can't even imagine. Is this how I repay my father-in-law, who believed in me when no one else would? On my wedding day, I gave him my word I would never do anything to hurt his daughter.

"I already told you that Sally's father is close friends with Jared Morgenstern, my boss. I owe my whole career to that man. There's not a chance in hell he would keep me on. My in-laws? They'll hire a high-priced lawyer and take everything I've got. Worst of all, they'll keep me away from Charlie."

"Danny, I'm not downplaying any of that," I heard myself saying. "But there are ways. You're great at what you do, and you'll land at another agency. The courts are more receptive to father's rights, and we'll hire a good lawyer. It won't be simple, but..."

"Yeah, maybe, but how would we live?" Danny interrupted. "The courts will seize most of my earnings. You know that. Even if we could live together, do you want to be financially responsible for both of us and pay the lion's share of our expenses? And do you honestly want to take Charlie on? He's such a high-spirited little guy."

I put my finger to his lips. "I'm not naïve enough to think for a second this won't be challenging. I'd tell you it isn't worth it if I loved you less selfishly. But I think it is. You can't spend the rest of your life with a woman you don't love. And I can't live without you for the rest of my life."

"You would really be there for me?"

"Of course. Don't let us get ahead of ourselves. One step at a time."

We shared a passionate kiss. Danny lifted my t-shirt and, in one swift movement, released my breasts from their constraints. When I looked down, my nipples were dark and hard. I fumbled with his zipper, and his cock shot straight out. I cradled it in my hand. We made love for the third time that day and fell asleep in each other's arms. Emotionally and physically spent.

What we had confessed to each other was monumental. Cutting ties with Sally and the McAllisters would be difficult, no doubt about it. But I would wait for him as long as I knew he loved me. I drifted off to sleep.

I don't know what jerked me awake a couple of hours later. An unfamiliar sound was in the room. It took me a minute or two to gain my bearings and identify it. It sounded like another person breathing, but that was impossible. Only the two of us were here.

The breathing became more pronounced. I wondered if I was still dreaming but knew I wasn't – and I was terrified.

"Danny?" I whispered. Deep in the throes of sleep, he murmured, "Hmmm?"

"I think someone is here. In this room."

He raised himself onto his elbows, and his body stiffened. His eyes widened with horror.

"Danny?" A jolt of adrenalin now shot through me as well. I instinctively reached for him while lifting myself.

We could make out the outline. Sally. Sitting in the room, watching us from a chair near the window, silhouetted in the artificial light, her face contorted in fury. I heard her breath-ing noisily through her mouth, soon punctuated by sharp sobs. For a few seconds, nobody dared move.

"Sally, what are you doing here? Where's Charlie?" Those were Danny's first words, and I could almost smell his fear.

"At my mother's. I wanted to surprise you, and we could make a weekend of it, driving to Sedona. I've planned this for some time, got the okay from Jared, and reserved a few days at a hotel there. Everything was planned. I even called ahead and arranged to pick up a key to your room here. To make it a real surprise. Surprise! Well, the joke's on me. Tell me – does this slut come as a bonus with your package hotel rate, or did you pay extra?"

Danny pulled away from me. I lay there, as naked and alone as I've ever been, with my heart pounding. I started getting up, and he gave me a curt warning: "Joanna!"

I watched the comprehension begin to dawn on her face. "Joanna? So this is the Joanna that Evan was teasing you about at his farewell dinner? The video girl? You told me Evan was an asshole, and you had only met her a couple of times. But Evan wouldn't let the joke drop.

Sally glared at Danny and then at me. "How long has this been going on?"

Neither of us answered.

"I'm asking you," she said through clenched teeth. "How long?"

"Sally…," Danny began.

"You fucker. You damn bastard. How dare you! You asked about Charlie. You're never going to see him again. I'll make damn sure of that."

She whirled toward me. " And you? Get the fuck away from my husband. Get out of my sight. Now!"

I grabbed my clothes and raced into the bathroom, leaning against the door, heaving. I could hear a loud slap and Danny's pleading voice.

"Sally, I'm sorry. I'm so sorry. Please. Can we talk? We've got Charlie to think of. Let's talk, please?"

I sat on the cold marble floor and rocked myself in a fetal position. I fixated on a small fissure on the floor and listened to the voices rise and fall in fury. Then the voices dipped. I couldn't make out everything, but I got the gist.

She would be heading home, and somebody would change the locks by the time he arrived. He was an ungrateful son of a bitch. She would make sure he would suffer every bit as much as she was right now. Danny's voice was soft, cajoling, pleading. Soon, they both were whispering.

I went into a fugue state until Danny knocked on the bathroom door. His left cheek was deep red where she slapped him, and his eyes were dull and puffy. I didn't dare reach out to touch him. In a monotone, Danny told me I should go downstairs, book another room for myself, and ask them to charge it to his account. He needed time to talk with her, and he'd join me in an hour or two.

I didn't ask questions. I just did what he asked. My suitcase was mostly packed since we were supposed to leave late in the morning. I threw the last few items into it. I averted her eyes, which I knew were watching me every step of the way.

The night clerk looked at me sympathetically. I guess he suspected my lover and I had had a fight. He had seen it all before – and silently handed me the key to the new room.

I spent the whole night awake and shaking, staring at the door. I witnessed the first pink glows of sunlight enter the room, and I still waited. But Danny never showed up.

He called mid-morning, and I could tell she was listening to every word he was saying.

"Joanna, you left your plane ticket in the room. I gave it to the front desk. And I called the airline to reschedule you on a 2:15 flight. It would be best if you went home now. I've been so selfish. Sally says she's having another baby. Things are complicated. I can't see you anymore. I'm sorry."

"A baby?" I asked. "After all this, you and Sally are having another baby?"

A long pause intervened. "I…" he said and fell silent.

We both breathed shakily.

"I am so sorry," he whispered miserably.

# CHAPTER 28

**DANNY**

As a kid, I learned how to remove myself from the hurt. My mind would turn off like a TV with an on/off switch. All the noise would suddenly cease. I'd drift far away to where no one could touch me or cause me pain.

That's what I was doing with Sally as we left the Biltmore. I could still hear her crying, blaming, and yelling. I was in a bubble where her words couldn't reach me.

Joanna was already a far-off dream. I had blown it with her, and I already missed her unbearably. While packing to leave, I discovered a scarf she had left behind. I placed it in a compartment in my suitcase that Sally wouldn't notice.

We went downstairs to check out. Standing beside my glowering wife instead of the smiling woman I came with felt surreal. I was trapped with Sally for life.

"Was everything all right, sir?"

"Oh, yes. Thanks."

Sally and I drove to Sedona and checked in at the Enchantment Resort. No doubt, we were the most miserable couple in the lobby. It was an incredible place. Exposed wood beams, Native American art, and stunning views of the red rocks that Sedona is famous for.

We unpacked our suitcases. I cleared my throat. I was now on autopilot, forcing myself to form the words I knew I was expected to say.

"How are you feeling? I mean, with the baby and all. How far along are you?"

"Why should you care?" she said.

I winced, knowing I deserved her contempt. The marriage wasn't working, but still, she didn't deserve this. Later, I suggested we have dinner at the spacious outdoor patio. I asked for a table with a view of the mountains. She wiped the tears away during the whole meal, occasionally spitting out a sarcastic comment.

I couldn't take another minute of this poisonous atmosphere without trying to talk.

"Look, I know I've been a shit. I'm very sorry. I never intended to hurt you so badly."

She looked at me as if examining a toad.

"I can't change what I did. I know I behaved despicably. You have every right to be furious. But we need to try to move forward. If not for our sake, then for Charlie's sake. And the new one. We need to consider them."

"As if it matters to you."

"Come on, Sally. Let's at least try a little. I get it. I did something horrible. I was selfish and unthinking, and I hurt you badly. It will take me time and effort to earn your trust again. What can I do to start making it right?"

She looked directly into my eyes. "For starters, I want you to promise to never, ever see that slut again. Then I want you home each night, right after work. I need to know where you are every moment you're not home. Do you agree to that?"

'Uh, okay," I said sheepishly. Things were going to be pretty stark at the Monahan home.

"Also, I spoke to my parents earlier today on the phone."

Uh oh, I thought. Now the shit is going to hit the fan.

"Don't worry, I didn't tell them what happened. I didn't want to get into this whole awful mess with them. I told them we were having some marital problems. Mom and Dad think the world of you, by the way."

"I think the world of them, too, Sally. I really do."

"Anyway, they want to help us. My father is signing us up for a Marriage Encounter workshop. We'll go the weekend after we get back."

"What is a Marriage Encounter workshop?"

"We will be putting our whole life into God's hands. With other couples. For the whole weekend."

"Umm, okay."

"Let me be honest, Danny. I don't trust you. I don't know if I'll ever be able to trust you again. But I don't want to give up on this marriage. We made a sacred commitment to God when we took our vows."

"Okay, I'd be happy to go and do this Marriage Encounter thing with you," I said. It looked like from now on, my life would be dedicated to making the best of things.

"We'll see if it works."

We flew home and tried to put on a good show when we picked Charlie up at the McAllisters. Her parents eyed both of us cautiously. They knew something was wrong. I busied myself with my son, listening to Sally's description of our stay.

"Oh, it was gorgeous," she said. "The red rocks, the pools, the desert sun. Mom and Dad, you'd love it! Maybe you could go there for your next anniversary."

She was putting on quite the performance. Oddly enough, I felt sorry for her. I understood what an effort it had to be.

Sally and I spent a tense week together. We said little to each other for fear of demolishing our fragile peace. I went back to work and put on a performance for my boss, Jared.

"I'll never forget Sally showing up at my hotel room," I said. At least that much was true!

"She said you were in on it. What a wonderful surprise. And to keep the secret for so long!" I could have won an Academy Award for best performance.

Every evening, I dutifully caught the 6:33 train home. We were the perfect family. Sally would have dinner ready. I'd compliment her on the meal. We'd ask Charlie about his day. We'd turn on the TV and sit there gloomily when we got him into bed. Neither of us cracked a smile despite the obnoxious laugh track.

On Friday, after I got home from work, Sally and I dropped Charlie off at his grandparents and took the short drive to the marriage encounter. We were greeted with a huge banner that read, "God Loves Marriage."

Other couples, many holding hands, streamed into the room, whispering excitedly. We took our seats and waited for the pastor to deliver his canned spiel. This was going to be like going to church on steroids.

A gray-haired man with a pockmarked face, dressed in a black cassock, took the podium. "Welcome." He raised his hands to us.

"I want you to know, within each of you couples, there is a divine energy of love. When there is sharing between husband and wife, love will be released. It happens through the communication of your feelings. As you share, you will come to the discovery of God's vision of marriage. You will be called to unite with each other in His holy presence."

Sally looked rapt and clasped my hand tightly. I couldn't wait to mimic all this for Joanna. But wait, Joanna is out of my life. How could I have let that happen?

We were assigned to a couple named Bernadette and Thomas. They would accompany us for the rest of the evening. They smiled smarmily and hugged us.

"We're so glad you're here!" Thomas said. "You've taken a positive step. There's nothing to be ashamed of. Every couple faces deep disappointment at one point in their marriage."

"You'll feel yourselves growing here," Bernadette continued. "Marital preparation for the wedding gives couples all the doctrinal answers. Yet it leaves us woefully unprepared for life's very real problems."

"Once upon a time, we, too, faced a fork in the road in our own marriage," Thomas said.

"Oh yes," Bernadette said. "It's true. Well, now you know. Believe it or not, we sat where you are today."

"We learned something important during our Marriage Encounter," her husband added. "The gift of love became fruitful only with the discovery of the place of God within our lives."

"Oh, just think of the joy of living each day as a godly couple, with your life blessed by Jesus and His eternal love," his wife added.

Could I listen to any more of this crap, I wondered.

The pastor was back at his podium. "The grave sin of divorce infects everyone around you," he said. "It's time now to turn to Christ and ask Him to help us."

We received our first assignment. We had 10 minutes to write our deepest feelings about the following topic: What were our hopes and dreams for the future? What can we as a couple do to make those hopes and dreams become a reality?

We each received a notebook to write our answers in. Sally opened hers immediately and began to write furiously. At one point, she had to shake out a hand cramp. Every few minutes, she turned to a new page.

I opened my notebook and sat there, looking at the blank page. I couldn't think of anything to say. Finally, I eked out a few thoughts. When they asked us to stop, I had produced a pitiful half-page.

All the couples gathered together and asked to read our entries. Sally stood up and read hers with zeal.

"My dream for the future," she began, "is to glorify God and to honor Him forever."

Bernadette beamed at her.

"Reaching that goal," Sally went on, "depends on a healthy relationship centered on trust. Without trust, there is nothing." She turned to me.

"We need to make each other a priority. Communicate openly about our feelings. Create hope and a future by striving to love each other the way God loves us."

She was not specific on what that future would be. "We must form a love that forgives, serves, perseveres, and celebrates. We will watch our son Charlie grow up to become a godly man who feels secure in the love his parents share. We will create a life filled with family and friends, experiencing fun times together – from family vacations to the beach to dinners and movies."

Her contribution was met with loud and approving applause from the other couples. Sally, Bernadette, and Thomas turned expectantly to me.

I stood up, shifting back and forth. "Sharing your dreams together is important for a good marriage," I said. "I'd like to reawaken the passion we had in the beginning."

I could see Sally wincing.

"I have learned from experience the future is not assured." I continued. "For the present, I'd like us to share accomplishments and grow individually and together."

I closed my notebook, sat down, and received a smattering of applause.

"That's it?" Sally whispered and glared at me.

In truth, I couldn't imagine a future where Sally and I would be excitedly working together, embracing what lay ahead of us. All I could envision was more of the same.

Sally was starting to cry.

"We have a lot more ahead this weekend," Thomas told her helpfully.

Bernadette nodded encouragingly.

In the next two days, they prodded us – sometimes aggressively – to declare what we loved most about each other. What things could we work on to strengthen our marriage? How could we improve our communication skills? How did we function together as a couple? What did trust look like for each of us? What did passion look like?

At the end of the weekend, each couple stood facing one another. Each solemnly promised to become better partners for the other.

Sally appeared exhilarated, but I was relieved. I realized our attitudes toward the world were opposed. Sally believed her life had purpose and meaning, driven by God's love. I knew first-hand that much of life was purposeless, that we seized happiness where we could get it.

Sally didn't know it, but for me, working on our marriage was the last thing on my mind.

# CHAPTER 29

## JOANNA

Later, after the endless plane ride home, all the wrenching tears, all the sleepless nights, and the deadened days, I heard from Danny.

I had just begun to piece my life together. It hadn't been easy. It took everything within me to go through the masquerade at work. To pretend I was fine, and all was okay.

Of course, it wasn't. Danny had broken me in all the most tender places. Nothing in my life was giving me joy. The emptiness was so intense that sometimes, before bedtime, I'd go out and roam the streets. I'd stop at the local Borders Bookstore, grab a coffee, and sit there leafing through books until closing time. Anything to not be alone.

Going to work and meeting friends was a burden. I had to pretend everything was fine. I figured I'd never hear from him again. But I yearned to call him. I taped affirmations to my phone: "You are strong. You will get through this."

Weeks past. I had finally begun getting my life together when he called.

"Hey. It's me."

"Yeah?" I said in a small voice. There was a long silence.

"You probably never wanted to hear from me again. I wouldn't blame you. But I have a few things to say if you're up to it. Or would you rather I hang up?"

I should have said yes. Instead, I answered, "No, go on."

"When Sally showed up in our room at the Biltmore, it was a nightmare for me. For you, too. You and I had just begun talking about a future together. We didn't even have a plan yet. I wanted out of the marriage, but not how it played out that night. Not until we had some certainty."

"Hmm," I said. If Danny thought I would make it easier for him, he thought wrong. He had put me through too much pain.

Danny continued. "When she told me she was expecting, it felt like prison bars were closing in on me. There was no way I could leave her like that. I didn't know what to do.

"You were steps away in the bathroom, hearing everything we said. I wanted to leave her and come to you. But I needed time to talk to her and process everything. After you left the room, she and I talked all night. Then I called you in the morning."

A pang went through me when I remembered that phone call.

"I thought I was doing the right thing. But how could anything be right if it felt so awful? I was so confused. I

160

agreed to go with her to the place she booked in Sedona – The Enchantment Resort. It would have been remarkable under any other circumstance – if you and I went. With Sally, it was awful.

"Sally held nothing back. One of the worst things she hit me with was that I was a carbon copy of my old man. 'The apple doesn't fall far from the tree,' she said. She could never trust me again – not with her or Charlie. On and on. I was hoping she would tell me it was over, but she didn't. She's a good Catholic, and divorce wasn't her way.

"After a few miserable days, we flew back to White Plains. Went to a Marriage Encounter – my father-in-law's idea. Sally, of course, loved it, but I found it ridiculous. I stayed sane by imagining how you would laugh when I told you about it. Of course, that wasn't to be. A month after we got back, she had a miscarriage. She blamed me for that, too. The miscarriage meant the baby issue went away, and it will now be gone forever.

"I have no interest in ever having sex with her again. I know I implied we had stopped sleeping together. It did happen – very rarely but on occasion. During those times, I pretended it was you so I could get myself aroused. Now, I can't even look at her. I can no longer pretend we're truly husband and wife."

"Oh, Danny," I said.

"Joanna, I can't be with her. So here's what I want to know. I plan to tell Sally I'm leaving. I don't know what will happen after that. What I'm about to ask you is unfair, but will you be there for me once it's over? I don't know if I can go through this alone.

"I'm a shit for laying this on you. But I'm doing it anyway. Were you serious when you said you'd love me no matter what?"

"Of course," I whispered. "Just be sure it's what you want."

# CHAPTER 30

## DANNY IN THERAPY

"Really nice to be back. Meant to tell you – great place you've got here." I said to Walt, looking around the room. "Makes me feel right at home. The 1950s couch, the dime store picture of the forest, the dim light. Maybe you can give me some how-to-decorate pointers later."

From Walt's thin smile, I achieved my objective of making him uncomfortable. Today, he would get the complete Danny Boy treatment – the humor and mimicry. It almost always worked to give me the upper hand. If it made him squirm – well, that's what shrinks get paid for. I was tired of showing up each week with him acting like he knew me more than I knew myself. He didn't.

He quickly put me in my place. "Nice evasion tactic. Do you recall what we talked about the last time you were here?" he countered.

"You told me childhood is about survival," I said. "Well, I survived. It wasn't pretty, and I could have done it better. But at least I walked away knowing what I wanted. Case in point: Joanna and I are together."

"That sounds like a good start," Walt said. "How is it going with her?

"Who knows how it's going? I'm sure you have the answer. Lay it on me."

Walt sighed. "Danny, I've been in practice for over 25 years. And no, I don't have all the answers. We could discover the answers together. But first, you need to lay down the armor. I realize that's hard to do. The feeling of unworthiness goes hand in hand with childhood trauma. Are you willing to try?"

"Look, let me get one thing straight. My childhood wasn't any fairy tale. But it wasn't that traumatic for me," I shot back. "It was traumatic for my mother. Not me."

"Is that how you remember it?" Walt asked.

"Yeah. That's how I remember it. My father gave me tough love. Sometimes, he overdid it. That's it. End of story."

"I call it by another name. Abuse. You are shielding yourself in denial. It's not going to work. That shield will keep you from ever truly trusting anybody. If you can't trust, you can't connect."

"Interesting theory," I said dismissively.

"Danny, hiding your feelings doesn't equate to mastering your feelings. It's going to take some courage to confront them. I promise you this: if you can do that, you can take away their power."

"Walt, is this some 'Lord of the Rings' fantasy? I have to perform feats of courage, confront Sauron, and take back the ring?"

"Well, if you put it that way. Sometimes, a person needs to confront what is scary."

"Oh, is that right, Walt?" I was angry. "What the fuck would you know about childhood trauma? Probably your parents smothered you with love because you were…"

I didn't like where I was taking this. Still, I gestured at his wheelchair.

Walt shook his head. "You think I can't possibly know what it's like to grow up with an abusive father? Here's where you're wrong. Do you want to know why I'm in a wheel-chair? I don't tell the story to most of my patients. Unless I feel it can do some good. I'm going to share it so you'll know you are not alone.

"So let's go there together – back to my high school prom. I was dating a girl named Emily. She and I had both been accepted by Cornell and were so excited. We'd be graduating soon, and then we'd be going into pre-law. We joked about starting a practice together.

"It was going to be a late night. I couldn't drive home; I didn't have my driver's license yet. I had skipped a grade and had not yet reached driving age – as you know, 18 in New York.

"My father told me not to worry; he'd pick us up. Now that had me nervous. My dad would regularly drink heavily. He was pretty good at holding his liquor, but not that night. On the way home, his car veered off the highway and hit a tree, going 75 miles an hour.

"Emily was killed outright, and I broke my spine. I never regained the use of my legs. I had to go through years of rehabilitation. I've never stopped feeling guilty for letting Emily get into that car. I gave up the idea of a law degree and entered the field of psychology."

"Jesus, Walt," I said. I felt like a total asshole.

"So you see," he continued." I know more than you think I do about repressed guilt. It takes courage to face guilt head-on. I'm asking you straight out: when are you going to stop making excuses for your father? He was a damaged man who torpedoed his own life. He's well on the way toward torpedoing yours."

"My father...," I faltered. I stopped and stared down miserably.

"This may be the toughest thing anyone has ever asked you: Do you have what it takes to investigate the unresolved pain you've lived with for most of your life? Right now, in the privacy of this room, you can find out what is keeping you from claiming your happiness. Happiness, by the way, that you deserve."

A lump formed in my throat. I could not force the words out.

Walt smiled. "It's okay to nod your head."

I nodded. "I'm scared," I said.

"Of course you are. You wouldn't be honest if you said otherwise. But if you can summon the will to examine what you went through, you'll feel a sense of release. We can do that together, Danny."

For some crazy reason, I believed him.

# CHAPTER 31

## DANNY

Leaving Sally was challenging, but I had to do it. I didn't love her anymore. I sat her down one evening and told her it wasn't working between us, and I would be renting a small apartment nearby. I couldn't go live with Joanna. Cohabitating with her wouldn't play well in divorce court.

Sally reacted in shock, crying, yelling, and ultimately, screaming at me to get out. I hastily packed a suitcase.

Going through that scene took everything out of me. Facing her father, though, would be the tough part. I loved the old guy. He believed in me when no one else did. I had looked him in the eye and promised him I'd always be there for his daughter. Thinking about facing him and telling him I was bailing out made me cringe.

I took the cowardly way out. I kept moving when I drove to the house to pick up more of my clothes and saw his

Cadillac parked outside. Still, I knew he would call me sooner or later. One day, the phone rang, and it was him.

"Hello, Danny."

"Uh, Dr. McAllister?" I had just gotten off the john and had raced to grab the phone.

"Are you free for breakfast on Saturday?"

"Well, uh, sure."

"Let's meet at the Darling White Plains Diner at nine. You know where that is?"

"Of course. I'll be there." I hung up and hitched up my pants. I took deep breaths and tried to rehearse what I'd say to him. How on earth could I make him understand why I had to leave?

As soon as I entered the diner, I could feel my heart rate soar. I wished I could turn around and walk back out. My father-in-law was already seated, looking contemplative, with a cup of coffee on the table before him. He examined me as I walked toward him. I was about to reach out my hand to shake his, as I usually would, but at the last minute, I decided not to.

"Sit down, Danny."

I pulled out the chair across from him and lowered myself into it awkwardly.

"You think I called you here to dress you down," he said. "By God, part of me wants to do that. Because you screwed up, Danny. You gave into temptation without regard to Sally or Charlie."

I looked for a place to focus my eyes. I watched a waitress approach the next table with a cut-up chicken. At that moment, I sure could sympathize with that dismembered bird.

"We could talk about all the whys and wherefores of what you did. But what is necessary at this point is to turn to our Savior. Jesus can heal in times of trouble. He can help you, Danny. You just need to open your heart to him."

My throat issued a strangled noise.

"You probably think I can't possibly understand what you did. Oh, but I can. Back when I was your age, I had four young children at home. Another on the way. Two had the sniffles, and one was having a meltdown. Maude needed my help, and then I had to put in a 16-hour shift at work.

"At the hospital, there was this nurse. I've never told Maude about her. She was young and fresh-cheeked and blonde. She'd bring me a warm muffin in a paper bag each day and hover over me as I ate it. I could see the desire in her eyes! Lord, how she worshipped me. She'd say things like, 'Dr. McAllister, I just saw Johnny's mother. She said to tell you she'll keep you in her prayers every day of her life for saving her little boy.' She made me feel like a hero."

My father-in-law's eyes got a little dreamy. "All I needed was to say the word; she would have given me anything I asked."

I tried to imagine a young Dr. McAllister frolicking naked with a blonde nurse. It distracted me from feeling like the cad I was. How would he have seduced her? Regale her with his exploits in the operating room and then take her to the linen closet for some fun?

"Then I had an awakening," Dr. McAllister continued. "I was in the doctors' lounge, drinking strong coffee to bolster me for the all-night shift. The nurse would be assisting. I thought about how the devil had tempted Jesus. He'd been fasting for 40 days and 40 nights in the Judean desert."

My eyes glazed over, but Dr McAllister didn't notice.

"The devil took Him to a high mountain, showed Him the world's kingdoms in their magnificence, and said, 'All these I shall give to you if you will prostrate yourself and worship me.' Jesus resisted. He chose to depend on his Father to satisfy his deepest hunger."

My father-in-law turned to me. "Danny, you are at a crossroads. If you are willing to ask Sally for forgiveness, I believe she will take you back. We can work to put this behind us and go on as if nothing happened."

The waitress came with her ticket book in hand. "Ready to order, folks?"

"No, we'll need a few more minutes," he said and turned back to me.

"Son, if you can summon up the courage, you will be rewarded a million times over for what you decide. When you and Sally are grandparents, you will be able to take comfort that you made the right choice all those years ago."

I tried to imagine Sally and me as grandparents, holding hands and watching the grandkids romp around the playground. Would she still be wearing the same sweats?

"But if you leave Sally for good, do you think your son will continue to adore you? And that woman you've been consorting with, do you think she would stay with you? She doesn't have an ounce of Sally's loyalty and commitment."

Joanna has no loyalty and commitment? I thought of all the indignities she had put up with and how her love was still there for me.

"If you give in to lust, you'll never be right with the Lord. I don't have to remind you the Church considers marriage to be a sacrament. If you choose to continue to hurt my daughter, I can make this promise to you. I'll make sure you regret your decision for the rest of your life. That's just the way it has to be."

He stood up, put some money down on the table to cover his coffee, and grabbed his coat. "You don't have to give me your answer now, son. I don't suspect you have much of an appetite. Go home and think about it. Pray on it. I know in my heart you'll make the right choice."

I left the Darling Diner and headed back to my apartment. It was small and sterile and would never feel like home. I tried eating a few bites of a left-over sandwich but felt sick to my stomach. The vision Dr. McAllister painted was bleak. I couldn't forget his warning – that he would make sure I would regret my decision for the rest of my life. I felt shamed and chastened despite striving hard to keep an emotional distance from him. The truth is, I still respected my father-in-law enormously, and it was painful to know I had disappointed him. I could try to shield myself from the truth as much as I could, but deep down, I knew I was not half the man he was.

The phone rang. It was Joanna.

"Just want to see how you're doing."

"It was bad."

"I was afraid of that. I can come right over if you want."

"Thanks, but I'm spent. Need to get some sleep." I didn't want her to see me like this.

"Okay, I understand. Call me if you need me. And don't let him get to you. We'll figure it out."

Sleep eluded me for hours. I finally dozed off but had a nightmare. Dr. McAllister was standing in a wide-open desert, holding a burning torch in one hand and the blonde nurse in the other. "Be strong," he told her. "I am sacrificing you to the altar of Jesus." She went up in smoke.

He meant well by suggesting I turn to Jesus. But where was Jesus when my old man came home stinking drunk, pissed off my mother hadn't made dinner for him? That night, he knocked one of her teeth out. She lay there weeping, with Jesus nowhere in sight.

It's easy to believe in Him when you're a well-to-do doctor with a perfect family, revered by the whole city. For me, it would take a lot more effort. As a child, I had tried praying and then praying some more. No Jesus then. He must have been sleeping on the job that night.

Dr. McAllister was right about one thing. I was at a crossroads. I could move in with a remarkable woman offering me the kind of love I never would have imagined. Or I could do what he called the right thing and stay with Sally. Every day, I would lose a little more of myself as the ghosts of my past caught up with me.

I paced around the apartment the next day. One way or another, I needed to pull myself together and focus on my work. I couldn't stay paralyzed like this. I decided to talk it out face-to-face with Sally in the late afternoon.

I drove over to our house. The place held a lot of memories. The balcony we put in five years after we were married. The new skylights we installed last year. The gray-stained hardwood flooring that replaced the old carpet.

I let myself in with my key. I saw pieces of Charlie's train set strewn across the living room. That took me aback. The Sally I knew would have demanded Charlie pick them up. Over in the dining room, I could see plates with half-eaten food on the table.

Sally walked into the living room to greet me. She shuffled quietly like an older woman. Her eyes were puffy, her hair was limp and needed washing, and her skin appeared ghostly pale. My heart went out to her.

"Sally," I said softly.

She looked at me, and I could detect a flash of hope in her eyes. Her father had probably told her I would be giving the marriage another try.

"Sally. I'm so sorry. You must believe me. I never intended to hurt you. That night in Phoenix was one of the worst nights of my life. I had no right to put you through it. I was a bastard and a coward."

She stared at me, hopefully, waiting to hear more.

"I think you know the last couple of years haven't worked for either of us. I don't want to make you miserable any longer. You deserve so much more than what I can offer you. I promise to do everything possible to make this easy for you."

She frowned at me. Now, our conversation was going differently than she expected.

"Tell you what," I said, "you can keep the house. We both love Charlie. We can move forward as two adults who care about each other and not get caught up in this bitterness."

All of a sudden, Charlie flew into the living room. "Daddy!" he yelled out and jumped up on me.

"Nice to see you, little buddy!"

That's when Sally lost it. "Charlie! Pick up all these toys and take them back to your room. Me and your father need to talk."

His face puckered. "No! I want to stay here and see Daddy!"

I reached over to calm him down. But Sally began screaming.

"Charlie, get to your room! Now!"

Our frightened little boy dashed away, slamming his door.

"You didn't have to do that," I said. "He's confused and scared enough as it is."

"Oh, and who did that?" Sally said. "You disappear for a couple of weeks and now want to be crowned Father of the Year? You spent your childhood wishing you had a stable family like mine. Now you're ready to put our son through what you dealt with."

That hit me where it hurt.

"Give me some explanation, Danny! Tell me why you're so hellbent on tearing our marriage apart. Did you get bored with me? Or did you get too big for your britches? My father got you that damn job. And now you're fucking every girl in sight!"

"Sally, please," I said.

She came at me, her hands clenched. I had a flashback to my childhood. My parents were fighting in the kitchen, and I was trying to get somewhere safe. I raised my hands to protect myself and lightly pushed Sally away.

She stepped back onto one of Charlie's train pieces and fell, hitting her head on the edge of the coffee table. She lay there silent, and all time ceased.

"Sally!" I yelled. I rolled her over. She was breathing but unconscious. I ran to the phone on the kitchen wall and called 911.

The EMTs were there in a flash. They quickly assessed the situation and stabilized Sally's head and neck. She stirred and moaned. Charlie stood in the hallway watching, tears still rolling down his face.

"What is the lady's name?" an EMT asked me.

"Sally Monahan," I said. "She's my wife."

He turned to her. "Sally, you're going to be okay. We think you have a concussion. We will transport you to the hospital and have a doctor check you out. If you like, your husband can ride with you in the ambulance."

My wife's eyes flashed. "No! I don't want him with me!"

The technician seemed to understand the situation. "We'll take you out of here. You'll be okay."

I picked up Charlie. "Mommy took a fall, and they need to check her out. She'll be home in no time."

But the gravity of the situation was sinking in. The EMTs were going to the same hospital where my father-in-law worked. He was going to see his injured daughter and would leap to the worst conclusion.

The EMTs left with Sally. I stayed with Charlie at the house. At first, I couldn't console him. He cried, made high-pitched noises, and circled aimlessly around the living room. Finally, he lay his head against my chest, raising it every now and then and banging it down hard against me.

"What if I order us a pizza for dinner?" I asked. "You and I can watch TV. What do you say?"

Charlie looked at me with mounting interest. He sniffled several times and mumbled, "Okay, Daddy."

"Thatta boy," I said, "I love you so much."

As we waited for the pizza, I heard a key turning in the lock and the front door opening.

"Grandpa!" Charlie called out.

Dr. McAllister held his arms out to Charlie. "Come here, big boy!"

Charlie ran over and flew into his arms.

"I just left Mommy. She's all right, and she told me to let you know she loves you. She'll be in the hospital overnight, and then she'll be back! You're going to stay with Grandma and me. Grandma went to get you chocolate chip ice cream. Your favorite. Mommy said it would be okay for you to have two scoops! So let's get you packed up."

"But Daddy's ordered pizza," Charlie said.

"Don't you worry? We can get a whole pizza too!"

"Can Daddy come? He won't have anyone to eat it with."

I turned to Charlie and managed to smile. "It's okay, Charlie. I'll put it in the refrigerator for you to eat later. Why don't you go to your room? Pack up your duck T-shirt and those pajamas you like. And don't forget your toothbrush. Come on, go and get ready."

Charlie hesitated a minute. I gave him an encouraging nod. He skipped off to his bedroom, leaving me and my father-in-law alone.

Dr. McAllister was silent. He clenched his teeth, and the veins on his neck stood out.

"How's Sally?" I asked.

"She has a mild concussion. She is staying overnight for observation." His voice got harsh. "Did you have something to do with this?"

"It was an accident. Sally was angry and…"

"She says you shoved her right onto the edge of the coffee table."

"I didn't shove her," I said. "She was coming at me, and I pushed her back very lightly. She tripped over one of Charlie's toys and hit her head on the coffee table."

"Don't give me that crap, Danny. I witnessed enough during my internship to know how these things occur. The husband argues with his wife. He gets angry and pushes her down. Out-of-control husbands can become quite violent. Their injured wives end up in the ED."

Don't I know it, I thought. I flinched and said, "No, I would never...it didn't happen like that. Dr McAllister, you've got to believe me."

"I'm supposed to believe you, my cheating son-in-law? Or believe my daughter, who has been putting up with your shenanigans for months? Nothing seems to have registered at all – not the Marriage Encounter, not what I said last Saturday."

"No, wait. I came over here to talk with Sally. To reach an agreement."

"Don't interrupt me, you soulless bastard. Here's what you're going to do before Sally comes home tomorrow. I want you to gather all your clothes and personal belongings. I want you out of here. I don't want any trace of you when my daughter returns."

"You can't ask me to do that," I said, trying to act calm. "It is, after all, my house."

"Your house?" he said. "Who the hell do you think paid for it? I took care of the down payment, which was, I remind you, over 50%. The first time I laid eyes on you, you were a big nothing. The son of a felon, barely able to raise your head and look me in the eyes, with no real concrete plans or direction."

"Wait, one minute there," I stammered.

"Do you think Jared Morgenstern would ever have hired a wet-behind-the-ears kid with little going for him if I hadn't interceded? Jared and I go way back. Do you think he'll keep you when I tell him everything you've done?

"I wish to God she had never laid eyes on you. In case you don't know, adultery is still against the law in New York. You can kiss Charlie goodbye. We'll give Sally and him all the support they need. Once Charlie fully understands what happened, he'll never want to talk to you again."

Charlie was standing at the doorway, looking at Dr. McAllister and then at me.

His eyes welled with tears. "Why are you two fighting?"

"I'm not fighting, Charlie," I said.

Dr. McAllister fell to one knee and beckoned Charlie to come to him. "Let's see what you have in that backpack."

Charlie hesitated and looked at me. I motioned him to go to his grandfather, and he went.

Dr. McAllister opened the backpack. "A T-shirt, pants, pajamas, toothbrush, book. Yep, it looks like you packed well. Now say goodbye to Daddy, and let's get you some chocolate chip ice cream."

My son ran over to hug me. I whirled him around twice and took a few more moments with him before I let him go.

180

"I love you," I whispered. "You be good, and I'll see you soon."

They both left the house. Charlie got into the front seat of the Cadillac. The taillights went on, and the car backed out. Five minutes later, the pizza arrived. I got the trunk down from the attic and began filling it with my belongings. My hands were trembling.

I went to the kitchen and dialed Joanna's number. She answered on the first ring.

"Danny, are you okay? Where are you?"

"I'm over at Sally's. She had an accident and had to go to the hospital."

"What? What happened?"

"She tripped. She has a mild concussion. I'll tell you about it later."

"Oh. Where's Charlie?"

"My father-in-law just took Charlie back to his place."

"Oh, Danny," she said, and I could feel her love caressing me through the wire.

Then I uttered the three words I had never said in my life.

"I need you."

# CHAPTER 32

## Joanna

For the first time since I met Danny, I truly got a glimpse of the lost-looking, vulnerable, and scared little boy Maureen had told me about.

Danny had just called and told me he needed me. I sprung right into action. I told him to take the train to Grand Central, and I'd meet him there. I didn't want him to be alone a second more than he had to be. It was a rainy night, and I waited in a cab parked on Lexington Avenue to take Danny back to my home. When he emerged, he looked more wrecked than I had ever imagined. It was a whole new Danny. I had always seen him with his guard up.

I reached out to hug him, and he flinched. He looked like some miserable refugee from a war zone, hoarding every ounce of his energy to survive. During the ride, I watched him wearily and squeezed his hand. He sat there inert, hunched over, his eyes unblinking. He had withdrawn into his cocoon.

At my apartment, he went directly to my bedroom without speaking a word. I threw the comforter back, helped him remove his shirt and pants, and tucked him in. He lay in a fetal position, punctuating his breathing with an occasional moan.

"Get some rest, Danny. I'll be right in the next room if you need me."

He didn't come out of the bedroom. A couple of hours later, I went into the room and crept into bed with him with my clothes on. I was careful not to touch or wake him.

"You're not alone, Danny," I whispered. I didn't know what else to say.

When we woke up Monday morning, it was already past 9:30. He immediately reached for his clothes and started getting ready.

"You can't go into work like this," I said. "Call the office and tell them you have a fever and think it's the flu. You need some time."

He nodded, went into the kitchen, and called his work. His voice sounded so dull I'm sure whoever answered was convinced he was truly sick.

I rustled up an omelet and set it before him. He picked at his plate half-heartedly, then abruptly headed back to the bedroom. I came in and told him I had to go to the office for a few hours. I would stop off and get something for dinner.

"If you need anything, anything at all, just call," I said.

He nodded vaguely and shut his eyes.

I did a few simple things at work. Then I told my boss I was expecting a repairman and needed to work from home. On the way back, I stopped at Gristedes and filled my shopping cart with various cheeses and hard sausage and prepared dinners.

When I got back, Danny was sitting in the living room, holding a cup of coffee and staring into space. I put away the groceries and cautiously sat down in a chair across from him.

"Do you want to talk about it?" I asked.

He looked up from his coffee. There were dark circles under his eyes.

"I know it must have been awful," I continued. "You're hurting. What do you need from me? How can I help?"

When he began to speak, his voice was raw. "What have I done?" he said. "How could I have screwed up this badly? What must Charlie be thinking? I have no idea how to make this right."

I got up, grabbed both of his hands and led him to the sofa, where we could sit together.

"We are going to take this one day at a time, okay? First, we need to get the stuff you took from the house. Did you leave it in your car outside the station?"

"Yes," he croaked.

"Not a good idea. Give me the keys to your car."

He pulled them out of his picket and handed them to me.

"I'm going to get your stuff now. My friend from White Plains is downtown tonight, and she's headed back. I called her earlier, and she said she could drive me to your car. I'll retrieve your car and belongings and drive back here. and we'll unload. Okay?"

"Okay. Thanks. Joanna, I…"

"Shh. You know you can stay with me as long as you want. Forever would be fine with me."

That got a smile from him.

"I know you don't feel like it right now, but you need to speak to a lawyer and find out how to protect yourself. You need to be able to see Charlie. I know a good attorney. One of the partners at work broke up with his wife last year, and I'll find out who he used."

"I don't know if I'm ready for that."

"At the least, you need to contact Charlie. It would be good if you could see him. You need to let him know you'll be there for him."

"I guess you're right."

"I wish I could stop your hurt," I said. "I love you. You're the best man I've ever known. I want you to know you'll never be alone. Whatever Sally and her family do, you're going to stand strong. I know you have it in you."

# CHAPTER 33

**DANNY**

I don't remember too much of the next few days, but I do remember calling Joanna and saying I needed her.

She reacted fast. "I'll pick you up at the station. What train will you be on?"

It took all the energy in me to get to the station and board the train. I was full of regret. What could I possibly have been thinking, to throw away the only stable life I ever had? After I took my seat, the ghosts from the past danced around me, mocking my stupidity.

First came my father's tobacco-cracked voice. "So, Danny Boy, you thought you were better than the old man?" His laugh sounded like a rattle. "Let me tell you something about people like you and me. No matter how hard we try, we're bound to screw things up."

"I'm not like you," I shot back.

"You're more like me than you think. Remember how you got booted out of school for breaking that kid's arm? Congratulations, you've graduated to breaking a woman's heart, just like I did with your mother. You're a loser, kid. You always were and always will be, no matter what you do."

Then my mother came into focus. "You never called after you left. You thought you were better than us. Hitched your wagon to those highfalutin McAllisters. I always knew it would never last. Sooner or later, they'd discover who you really were."

My thoughts turned to Joanna. Did I truly know her? The sex was fantastic, and she adored me. But how would she feel when she had me day after day? Would we get sick of each other? Would we start bickering about who's going to pay for dinner this time? About who's going to clean the kitchen countertop?

Joanna hated to have anything out of place. Would she go crazy if I left my shoes on the floor? If I brought Charlie over, and he made a mess? My heart broke when I thought of Charlie. What would he think when he returned from his grandparents and all traces of me were gone?

The train pulled into the station, and I got ready to disembark. When Joanne picked me up, I just felt tired. More tired than I've ever been in my life. I couldn't focus, and I couldn't talk. When we got to her apartment, all I wanted to do was sleep and forget the whole miserable mess I had created.

Joanna picked up on my mood and gave me plenty of space. But I still felt ashamed. This wreck of a man, not the

Danny she had fallen for. I had no idea whether she could ever put up with the Danny who sleepwalked into her place that night, and if she couldn't, where would I go from there?

# CHAPTER 34

**DANNY**

I needed to let Joanna see a more decisive Danny. So I made an appointment with John Wagner, the attorney recommended by Joanna's colleague. His office was in a new steel and glass high-rise. The elevator whisked me up to his office on the 37th floor. I reported to a well-coifed woman in her early 20s, perched on a swivel chair at the front desk.

"Welcome, sir! Something to drink? Gin and tonic? A splash of Scotch? We also have non-alcoholic drinks. Coffee, perhaps, or soda?

"I'll just have coffee, thanks."

"Coming right up. Have a seat. Mr. Wagner will be with you in a few minutes."

I sat down and checked out the poster-sized pictures on the wall. In one, Elle Macpherson was in a bikini on a beach, opening the passenger door of a Chevy Camaro. Another was a closeup of Joe Montana holding a football over his head, ready to throw. Then came a scantily clad Jerry Hall leaning backward on the hood of a Pontiac Firebird.

The receptionist came over with the coffee and took a practiced look at me.

"You're going to find Mr. Wagner is great at what he does. He's been practicing divorce law for 23 years." She set the coffee down in front of me.

"Thanks," I said, picking up the cup. I shifted in my seat uncomfortably. Being here felt like an admission of failure. Whichever way I looked at it, I would be walking out on my wife and my kid. Would a good guy do something like that?

"You must be Daniel Monahan!""

I looked up. A slight man in his 50s was approaching me. He had on aviator glasses and a full head of black hair closely cropped and combed back neatly.

"John Wagner," he said. "Pleased to meet you."

He was dressed in a three-piece suit with a handkerchief neatly tucked into the breast pocket. His black shoes positively shone. He stretched out his hand.

I stumbled up from the chair and shook his hand. In my rumpled oxford-cloth short and chinos, I felt out of place.

He examined my face while shaking my hand. "Nice to meet you. May I call you Dan?

"Actually, I go by Danny."

"Great! You can call me John. Let's go into my office." He turned and directed me through a door. Walking around a big desk at the center of the room, he motioned me to the chair in front of him. I sat down and looked at the diplomas lining the wall behind him. Yale University. Then University of Pennsylvania Law School. Not bad.

"Now, I know this must be difficult time for you. We'll try to make it as easy as possible."

I nodded. High stacks of files were piled up on the desk. A large wall clock behind ticked slowly away. Every minute I spent here was adding to my bill. Joanna told me to expect to pay at least $10,000 when all was said and done. About two months' salary before taxes.

"First, I'd like you to summarize your story. Tell me what brought you to me."

"I don't know where to start, really. Sally and I have been married nearly 15 years. We have an eight-year-old son, Charlie. We own a house in White Plains. My wife is a teacher, currently working part-time. I'm a senior account director at the ad agency Cooper, Masters & Young."

"Oh yes, I've heard of it," the attorney said. "What kind of salary are you pulling in there, Danny?"

It didn't take him much time at all to get to the bottom line. "About $75,000 a year," I said.

He nodded appreciatively. "Looks like we have some room to work with. From a budgetary standpoint, I mean."

"What is your rate, John? I hear you guys charge by the hour."

"Yes, well, my rate is $175 an hour. Plus incidentals."

I felt a little sick. "What do you think the total bill would be for me? I heard I should expect something like $10,000. Is that a good ballpark estimate?"

"Oh, I can't tell you that yet. I have to find out more about your case before I could even give you an estimate. They don't make divorce easy in this state. So let's find out more. You've sketched your basic circumstances. Tell me, what brings you to my office? Why do you want to get a divorce?"

"Well, I fell in love."

"Aha! And that means you fell out of love with your wife?"

"Yes. I didn't want it to happen. Believe me, I really wish we could have made it to the finish line. The last thing I wanted was to...to find myself here."

"Of course." John Wagner played with his gold pen. "I assume you want to keep part of the proceeds from your house and be able to see your son regularly. And you'd like to keep the alimony and the child support reasonable."

"Yes, that's right. I don't want to be forced to pay a lot, especially considering my job may be on the line." I laughed nervously.

"Oh?" He did not look happy. "Sorry to hear. Now, I think we're getting to the point where I need to ask, are there any, umm, complications in your life that will make our case more difficult?"

"Well, I am still seeing Joanna – the woman I've been involved with – but not actually living with her. I found a small apartment close to home. If Joanna and I cohabited, it would make it harder to see my son, I guess."

"Yes, that is usually the case. Tell me, did you come forward to your wife about your relationship with Joanna? Or did she find out on her own?"

"Well, my wife found us together. You might say we were caught in the act."

The attorney shook his head and looked glum. "Anything else you'd like to bring up?"

"Um, my wife is alleging I knocked her unconscious the last time I was at the house. But that's not true!"

"Go on."

"I inadvertently pushed her. Lightly. She was very angry at me, coming at me with her fists. I was only trying to ward her off. She lost her balance and tripped over one of my son's toys. She ended up hitting her head on the side of the coffee table."

"Hmm." John Wagner narrowed his eyes. "But she's going to allege you pushed her down? With malice, I assume."

"Yes. I think she's going to stick with her story."

"But okay, you can still show the court you are not a violent person, correct? Other than this one incident, which, of course, you are disputing, you have never harmed your wife?"

"Yes, that's very true."

"Well, that's nice to hear! Might there be other violence in your life?"

There was, of course. I didn't want to get into it.

He sensed my hesitancy. "Danny, I don't need to tell you that as your attorney, I will need to know everything that has happened to you. No matter how bad. It will come out in the trial if it doesn't come out here. We'll be accused of covering it up."

Okay, I thought, so here goes. "My father was incarcerated for domestic violence. Against my mother. It happened when I was 14 years old."

Stunned silence. "Hmm, well, let's set that aside for now. Anything else?"

"I am very different from my father. But there is one incident I need to tell you about. I broke a kid's arm at high school and got expelled. It happened at my Catholic high school, and I did it because of being bullied on account of my father's incarceration. But I moved on. I became a very good student and went on to college."

"Okay, okay. We'll work with that." John Wagner looked a little pained. "Let me tell you straight, we have a challenge ahead of us. New York is a no-contest state. Adultery is still considered a crime here. In all likelihood, Sally will file a petition with the court alleging adultery as the grounds for divorce. She might add in an abuse charge. You will be served with a petition, and we will have a certain time to respond. Okay so far?

"Well, yes, okay."

"If we contest the divorce, the case will go to trial. If not, the court will typically hold a hearing. Once that happens, the court will eventually issue a decree of divorce. Got it?"

"Yes."

"You have a few options. Frankly, none of them will likely apply to your situation. First, you could reconcile with Sally. But it sounds as if that's not something that's going to happen. Divorce can get pricey, so if you have any doubts, or want to speak with a marriage counselor first, now is the time to say so."

"No, not really. We've tried something like that already."

"I see. All right, second. If Sally is also guilty of adultery or other marital misconduct, or if she hasn't been an attentive mother, I could argue you are not the only one at fault. Would that apply?"

"Um, no. Sally's been a good mom."

"Third, you could claim undue hardship. For instance, if you are financially dependent on Sally or her family the court would factor that in."

"Her father put down the money for our house, and he helped me get my first job at the agency. Dr. McAllister is very well-known neurosurgeon. My boss is a close friend of his. That's why I'm not sure I will keep the job."

John sighed. "Danny, I'll be straight with you: this is not going to be an easy case for us. How about Sally? You said she had been teaching part-time, but at present, is she primarily a homemaker? If so, you might have to provide alimony."

"She has a degree in elementary education. And yes, she's been working part-time and continues to do so to take care of Charlie. He has ADHD and…"

The attorney couldn't quite suppress a groan. "I get the picture. The chances are you'll have to pay child support and probably alimony for a couple of years. I'll try to minimize the alimony since she does have a professional degree and there's evidence her family can back her up financially. But you are still the responsible party.'

"What about Charlie? Will I be able to see my son?"

"If you want to have at least partial custody of him, you'll need to set up a room for him in your apartment. It will help if I can argue you already have a residence in place with a room for him."

"I do, but it's a one-bedroom. I'm renting it on a monthly basis."

"I suggest you consider a larger place with a separate bedroom that you furnish specifically for your son's visits. As soon as you receive the petition for custody from Sally, I will immediately file a writ to get you temporary visitation. I'll also try to subpoena Sally's hospital records. Hopefully, we can show you did not cause her accident.

"One more question. Can you gather some friends or family members willing to give depositions about your character and your loving relationship with your son?"

My mind started racing. I couldn't think of a soul – not at work, not in my private life. I could bring Maureen, but Sally would say she was hardly ever at the house. Joanna? Of course not! In the past 15 years, the only people we hung out with were the McAllisters and Sally's close friends. She even knew the neighbors better than I did.

"No," I said miserably. "Most of the people I was even a little close to are connected to my wife."

John gazed at me sympathetically. I could imagine him thinking, "poor bastard." Then he rested back in his chair.

"Okay, we'll do our best with what we have," he said. "I'll caution you; your wife's lawyer will try to do a number on your head. Spurned wives usually start by asking for the moon – nearly every cent you've got. Let me worry about that so we'll get an agreement that works for both parties. In the meantime, I need a full accounting of all the property and assets you have, Both individually and jointly. The information will take some time for you to get together, so I suggest you start right away."

He hesitated and locked eyes with me. "Divorces can get very heated. But you need to relax. I've taken on even tougher cases than this. It all gets settled in the end. Today's consultation fee will be $500. We'll be in touch soon."

# CHAPTER 35

**DANNY**

If I ever hoped Jared Morgenstern would be an impartial party with my impending divorce, I was quickly disenchanted. What did I expect? He was Dr. McAllister's best childhood buddy. Jared now stopped by spontaneously at my weekly team recap meetings, hoping to unearth some reason to fire me. He'd stand in the back of the room glowering at me, with his mouth puckered as if swallowing a roach.

During a break, I turned to him as one team member set up the slide projector. "Jared, do you want to tell us what you think? Give us that wisdom we count on you for!"

He sat there stone-faced. "No, I don't think I'll add anything right now."

A team member dimmed the lights and started the slideshow about tactics for the Proctor & Gamble account, our largest client.

A pie chart displayed the kinds of ad-buys for P&G: Print 10%, Radio 5%, Television 80%, Other 5%.

"Danny?" A disembodied voice called out in the dark from the far side of the room.

"Yes, Jared?"

"Why such a tiny sliver for print? A hell of a lot of people read the Sunday paper alone, not to mention the magazines. That's a huge market."

"Well, that was what P&G asked for. Reba Knauss herself said she wanted us to focus on TV. She's concerned newspapers are primarily read by an older segment, and Pantene's target audience is young women. She's very big on building a larger reach with a more visual impact. And she wants to showcase the vibrant colors of the packaging. Can't do that with newspapers."

"It seems a little skewed to me. And yes, you *can* do that with the Sunday newspaper magazines."

I met with him later in his office. "Why don't you ask Reba what she thinks about print?"

"Will do."

"I understand you have a very *special* relationship with her."

He had to get his jab in there. Dr. McAllister probably told him I was fucking every good-looking woman in sight, even though my relationship with Reba remained pure business.

"Reba and I see eye to eye, and that can only be good for the agency," I reminded him.

"That's fine. But we don't want our most important client to miss the opportunities that present themselves in newspapers and magazines. Just a 5% adjustment in the media strategy could help us expand our reach to older women, particularly if we go for the Sunday magazines."

"I hear you, Jared. I'll ask Reba the next time we meet." In fact, I did ask Reba, and, of course, she had no interest in moving any ad dollars from TV to print.

My working atmosphere now seemed lined with minefields. I was determined not to give Jordan any reason to let me go. I needed to hang on for a while, at least through the divorce. For the moment, that seemed very possible. My client was satisfied with me. I was admired by my team. I just had to make sure nothing went wrong.

But things did go wrong. Spectacularly wrong. Before that, though, it looked like things might work out. As if.

Jared popped his head into my office one morning. "Have a sec, Danny?"

I walked behind him down the long hall to his office. I had no idea what he wanted. Whatever it was, I couldn't imagine it being good.

So I was pleasantly shocked when he began by saying, "Good news, Danny". He actually offered a ghost of a smile before quickly flattening his expression. "I just got off the phone with Joe Pepperman and his head honchos." Pepperman was the senior vice president of marketing at P&G. They are very happy with the metrics from our last campaign."

"That's great," I said, and boy, did I mean it!

"So happy, in fact, they want to give us a shot at some more business. I'm about to receive their request for proposal. P&G is about to expand its line of men's grooming products under the Old Spice umbrella. Pepperman wants an established partner to handle the launch.

Jared stopped and considered me. "Reba Knauss specifically asked for you," he said. "Do you want to lead this thing?"

"Oh, yes, I'd be honored." I felt as if the weight of the world suddenly disappeared. My impending divorce, my estrangement from the McAllisters, my worsening relationship with Jordan. Everything would work out after all.

Then he got somber. "I'll be honest. I would not have picked you to lead this project. Now, I know you've been going through some *personal* issues. The less said about that, the better. I need to know Old Spice will have your complete attention and focus."

"Yes, of course," I said.

The challenges of this new assignment would be hefty. There would be plenty of blood, sweat, and tears before the presentation. Meanwhile, Sally filed for divorce, and I had to scramble to get my end of the paperwork ready.

The McAllisters had retained Thomas J. Gallagher, partner at the law firm of Gallagher, Keyes, and Thompson, the top Catholic divorce lawyer in New York City. When I told John Wagner, he whistled.

"They're going with the top guns," he said. "Gallagher is damn good and knows his stuff inside out. He's a real pro. We can't afford any blunders."

First and foremost, we needed to set up visitation with Charlie. Sally didn't want me to see Charlie at all. But Charlie had made it clear he wanted to see me. As I found out later, he was acting out in all sorts of ways.

Sally finally relented. Gallagher told my attorney I could visit Charlie but only in a supervised setting for a limited number of hours.

"We have to make absolutely sure everything goes right with these meetings," John Wagner told me. "No late shows or no shows or rescheduling. The court needs to believe Charlie is the most important person in your life."

"Of course he is," I said defiantly.

I was putting in a good 12 to 16 hours a day. I arrived at the office early and sat at my desk for hours – often until midnight – bleary-eyed and disoriented. Many times, I didn't bother going home. I just slept on the uncomfortable office couch without changing clothes, showering, or washing my hair.

Joanna called me one morning after one of these near all-nighters.

"Hi, I missed you last night," she said. "Missed your body next to mine."

"Me, too. Going through hell right now."

The next night, she showed up at my office late while I was toiling away all alone. She brought dinner she had picked up at Zabars. I hugged her but didn't have an extra minute to talk. She reached out and touched the dark circles under my eyes, kissing me gently before leaving.

Those few moments were a highlight, but the next day, it was more of the same. Leading the project meant dealing with other personalities on my team who were under as much stress as I was. Just when I thought I was making headway in developing a plan of how we would meet P&G's ROI goals and measure its success, my creative director, Bob Bolsen, barged into my office.

"Look Danny, we've got to talk now," he said.

I sighed. "Okay, what's up"? I was exhausted. I had spent the past few hours digging through my personal files to find tax statements going back five years.

"You gave me full authority to use my judgment in coming up with something innovative," he said. "Then, when I do something that will blow the client's socks off, all I get is pushback from you. All the creatives are demoralized. My art director is about to quit. You know I like you, man. But what gives, Danny?"

"Bob," I said through gritted teeth, "you handed me a campaign that's not targeted to our market. We're trying to reach a lower-income demographic. Your average Joe."

"I keep telling you, when people look at an ad, they want to aspire to a higher version of themselves. What don't you get about that, Danny?"

"I still think it misses the mark," I said. "I appreciate all the hard work, but Bob, it's not making it. I know what I'm asking, but I'd like you to give it one more try. How long will it take you?"

"Danny, I've been up all night for the past week. I don't even remember my wife anymore. Bunny thinks I'm having an affair. I have just so much in me."

"I hear you. We're all working really hard. Let's try to hang in there. We'll win this business. Then we can go celebrate and get back to our normal lives."

In spite of these tensions, the presentation began to come together. Bob and his creatives developed a series of amazing storyboards. Each one emphasized that Old Spice body wash was not just for old men but for men of all ages. For men who wanted to feel confident in how they smelled whatever they were doing – playing sports, working out, or trying to score with women.

The next day, Bob and his assistant, Frieda Lu, came triumphantly into my office.

"I think we got it!" he told me.

Frieda unveiled a board showing a cowgirl riding on a horse.

Bob narrated. "This beautiful cowgirl reins in her horse next to a virile cowboy. He's paused to view the mountainous road ahead."

Frieda flipped to the next board. "Flirtatiously, she whispers that she loves his scent," she said. "What the heck is he wearing?"

Frieda flipped again. "When he tells her it's Old Spice body wash," Bob said, "she's awestruck. So much so that she

204

winks and asks if he wants company on the trail ahead. They ride off together in the sunset."

"You nailed it!" I cried, giving Bob a high-five.

The media plan arrived on my desk afterward. It had a balanced mix of TV commercials, print ads, radio spots, outdoor advertising, public relations, and sponsorship of sporting events. The emphasis centered on TV.

My team had done it. They had put together an indisputable winner. Now it was up to me to bring this baby home by presenting it. It was less than 24 hours until showtime. I headed home to get a good night's sleep.

Lying in bed, my mind was focused on the dozens of last-minute details. Did the creatives include the last-minute revision we had discussed? Did I go far enough in my executive summary? Are there other metrics I should have introduced?

I tossed and turned, but I woke up energized. By mid-afternoon, the presentation would be behind me. That evening, I would see Charlie. The rest of the week, I would be at Joanna's. I arrived at the office early. It was buzzing with activity.

Jared was revved up. "Hey, Danny, are you ready for the win?"

"Hell, yes I am!" I said joyfully. This would be the final lap.

Bob Bolsen gave me a V-sign. "Let's knock 'em dead, Danny!"

Team members were making sure everything we needed was packed and ready to bring to P&G.

Then came the call that would change everything.

It was Sally. "Danny, a change in plans. I have an impacted wisdom tooth. Periodontist's schedule is packed but he's fitting me in. I just ordered a taxi and need to take off."

"Sorry to hear, Sally. I'll pick up Charlie after school and take over."

"Not so fast. I also just got off the line with the school nurse. Charlie's been throwing up. She says he has a fever. He needs to be picked up, and you need to go there right now."

"Now? Sorry, not possible. I have a huge presentation in less than two hours at P&G."

"Well, get someone else to it. Danny, he's your son too!"

"I can't. I'm the one who's leading the presentation."

"This is Charlie I'm talking about."

"This thing is a big deal. They've called in the top brass. Look, it will be over at four and I'll rush right there."

Sally swore under her breath "That's not good enough, Danny. You keep asking for more time with Charlie. The one time – the *one* time – I need you to pick him up, you tell me you can't do it."

"I want to do it, Sally. I have a presentation and my job is on the line if I don't deliver. Do you want me to lose my job?"

"Frankly, Danny, I don't give a shit about your job. I've heard enough about your 'big presentations' when what you were really doing was bedding down with your slut. You need to take care of Charlie."

"Sally, can't your parents do it? Or your sister? Can one of them go over there?"

"No. My parents are away for a couple of days at a medical conference. And Kathy is working. It's the middle of a work week."

"Well, what about a neighbor? Or a friend? Surely there's someone."

"No, Danny. I have no time to call around. Why don't you do it?"

"You've got to understand. I can't blow off this presentation."

"Yes, you can, and you will."

"This is crazy! Are you setting me up? Just be reasonable, Sally."

"Look, the taxi is already here. I don't care how you do it. You handle it. You better find someone or believe me, I'll let my lawyer know what a crappy father you are. I better not find out that 'someone' is your slut. Get the hell over to that school and take care of Charlie!"

She hung up. I tried calling her back, but the phone rang and rang. I tried calling my attorney, but he was in court. Time was running out. I dialed the number for the school and was connected with the school nurse.

"You're Charlie's father?" she said. "Yes, I have him. When can you get here?" She paused to listen to my answer.

Her voice reeked of disapproval "Okay, you're tied up. Well, he can stay here for a while, 'til 3:30 at the latest. Then I need to leave. Can you make it by that time?

The presentation was scheduled to begin at 1 pm. Even if all went well, it wouldn't be over until 2:30. Questions and answers afterward would mean a longer delay. That gave me less than an hour to take a cab to White Plains.

Bob Bolsen was knocking on my door. I gestured him away. Who else could I call? I tried a few of my former neighbors, but no one picked up. I couldn't ask Joanna. There would be hell to pay if I did.

Then I thought of Maureen. I got through to her, and I explained the situation. She sighed. "It's not the best day, Danny Boy. But I hear you. Give me a sec to think this through." I held my breath.

"All right," she said, "I've moved things around. I can pick Charlie up around 2:45 or 3:00. I'll take him to your apartment and wait for you. First, I'll need to get your key. Can you leave it at your reception area?"

I agreed. I called the school back and asked to speak to the nurse again.

"A friend will pick up Charlie," I said.

"A friend?"

"She's someone I've known since childhood. Her name is Maureen Boyd. She'll be there by 3."

"It's unusual not to have a parent come in these situations. Right now, Charlie has a temperature of 101.5. He really shouldn't still be at school."

"I'm sorry, it's the best I can do."

I hung up with a sigh. I could also hear a rising chorus outside my door: "Danny! Almost time to go. "We're all waiting for you." "Danny, we need to review this section more time."

I opened the door. "Could you guys please wait a second?" I asked. "I'll be right back." I hastily wrote a note and took it and my key to the reception area, then stopped in the men's room to relieve my aching bladder. Leaving the stall, I took a moment to look into the mirror.

"Danny, Danny, you need to get a grip," I said to the frantic-looking man staring back at me. My hair was disheveled, my eyes were wild and bloodshot, and a canker sore was forming on the left side of my lip.

I splashed some water on my face, tried combing my hair with my fingers and adjusted my shirt. Even so, I imagined I looked disheveled and harried. So many things could go wrong. What if Charlie's fever rose before Maureen could get there? What if he refused to go with her? He'd only met her once or twice, and Sally always cautioned him about trusting strangers.

I raced to meet up with Jared and the team. We all took the elevator down to the lobby, went out on the street, and started hailing a few cabs for our ride to P&G's New York offices.

Bob Bolsen climbed in next to me in the back of a cab. He peered at me with concern. "Danny, you don't look too good. What's going on, my man?"

I felt the sweat pouring down my neck. I wasn't used to wearing a coat and tie. "Just a last-minute thing. I'm definitely ready. On all cylinders."

We piled out of our cabs with our presentation materials and made our way up to the P&G offices. There we were greeted by a young receptionist.

"Welcome, Cooper, Masters & Young. We're expecting you. Unfortunately, Mr. Pepperman has been delayed by a last-minute call from Cincinnati. In the meantime, won't you please sit down? It should only be a few minutes, I think."

Jared sat across from me, assessing me with narrowed eyes. I stared at the clock overhead. It ticked on for 15 minutes, 20 minutes, 30 minutes. This presentation would obviously be running late. How would I know Charlie was going to be safe in my apartment? I had no way of contacting Maureen.

Finally, 45 minutes after we arrived, we were ushered into the meeting room. Joe Pepperman and his team greeted us. I locked eyes with Reba. She looked a little worried and motioned for me to straighten my tie. Then she gave me the V-sign.

"I'm sorry I was late," Pepperman said. "Urgent business matter back in Cincinnati."

My whole team sat down around the conference table, facing the P&G executives. I waited as the folders were distributed and storyboards mounted on their frames.

"Are you sure you're okay?" Bob whispered to me, his eyes flashing. "Danny, whatever you're dealing with, you've got to focus."

"I will!" I shot back. I could hear some coughing and shuffling. I arose with confidence I did not feel and started the presentation.

"Most of you know us," I said. "We've been loyal partners of P&G for years now, and we couldn't be more grateful to be here today. I want to introduce my first-rate team now." I could see them visibly relax as I ran through each one's qualifications. Old Danny Boy was back!

"The way we see it, many men out there are reluctant to use body lotion because they associate it with not being very manly. How do we change their perception that Old Spice body lotion is not a feminine product while at the same time differentiating it from brands they already know, like Nivea and Dove? Those are the two top-of-mind challenges we confronted when our team put together the campaign that I'm proudly about to show you."

Joe Pepperman looked pleased. I was off to a good start, but was it just me? It felt stifling in the conference room. I took out my handkerchief, furtively mopped my brow, and continued.

"Now, I don't have to tell you, according to a recent survey, only 12% of men in the United States use body lotion. That gives us a big field to convert to the benefits of softer skin, reduced body odor, sun protection, and relief from dry skin. But how?"

I began to hear a dull buzzing in my ears. It felt so hot! I tugged at my tie. Jared was muttering to himself. Reba looked concerned. I plunged ahead, presenting statistics about the segments most likely to be receptive buyers. I touched on all of them: men who want to look their best, men with dry skin, and so forth.

I actively tried to hide the physical distress, which was increasingly becoming evident. I knew my sweating was becoming more pronounced. My breath was ragged, and I felt an ache in my chest. I was now dreadfully afraid I was going to pass out. So I quickly passed the baton,

"There's a lot more I want to talk about today. But first, let me introduce you to Bob Bolsen, our creative director extraordinaire. Most of you know him for the excellent work he and his creatives have done for P&G."

Bob sharply twirled his head. This was not part of the rehearsal. I was supposed to review the challenges, objectives, goals, and target audiences. By doing so, I'd pave the way for him to introduce the key messages. He recovered quickly and launched into his segment. "Umm, as Danny was saying ..."

I took a seat and felt even more lightheaded. The last thing I remembered was the storyboards going up. Then darkness.

The next thing I knew, I was waking up in an emergency room. EKG wires were attached to my chest, and a monitor was beeping away. What time was it anyway? How did I get here? What happened in the presentation? I needed to get up – I was sure of that – and get to Charlie.

I raised myself up on my elbow. The resident-on-call gently pushed me back.

"Relax, Mr. Monahan. You're here at New York Presbyterian. Our EMS team brought you in about an hour ago, and you've been in a semi-lucid state. We thought you might have suffered a mild heart attack. The good news

is your EKG and bloodwork are all fine. I'm your doctor,
John Rizzuli."

"What happened with my presentation?" I croaked.

"Your presentation? Well, I wouldn't worry about that.
The important thing is you're okay. I want you to relax."

I raised myself with my elbows. "I can't stay here. Need to
get to Charlie."

"Who's Charlie?"

"My son. I was supposed to pick him up from school."

"Well, okay, we can try to help you with that. Is there
anyone we can call for you? To let them know you're all right,
and to see about your son."

"Yes, uh, Joanna Sjostrom." I gave the doctor her number.

"I want to keep you here for a while longer to monitor
you. If everything continues to check out, you can go home.
Tell me: have you been under undue stress lately?"

I gave a sarcastic laugh. "Stress? Oh, just a bit. Look, can
we at least get the paperwork started?" Almost by command,
a staff member appeared with some papers in hand. The doctor continued to go over my vitals as I signed sheet after
sheet of post-visit instructions.

Joanna arrived while I was completing the last of the dis-
charge papers.

She hugged me. "Oh, Danny, are you okay?"

"Yes, I'm fine," I said. But I felt close to tears.

"I called your apartment and spoke to Maureen. She has
Charlie there. He has a fever and is very cranky. She said to

tell you she's been through this before with her daughter and not to be unduly concerned."

"Can she stay there a little while longer? "

"Yes, another hour or two, she said."

Joanna ordered a limo for us. She helped gather up my things and called Maureen back to let her know we were on our way. Only when the limo came and we took our seats did she finally ask: "Danny, what's been going on? What happened today?"

I gave her a crooked smile. "Well, I blew it. I felt faint and someone else had to finish the presentation. I have no idea how it turned out. But I can tell you this: I'm done for. They were waiting for some reason to get rid of me. Now they have it."

"Oh babe."

"Sally called right before we left for P&G. She had some dental thing going and told me I needed to pick Charlie up right away – or else. Told me if I did not personally go get Charlie from school, she'd make sure it ruined my case in the divorce. I doubt I'll get any custody over Charlie. But otherwise, I'm honky dory."

"I'm so sorry."

"And what does this mean for us, Joanna? I'm going to have no job. No prospects, no money, no future. Why would you want anything to do with me?"

"Okay, you've had a horrible day. You hate yourself. You want me to join in? It's not going to happen. I love you, baby."

"But there's no job, and then my son."

"Let's not get ahead of ourselves. You don't know whether you'll lose your job. Or lose custody over Charlie."

"Oh yeah?"

"Tell you what. You're going to make sure Charlie is okay. After you get some rest, we'll figure out a way forward."

Joanna dropped me off at my apartment. I told her I would call her a little later. I watched her drive away, and I walked upstairs. Maureen answered the door.

"Shh!" she whispered, a finger pressed to her lips. "Come on in."

My son was lying on the couch on his back, mouth open, lightly snoring. His dark hair was plastered to his head. He looked relatively peaceful.

"I gave him a children's aspirin and got him to eat some soup and drink some water," Maureen whispered. "He's a good kid, but he's still not feeling well. And he's scared."

"Oh Maureen, I don't know how to thank you."

"Don't worry about it," she said. "I'm more concerned about you than I am about Charlie. I hear your presentation didn't go well. Sorry to hear."

"Well, them's the breaks, I guess." I tried to put on a smile.

"I'm glad to help. Tim is on his way to pick me up. He should be here any time now."

Shortly, Maureen's husband came to the door. She grabbed her sweater. "One more thing, Danny," she said. "Joanna's a keeper. You better not screw up."

Charlie slept fitfully for another hour and eventually opened his eyes. He stared at me for a minute and sat up. "Daddy, you're here!" he said, breaking into a smile.

And I was. I was there. If I were ever sure of anything, it was just that: I was there. After the horrific day I had gone through, for the moment, it was all that mattered.

# CHAPTER 36

## DANNY

I let Sally know Charlie would be staying with me overnight. She wasn't happy about it, but considering the hour was late and he had fallen asleep, she agreed.

The next day, Charlie's color came back but he still was running a slight fever. I made an appointment with the pediatrician and then called Sally again, arranging for her to meet us there. She was already sitting rigidly in the waiting room when we arrived.

"Mommy!" Charlie called and ran to her. Sally smiled and hugged her son before shooting me a poisonous look.

"He could have ended up in the hospital, you know."

"Sally let's not be melodramatic. His fever has subsided. It was a tough situation, but everything worked out."

"Okay. I'm not going to talk about it anymore in front of Charlie," she said.

We sat in silence. She was seething. I knew the silence wouldn't last for long. Of course, I was right.

"By the way, Jared called my father and said something about you going to the hospital. I wish you had told me. Charlie was sick! You were in no shape to watch over him last night."

"Thanks for the heartfelt concern, Sally. Great of Jared to let you know. Yeah, I had been working 16-hour days for the presentation. Your call, which came in two hours before I was set to take off, sure didn't help. Especially when we both know you were just being vindictive by insisting it had to be me and only me. I was dealing with exhaustion. Everything else checked out, and I'm perfectly fine. As you can see with your own eyes."

"Oh, poor Danny. Sixteen hours of work a day. That only left you with – what? – eight hours to fuck your slut. No wonder you ended up exhausted."

"Great, Sally. Right in front of Charlie. You're a class act. You know damn well I would never let anything bad happen to Charlie."

"Don't lecture me about class acts. After what you did."

Charlie was staring at us wide-eyed, his lip quivering. His mother was about to let loose some more touches of sarcasm when the pediatrician opened her door.

She stood there, arms folded, surveying the scene. Sally and me looking like we were ready to kill each other. Charlie behind us, rocking in his chair, his eyes filled with tears.

We shuffled in behind her. By now, Charlie was full-out bawling. The pediatrician spoke to him softly while examining him. She said our son had a respiratory virus. He'd be back to normal in a couple of days but the last thing he needed was stress. Sally and I locked eyes and each of us gave the slightest of nods. I knelt down and gave Charlie a big hug.

"You stay healthy now, little buddy."

"I really liked staying with you, Daddy. And that woman was really nice too. Can we do it again?"

Sally turned bright red. So much for not adding stress. She spat out, "Danny, I can't believe you. I've already told you that woman better not be anywhere around Charlie. Now I find out she's..."

"Relax, would you? He's talking about my old friend Maureen. Not Joanna."

Sally glared at me before slowly exhaling. "Okaaaay, Charlie. We need to get back. Say goodbye to Daddy." Grabbing his hand, she strode to the door. My son kept looking backward as she pulled him along.

Once I got back to my apartment, I took a few deep breaths. No way around it. I had to call work and let them know I couldn't come in for a few days. Emergency room doctor's orders. I dialed Jared's number and got hold of him right away.

"Danny," he said icily. "What happened yesterday? You're okay, I hope? Back home?"

"Yes, back home. Turns out it wasn't anything serious. I'm sorry about..."

Jared cut me off. "Good to hear. Listen, I hate to cut you off but I'm about to go into a meeting. I'll let the team know you're doing better."

"Oh Jared, one more thing. The doctor wants me to stay home and rest for a few days. Just as a precaution. I'll be back full force by Wednesday."

"Yes, I expected you would need a little time. Go on and take it. We should hear from P&G about their decision shortly. I'll let you know what I find out."

He hung up. I lifted the phone again and called Bob. I needed to know the worst of it – if the presentation ever achieved lift-off and if we had even the ghost of a chance.

"I tried pinch-hitting for you," Bob said. "As you can imagine, no one was focused after the EMS team took you away. Nothing like a little drama to dampen the mood. The P&G team couldn't wait to get rid of us. Reba was concerned about what happened to you. She said we should keep her updated."

"Damn. I guess we can kiss that business goodbye."

"Even worse, the agency presenting this afternoon is Lowe & Partners. I checked out some of their work. Danny, they're formidable. I really like their sleek design and their irreverent commercials."

"We're better than them."

"Yeah, we could have been. We had a fighting chance."

"I'm sorry, I let the team down."

Big pause. Then, "Look, man, you don't have to tell me. But what the hell happened with you yesterday? I've never quite seen you like that."

"I don't know where to begin. I've had a few tough weeks. I'm sorry."

He waited for me to say more, but there was nothing else to add. His voice softened. "Take good care of yourself, Danny Boy."

# CHAPTER 37

## JOANNA

Danny became a different person after the failed P&G presentation. The new Danny was badly hurting, with his life in flux. He was looking to me for help and guidance. Was I up to it?

We had been living in a bubble. A world of passionate lovemaking and the thrill of breaking all the rules to be together. We talked little about the past and not at all about the future. The present felt like a pretty good place to be. Now the present wasn't so enticing. But I knew if we could get through this rough patch, we could get through anything.

A couple of days after the presentation, Danny came to stay with me. We had agreed he would sleep over for a few nights. He arrived in a horrible mood.

"The agency wants to suck every ounce of blood out of me," he complained. "I spent nearly a month not eating or sleeping because of that damned presentation. I jeopardized my relationship with my son. How quickly they forget. I've raised their revenue by millions, just with the P&G account. Then I have an off day, and it's like, fuck you, Danny. Well, fuck all of them!"

I hated hearing him like this. "I get you're angry," I said. "You're right. People can be self-serving, and they can be cruel, and many aren't there when you need them the most. But there has to be someone in your life you can trust at times like this."

"Yeah, trust..." he said, with a distant and disdainful look. He was quiet for a minute. "How about me? Do you trust me?"

"Of course I do," I murmured.

He reached for me, methodically took off my clothes, and turned me on my side, never looking at me directly. He wetted his finger with his saliva and pushed it up my ass, first cautiously and then harder. I let out a gasp and wiggled with discomfort. His finger inched higher. I wasn't liking the sensation. It was as if Danny had morphed into a stranger I barely knew.

Danny didn't crack a smile. "Trust me now?" he said.

Uncertain what he was after, I nodded.

Danny caressed my inner thigh and my flat belly, and then caressed my special spot, rolling it between his thumb and index finger. He slid his fingers down both sides of my shaft.

"Good girl," he murmured. "You're really wet."

I was gasping for air, making sounds I'd never uttered before. Now this was what I liked! I arched my back, thrust myself into his eager tongue, and begged him not to stop.

But he stopped abruptly, walking over to the cozy chaise, and stared at me with his hands clutching his knees.

"You're not getting my cock tonight," he said. "I want to see you finish yourself off while I watch." I hesitated. "Go on. Do it!"

It didn't take much. I was so primed I only needed to stroke myself a few times, my hips rising and my breath coming in short gasps until I convulsively came.

"Good girl," Danny said again as I struggled to catch my breath. "You did what I asked but you're not about to get a reward."

I looked at him quizzically.

"Joanna, I'm going back to my apartment tonight. I'm not staying here. What you haven't realized up to now is I'm really not a very nice guy. I decide what to take and when to take it. Now let me ask again: do you still trust me?"

Tears welled up in my eyes. He was trying to destroy everything! A part of me knew that might happen if he felt threatened and pushed against the wall. But not to me. Not to the one woman who was on his side!

I had everything to lose. I blurted out, "I don't know what's going on with you tonight, Danny. You're very angry, and yes, I can understand why. So you're trying to tear it all down to prove yourself right. I mean all of it – even the good part with you and me. You're sabotaging us. I know this game because I could write the script on sabotaging. Well, give it your best shot. I'm not going anywhere."

His eyes softened a little.

"Yes, I trust you," I continued, "Even when you're hurting this badly."

"Why?" he asked, looking puzzled.

"Because…" I couldn't form the words. "I love you, Danny. When you're not acting out, you are the person I want to be with more than anyone else. You can't chase me away. I'm going to show you, not everyone is against you."

Danny nestled against me, his face half buried under my flowing hair. I soothed him as if he were a child. "It's okay, baby. It's okay," I told him. "I'm here for you. I promise I'll always be here for you. Sssshhhh. It's all going to turn out okay. Rest now."

I stroked him like I would a young child, running my fingers across his chest, pausing at the deep scar running across his upper chest. The one time I asked what caused it, he shrugged it off. I never did find out. He winced reflexively and then let himself be soothed by my caresses.

Danny never did make good on his threat to leave. He slept in my arms. Later we awoke at the same time and made love. This time, he was tender.

Until now, our time together was full of fleeting interludes, illusions, and the exhilaration of discovering each other. It was intense, and it was energizing. In the back of my mind, I always feared it couldn't last. Now, we were being put to the test.

I never gave in to denial. I knew half of the relationships like ours resulted in the cheating partner cheating again. I also knew Danny's heart and that he married Sally for the wrong reasons. He wanted to step into another reality. It didn't work, and now he was running scared. Like me, he would sabotage anything that would make him confront his feelings.

He had to be deathly afraid of losing what he wanted most. So he constantly pushed me away, hoping I'd end it and confirm his worst doubts about himself. But I didn't do it. At least, not then.

# CHAPTER 38

**DANNY**

I knew Jared Morgenstern would want to talk once I got back to work. I didn't expect it to happen hours after my return.

Jared came by in person and asked to see me immediately. He walked ahead of me back to his office. No smiles, no small talk. This would be like going to the nun's office back in school, except much more was on the line. My whole career, everything I had accomplished all these years at Cooper, Masters & Young.

I followed him into his office. He closed the door and motioned me to sit. From behind his desk, he cleared his throat and looked at me. "It's probably no surprise to you that P&G awarded their business to Lowe & Partners. They personally called to tell me. Isaiah Mustafa – you know, the former NFL wide receiver with the booming voice – will be the new face of Old Spice."

Jared leaned toward me. "A great idea. Too bad you didn't think of that. Lowe & Partners was going to be tough to beat. But I didn't expect you'd hand them their victory on a platter."

He got up and walked toward the window. "When Francis first told me about the divorce, he said you seemed to be having some sort of breakdown. 'He's not that way at work,' I told him. Yes, you were acting erratic and hurting Sally, who happens to be my goddaughter. But at work, your efforts for P&G were admirable."

He turned around and looked at me. "Since then, however, I've changed my mind. In the days you've been out, I interviewed everyone on your team. Most of them agreed you were not giving your all in the presentation."

That was a blow. I thought I had a good rapport with my team.

"They relayed that most nights, you fell asleep in the office. Some nights, I was told, you arrived at morning meetings bleary-eyed, as if you hadn't slept at all. The fact is you weren't giving clear direction. You weren't the captain of your own ship. In team meetings, they said, your mind seemed to be elsewhere. Some people said you were short with them and didn't give them the guidance they needed."

Jared came to an abrupt stop before me. "Look at you, Danny. You've got a contentious divorce and a child custody battle ahead of you. I'm not at all convinced you have the wherewithal to shepherd our largest account. Your performance the other day is clear proof."

"The P&G presentation, that was just a glitch. Overall, they've been happy with my work. I've increased billings significantly."

"Excuse me, Danny, I'm not finished. That day, I heard, you had some childcare issues. You were racing back and forth to reception minutes before your team had to pack up and leave. You were flustered and non-inspirational. Ultimately, you were unable to complete the presentation."

"It ended up being an unusually stressful time," I said. "I learned from it. It won't happen again."

"But it wasn't one bad day. There was the lead-up to the presentation. All the distractions were getting in the way of your work. Frankly, Danny, I don't see it getting any better. We lost a multi-million-dollar product extension. If I allowed you to continue in your current capacity, I believe our core business with P&G would be at risk."

He was gearing up for the final blow, and there was nothing I could do about it. Nothing I could say would change his mind.

"Danny, I'm asking you to go back to your office and pack up. HR will call you in the next day or two for your exit interview. Remember, all client information is property of Cooper, Masters & Young. Leave anything that's not personal in your office. Security will watch you pack and escort you to the entrance."

Here I was, about to be thrown out, as if I were a common criminal. And to never see this place again.

I got up. Jared continued talking to me. "We will offer you a generous three-month severance package. I had strong expectations for you, Danny. You were good at what you did. Francis was proud of you. I was, too. Then, for whatever reason, you took a wrong turn. You made some self-destructive decisions."

His body language conveyed that the conversation was finished.

"I hope you find your bearings again. Someday, when all this is behind you, I believe you'll be an asset to another company. Now, is there anything you'd like to say?"

"Would it matter if I did?" I asked.

# CHAPTER 39

## JOANNA

When I got home from work, Danny was already there, watching "Everybody Loves Raymond." He turned the volume down and looked at me with that soulful expression of his.

"Well, it happened," he said. "Jared fired me. For an extra warm and fuzzy touch, he had a security guard watching me pack and walk me out."

"Oh babe," I said, taking him in an embrace. "I'm so sorry."

"There's more, though. I've been adding up the numbers. Child support, alimony, $700 monthly rent on the apartment I barely use, utilities, insurance. I'm getting three months' severance, but when that dries up, I'm as good as screwed."

"Danny," I said, "you are one of the top account directors in the city. I'm so positive you are going to end up fine.

Maybe not at a big shop like Cooper, Masters & Young, but who cares about them?"

I ran my hand through his hair. "Tell you what. I'll put out some feelers for you, and you start making a list of people you know in other agencies. I know of an excellent head-hunter. I'll put you in touch with her. Just for tonight, let's not dwell on the next steps too much. Tomorrow, we'll figure it out, okay?"

Our sex life, once so passionate, had become practically nonexistent. Danny was preoccupied, depressed, and, I suspected, ashamed he had been laid so low. It didn't help that I had to get up early and go to work. By the time I ate my yogurt and got the coffee perking, Danny was just starting to wake up. Sometimes he wouldn't even be out of bed when I left.

Before Danny moved in, I would go out for a drink or hors d'oeuvres with friends. When I got home, I'd kick off my heels, put on some classical music, and unpack my latest Zabars find. Now I raced home to Danny.

My role was to bolster him up and tell him all was good, but his world was falling apart. Some nights, however, I felt too fatigued to hold a reassuring conversation with him.

Danny's problems were becoming my problems. I had begun taking liberties at work. Leaving unexpectedly, arriving tired and preoccupied. This didn't escape the notice of the partners. Bill, who had been my mentor and champion from the start, asked if he could have a word.

He was a big guy with salt-and-pepper hair and a hail-fellow-well-met demeanor. He reminded me of an overgrown teddy bear – friendly, cuddly, and benign.

Bill gestured for me to take a seat. "Joanna, I believe it's no surprise we've been grooming you to be a partner. I've got daughters. It's time we added a woman to the top echelon. You're a whiz at what you do, and the clients are wild about you."

I started to thank him, but he waved me off.

"Now, you can tell me to booger off because this is none of my business. But please indulge me for a moment. I know Danny Monahan. He's a likable guy, easy on the eyes, and a real go-getter. Hell, if I were a woman, I'd go after him too." Bill chuckled. "I've heard the rumors he left his wife and may be living with you. Is that right?"

"Yes. Is that a problem?"

"No, not really. No judgments here. It's almost the 1990s, and no one is going to run you out of town or paint you with a scarlet letter. But I know Danny was let go by Cooper, Masters & Young. He's radioactive right now. There's nothing Madison Avenue likes more than watching one of its super-stars take a tumble and explode."

"Danny's at a low point at the moment," I said. "I truly believe he'll end up somewhere. He's too good not to."

"Yes, you're right there. But the thing is, Joanna, there's more to it than that. I don't think this guy is good for you. Do you really want all the headaches that come with him?

The angry wife, the childcare, the bitterness? Look, he's already stressing you out. You've had to leave work early a few times in the past couple of weeks. That's not you."

"I'm sorry. I'll try to be more focused."

"I shouldn't pry. But I always imagined you with someone less volatile. Like that guy Gregg you brought to our holiday party. Someone steady and smart, with no baggage to bring to the table."

"I appreciate your concern for me, Bill. But I know what I'm doing. What Danny and I have is genuine."

"I'm speaking not as a boss but as your friend. Men like Danny are exciting at first. Soon enough, though, the glow begins to fade, and you end up in a world of hurt. You can get sidetracked from what you really want in life."

"Look, I promise I'll be careful," I said. "I hope you know you can count on me to keep up my end of things." I gently squeezed his arm while trying to exude all the confidence I didn't feel.

"Well, that's all I'm going to say. I respect you, Joanna. I'm sure you'll make the right choice."

As I left Bill's office, I was thinking, "Oh Danny, what's going to happen with us?"

# CHAPTER 40

**DANNY**

Just as my lawyer suspected, Sally and her family were going for blood.

We both knew they would nail me on the adultery charge. It was a slam dunk, with many affidavits from witnesses who had seen Joanna and me at My Place. Not to mention so-called work "friends" who were more than happy to collaborate with the defense.

They also noted a "suspicion of abuse," which Sally's hospital records supported. She alleged I pushed her, causing her to stumble and end up with a concussion, which was not true. But Sally stuck to her story.

Her family was eager to testify Sally was a good mother and the primary parent. I, on the other hand, was often absent from Charlie's school events and activities because I claimed (their word) to be at work. Sally's difficulty in conceiving and giving birth to Charlie and her embracing of motherhood contrasted with my so-called "hands-off" style of parenting.

My lawyer, John Wagner, read their charges to me and sighed. "Okay, most importantly, we need to neutralize this abuse allegation," he said. "Do not contact Sally or say anything about the case unless I'm involved. You'll want to keep records of every conversation you have on this issue. We need to vouch for your parenting abilities. Have you given any more thought to that list of relatives, friends, co-workers, and neighbors who can be character witnesses?"

"I have, and there's no one really," I replied. "My life has revolved around her parents, siblings, and friends. The parents of Charlie's playmates are closer to Sally than to me. And my relationships at the agency have all been kept at arms-length."

John Wagner looked pained.

"Of course, Joanna could vouch for me –"

"No! Not Joanna, for heavens' sake!" he said.

"Yes, I was about to say that. There's my old friend, Maureen. But she rarely saw me interact with Charlie."

My lawyer sighed. "We could arrange for you to undergo a psychological evaluation or even a lie detector test. Whatever you do, make sure you are honest, consistent, and cooperative."

"I can do that," I said.

"I might also remind her attorney about Family Code Section 3027. If she knowingly lied you were abusive, she would be subject to a variety of sanctions. She'd have to think long and hard about pursuing that claim."

"She'd have to admit to lying, and she won't. I know Sally."

"Getting her to admit to the truth might seem unlikely to you now," John Wagner said. "But when confronted with breaking the law, you'd be surprised how many wives change their story. So let's move on to the next topic."

He stood up, paced the room, and turned toward me. "I'll be honest with you, Danny. Right now, our best chance is to get your visitation with Charlie and ask for reasonable alimony. She does have her own source of income and then there's the financial involvement of her family. No one wins in a divorce, but we can minimize the damage."

"Whatever you can do," I said. "I just need to see Charlie. I don't want him thinking I'm disappearing from his life."

"They will probably demand supervised visitation. That means someone designated by the court will have to accompany you and Charlie at all times. This would continue until the judge is satisfied you can be alone with Charlie."

"What the fuck? Do they really think I'm a danger to him? I never lifted a hand to Charlie during his entire life, or his mother for that matter. I can't believe this!"

"Now, listen carefully. They'll argue this visitation will just be a precaution. In view of the evidence before the judge, they will have a strong case to get what they want."

Sure enough, Sally's attorney demanded visitation with court supervision and the judge granted the request. John Wagner met with me again to explain the details.

"The visits will start in a week," he said. "They would take place in a public setting after school, from 5 to 7 p.m."

I sat there silently as the news sunk in. Where the fuck was a court-designated supervisor when my old man was beating the crap out of my mother? And when I was left alone to deal with all of it? Who was protecting me?

"Danny, are you with me?"

"Yes, I'm with you," I said, simmering with resentment. "You're saying I'm supposed to sit there and pretend it's okay for some idiot to watch over me? Someone who doesn't know the first thing about me is supposed to judge my relationship with my own son?"

"Let it out now, Danny, because you must not – I repeat, MUST NOT – let the supervisor see one iota of your anger and frustration. You are going to be the most charming you've ever been in your whole life. Okay?"

"Got it," I murmured.

"That's what you have to do for now. If it goes well, we'll be able to get this supervised visitation lifted."

"How long will that take?"

"Maybe a few months. There is no way of knowing for sure."

"I have never, ever been violent with Charlie. He could even vouch of that."

"I know," John Wagner said. "But this is a game you're going to have to play. You are going to need to be calm and cooperative. I've had plenty of fathers let their anger overrule their good judgment."

"Okay," I muttered. "Okay!"

"Your goal will be to show the court-designated supervisor you're bonding well with Charlie. During these visits, be as positive as you can be. Be natural. Talk to him, play with him, ask about school or whatever he's interested in. In any case, you can't disparage Sally or draw Charlie into your issues with her."

"I understand. Anything else?"

"Yes. Make sure you're not late for the visit, even a minute late. Leave plenty of time in advance. This is no time for anything to go wrong."

# CHAPTER 41

## JOANNA

Danny sat around my apartment like a zombie.

I'd come home from my usual 10-hour workday, needing to unwind. But there he was, sprawled out on the couch, miserable and uncommunicative. I tried to soothe him with reassuring words, but he was scattered, inattentive, and unable to engage.

Then Danny got a break – a job possibility at Falcon Elliott, a big-deal ad agency. Its leadership had walked into a public relations fiasco, and they were looking for someone to help to make things better.

It all started when Falcon Elliott created an ad campaign for the popular TV show "Dynasty." It ran the word "Witch" over each photo of the show's three female divas, including Joan Collins. To make matters worse, someone in a leadership position sent a photograph of an African youth kissing a cow's backside to the woman who called their ads sexist.

JILL SHTULMAN

All hell broke loose that the agency was so insensitive and so contemptuous. Falcon Elliott seemed to be on a self-destructive tear and ended up being defined as not only misogynistic but also racist. In weeks, it lost $22 million in billings. Several key employees handed in their resignations.

The partners needed an experienced hand to help pull themselves out of the mess they had gotten themselves into. Someone suggested they reach out to Danny, who performed magic with accounts before his own fiasco. He went in for a job interview and came back looking energized.

"We'll have to see, but I think I got the job," he said.

That evening, we made passionate love. I caressed his face, his chest, even the scar that I assumed was caused by his father. He told me how grateful he was that I'd stood by him and said he adored me. I began to feel hope again.

The next day was a Saturday. He came up behind me and put his arms around my waist. "I have a surprise for you, babe," he whispered.

"What kind of surprise?" I wanted to know.

"It wouldn't be a surprise if I told you. Come, you'll need to dress up."

"Dress up for what?"

"We're going out tonight!"

I turned around and put my arms around him. "Oh Danny, I love you!"

"I love you too." He smiled. "Now get ready!"

I had just the thing to wear. A copper-toned midi-length silk slip dress that was lightweight, breezy, and seductive,

241

showing off my auburn hair and green eyes to maximum effect. I complimented the dress with a pair of Manolo Blahnik high heels that I had paid way too much for.

Danny came out looking dashing in his charcoal-gray suit and button-down pale blue Oxford cloth shirt. We hailed a cab, and Danny finally revealed his secret: "We're going to the Rainbow Room."

"I can't believe we're going there," I said. "I'm so excited! I've only gone once for some dreary business dinner." Even then, I couldn't help but be awed by the Art Deco style. The ceiling was adorned with chandeliers, the tables set with fine China and crystal, and the view was to die for.

"I've been there a few times myself," Danny said. "You know, with her family and all. Anyway, it's a great place. There is nobody I'd rather share it with than you."

I felt like a fairytale princess. The maître de ushered us to our table, and we were presented with a menu: Oysters Rockefeller, spinach salad with warm bacon vinaigrette, lobster tail with drawn butter, filet mignon with bearnaise sauce, and Danny's favorite, roast chicken with mashed potatoes and gravy. We were encouraged to leave some room for the chocolate soufflé.

Danny ordered a bottle of champagne. We giggled like children. He cradled my hand, and his fingers moved higher to caress my bare arm.

He held up his glass. "I want to thank you for standing by me."

I held up my glass, too. "Thanks. I know it's been hard for you."

"I guess I've been pretty hard to live with lately."

"Yes, you have, but it's all right. It's moments like these that make up for it."

"Joanna, I've got a feeling we've survived the worst," he said. "I'll be working again and I'm going to see Charlie starting on Wednesday."

"Oh, Danny, I love you," I said.

"I love you, and now things will be so much better," he said.

We were so absorbed in each other that we were startled when the flash of a camera went off. I looked up to see what idiot had interrupted our dinner. It turned out to be a well-dressed, middle-aged man in a dark suit with a military posture.

Danny gasped. "Dr. McAllister!"

"Nice to see your fortunes have reversed themselves," he said. His wife Maude was standing next to him with the camera, looking at Danny with an icy expression.

"This photo will be an outstanding souvenir," Dr. McAllister said to Danny. "You, dining with your, ah, *friend* in the Rainbow Room. The judge will be happy to see you have the wherewithal to pay the costs you've been contesting!"

Danny looked as white as a sheet.

"Enjoy your meal," Dr. McAllister continued. "The shrimp cocktail is a good starter. As I recall, that's what you always ordered when I was paying the bill." He turned his back on us and escorted Maude toward the door without looking back.

"Oh, Jeez, I should have known better," Danny said after they left. "This is the McAllister's favorite place to dine for special occasions. They always take along their camera to commemorate birthdays and anniversaries. Oh, of course – today is their anniversary! How could I be so stupid!"

We tried to recapture the mood, but it was impossible. Danny spent the rest of the meal looking at his plate. I could barely drink the champagne. Viewing the new risk of being caught on film, I knew Danny and I would not be going out again for quite a while.

The check came, and it was over $200. I knew it would be hard for him to come up with that kind of money.

"Hey, I can split this with you," I said.

"No, it was my idea and I'm going to pay."

"Danny, I'm sure you're going to get the job, and everything will be fine. But until then, you're going to need to go easy on the expenses."

"I said, I'm going to pay for it!" I was surprised at how angry he sounded.

Back at my apartment, he had returned to looking miserable.

"This divorce is going to be the end of me," he complained one evening.

"You've got to cheer up, babe," I said. I was beginning to get drawn into his negativity. This prolonged divorce battle wasn't good for him or me.

He went into the bathroom, and I heard him slamming the medicine cabinet and then the underneath drawer. I drew a sharp breath. "Danny, we need to talk. I think it's time you saw a therapist."

"I already told you I don't want to see a therapist. I have no interest in spilling my guts out to some guy who will be judging me."

"You need to talk things over with someone. You certainly aren't doing it with me."

"Oh, come on, Joanna!"

I'd raised the need or therapy a few times before and he had always resisted. But this time I sensed his resistance was flagging.

"You're just sitting around here looking morose all day. Seeking help would work in your favor in court. Isn't that what your lawyer said?"

I didn't let him wiggle out of it. I had someone in mind for him, a psychologist named Dr. Walter Berkowitz. He came highly recommended by a few people I knew. The next morning, I stood by Danny while he called Dr. Berkowitz and made an appointment for the next week.

# CHAPTER 42

**DANNY**

A few weeks after the Rainbow Room fiasco, I was offered a senior account executive position at Falcon Elliott. The position was a level lower than I had at Cooper, Masters & Young, and the salary was also less. They promised that if I proved myself, I could expect a handsome bonus, a title change as early as next year, and a commensurate salary increase.

I was asked if I could start the job the following week. I should have been elated, but the anxiety about meeting Charlie that weekend started taking over. It would be the first time I'd seen him since the paramedics came to take Sally away from the house. The court-appointed social worker would be present.

The meeting was at Butternut Woods Park. It had a pond and a nature center. I planned to briefly visit the nature center with Charlie before it closed for the day. We'd eat a picnic dinner I had put together by the pond.

I made sure to get there early and waited by my car. A black sedan pulled up next to mine, and the social worker stepped out. She had graying hair, was dressed in a crisp suit, and carried a notebook. Without acknowledging me, she walked around to hold the door open for Charlie.

He had grown in the couple of weeks since I last saw him. He broke into a big smile, leaped up, and raced into my arms. "Daddy, Daddy!"

My son buried his face in my chest. I could smell his familiar scent of grass and dirt mixed with bubble gum. "Nice to see you, little buddy," I said.

I turned to the social worker, put on a broad smile, and introduced myself. "Thank you for bringing Charlie," I said and shook her hand. I had carefully rehearsed the meeting so I could make a good impression on the social worker and get a good report. Be warm and fuzzy. Don't bring up Sally.

I needn't have worried too much. Charlie couldn't wait to share all his pent-up news, and it poured out of him. "Guess what? I made a friend on the class trip to the museum. His name's Oscar, and he taught me how to whistle. He lives just with his mom, but he sees his dad too. And I have a new teacher, Mrs. Drummond. But I don't really like her. She doesn't smile, and she gives out too much homework."

"I'm sorry you don't like your teacher, but I'm glad you made a new friend."

"It's good I met Oscar. Jon is still my best friend, but he has a crush on some girl. Yuck. So I don't see him as much anymore. He says he might go to Florida for Thanksgiving

247

to visit his grandma and grandpa. Oh, and the next-door neighbors got a puppy! I asked Mommy for one, but she said no."

"Well, I bet the Morrisons will let you play with the puppy if you ask them nicely. It will be good practice if you end up getting a dog when you're a little older. Oh, and about Jon? Girls aren't so bad. Maybe someday you'll like one."

"I guess. But I don't think so."

The social worker was taking notes, but that wasn't a problem. Charlie couldn't have been happier to see me. After visiting the nature center, we found a spot by the pond. I started unpacking the picnic basket. I had filled it with all the goodies I knew he liked. Tuna-salad sandwiches on croissants. French fries and pickles. Brownies with thick icing for dessert.

"Wow, Daddy," Charlie said. "Tuna-salad on those twisty rolls, like Mommy makes! And French fries and brownies!"

I peeked at the social worker. She was smiling.

"Oh, and Grandpa said he might take us to Florida for Thanksgiving just like Jon's grandparents, but he couldn't promise for sure."

"That will be fun! Grandma and Grandpa always show you a good time."

Charlie frowned. "It's not fun the way it used to be," he said. "When Mommy and I go over there? She always starts crying. Then, Grandma and Mommy and Auntie Kathy go off to the other room on their own. One time, Grandpa went with them. So I snuck over to the door to hear what they were saying. Grandpa was talking about you, and he used a word you told me never to say."

My son looked at me guiltily. "Mommy opened the door, and when she saw me, she made me go back to play with my cousins. But they don't act the same either. Cousin Sean told me you were going to hell for what you did. I hit him, and Mommy gave me a time-out, but he started it. Nothing is the same now."

The social worker's smile had disappeared. She was listening intently.

I hugged my son tight. Charlie seemed to sense our time together was ending. His eyes began filling with tears.

"Daddy, can't you come home with me?" he asked.

I'd also rehearsed for this. "Charlie, Mommy and Daddy have decided we can't live together. But you know the good thing?"

"What?"

"Both of us love you! That's never going to stop."

"But if you love me, why can't you see me more?"

"Charlie, I want that, too. More than anything in the world. Your mom and I are trying to work it out."

"But when can I see you next?"

"We're working on it. You know what? When I'm not with you, I'm thinking about you. Always."

"Really, Daddy?"

"Yes, you're my choo-choo-Charlie." I leaned closer to him. "Everything's going to end up fine."

"That's not what Mommy said." His eyes welled up with tears.

The social worker suddenly seemed more attentive. I needed to deal with this carefully.

"Um, what did Mommy say?" I asked.

"She said you found someone else. That you love her more than Mommy! Maybe...maybe even more than me? " Now he was straight-out sobbing. "She said you're not going to come home. Not ever!"

I hugged him. "Charlie, sometimes things aren't as simple as we'd like them to be. Grown-ups try hard, but they can mess things up. We're not perfect. But remember this: I love no one in my life more than you."

"Not even her?"

"No one. You never have to worry about how much I love you."

My eyes were welling up, too. The social worker looked touched.

"Daddy, I don't want you to go," he wailed.

"It's going to be all right, little buddy," I said. "I promise. Now, you need to go with this nice lady. Your Mommy and I will straighten things out. Can I get a big smile from you? Thatta boy!"

I hugged him one last time and got into the car. We waved at each other through the window as the social worker's car pulled away. Never had I felt so powerless before. The only silver lining was that the social worker would surely write a good report. Maybe my luck was going to change.

# CHAPTER 43

## JOANNA

Danny was on the way up again, but our relationship had started to take a hit. Doubts began to surface, and it was getting harder for me to ignore them.

I had mixed feelings about his new job at Falcon Elliott. On one hand, I felt happy he had landed on his feet. Still, I hated the agency and its casual disdain for women. I had experienced first-hand how this attitude could affect intelligent, upward-reaching women. Look what happened to my own opportunity when Danny's former boss Evan, a misogynist if I ever saw one, denied me the "win" after my presentation!

Anyway you viewed it, the agency's WITCH WITCH WITCH campaign came across as an insult. Of course, I knew Danny wasn't one of the "bad guys." His job, in fact, was to dismantle the old women-hating image and help build a new agency that could be respected. Still, I couldn't help but feel Danny had sold out.

On top of that, there was Charlie. Danny's negotiations for visitation were also going well. His first supervised visit had been a hit. His lawyer confirmed it: the social worker's report had been positive, and supervised visitations would probably be lifted soon. Still, the whole business with Charlie bothered me. Danny relayed that Charlie had asked him why he had left. It took me back to my own father's departure. How come he didn't love me enough to stay?

Wasn't Danny doing almost the same thing my father had done? Danny even looked like and acted like my father. They both were tall with reddish-blonde hair and not forthcoming. And despite myself, I was forcing history to repeat itself. I went from being the victim of my father to being complicit in taking away the love Charlie needed.

What if Danny wasn't the hero I'd made him out to be? I knew he had gone through hell as a child. It had left him mistrustful, walled off, and more than a little damaged. But hadn't he also cast away people who tried to help him? He pulled away from his mother. He left behind Sally and her parents, the people whom he once considered his saviors. What would it take for him to continue the cycle and cut and run from me?

To complicate things, I was the only one besides Maureen whom Danny could rely on. I couldn't pull the rug out from under him. I still loved him, didn't I? I felt exhausted, worn out, and unsure about how to right this flailing boat.

The good news is that Danny was energized again. We woke up together, had breakfast, and, if there was time, took a brisk walk around the neighborhood before catching the train to our jobs.

Still, two people living together in a one-bedroom New York City apartment wasn't easy. We had different styles. One of the first things he'd do when arriving home was turn on the TV or the stereo. For the most part, Danny thrived on chaos. His childhood had been filled with noise and drama. I liked nothing better than peacefulness. I loved curling up with a book or magazine or listening to the classical channel.

Danny wasn't big on going out, and I began to feel claustrophobic, spending so much time indoors. The Broadway scene was exploding – Sweeney Todd, Grand Hotel, and Prince of Central Park were ready to open – and my friends kept asking Danny and me to join them.

But Danny was not interested. Plays, ballets, and operas were just not his thing. At his core, he was a homebody and hated making small talk or pretending to be into events he'd rather pass on.

So, night after night, we stayed home, and the world continued without me. Danny said we could make our own fun. Maybe learn to cook together so we wouldn't have a need to get so much take-out food. But even our paltry attempts to take up that hobby had a way of boomeranging.

Danny was not careful with the things I loved. I collected crafts from my travels to Mexico. Among my favorite items was a pair of ceramic plates in vibrant colors, hand-signed by the artist. I had spent a small fortune on them and displayed them proudly on an end table. They were decorative and were not meant to be used for cooking.

Once, when I had to work late, Danny agreed to make dinner. It was one of the few dishes he could put together: homemade meatballs and spaghetti, smothered with Ragu Old World Style tomato sauce. When he served it up, he dished the spaghetti sauce onto the Mexican ceramic plates.

Fury rose in me. "Why are you using those? Why didn't you use the regular dinnerware?"

He looked dumbfounded. "I wanted to do something special. Why are you so upset?"

Months ago, I would have thought this incident was amusing. It would have become one of our jokes. Now, I only found it grating.

Danny was working long hours, too, and the lack of space began to take its toll on me. In the expensive New York City real estate market, I had managed to find a rent-controlled place in a trendy neighborhood. It had one spacious bedroom, a small den with large windows, a marble countertop, a Jacuzzi tub and a separate shower. I regarded it as my sanctuary.

I had set up the den with my latest purchase, a Kaypro computer. It sat on my roll-up desk. I also had a small table to hold my Xerox copier, a new fax machine, and a file cabinet. On the wall was an abstract expressionist painting by Jenny Holzer, another purchase that cost more than I should have spent.

There, I cocooned and did my best after-work thinking. I had a presentation due on Friday. I needed to spend hours holed up in my den, getting all the details right. But Danny got home before me, and his briefcase and tons of paperwork were strewn across the floor in my den.

I took a deep breath. "Babe, you know I've got the McCann presentation in just two days. I'm going to need my space. Could you please gather up your files and work somewhere else? I'm under the gun."

"Joanna, I've got a presentation, too. And it's important. Where would you like me to go?"

"Would it be too much trouble if you worked out in the living room? I need the computer this time. It's hard to get it set up again. The last time I tried, I lost a whole day's work on my floppy disk." I sighed. "I need my den tonight."

"Okay, I'll go to the living room," he said. He made a show of picking his things up. Even when he was in the other room, I could hear his Eagles tape playing and the occasional outburst as he checked over storyboards.

It took everything I had to try to be loving. At one point, I quietly walked out, put my arms around him, and kissed his forehead. "Love you, babe," I said.

He said nothing, staring at me as if I were the enemy. That night, we slept with our backs to each other.

I woke up and looked at him stretched out next to me. Such a beautiful man. He had given up everything secure in his life because of me. What kind of monster was I, having doubts at this late date? We had to get through it and work our way back to where we were before all this stress overcame us.

Still, a nagging voice whispered: Get back to what? We were two people who thrived on the drama of being together. We had lived in a space where we were sheltered in each other's arms and saw no consequences.

The truth was Danny only knew the Joanna I presented to him. Our life together had been about one person: Danny. I'd reassure him and make inquiries during the day to help him land another job. I'd help fill out and fax the paperwork his lawyer needed and comfort him after visits with Charlie. I'd shop for second-hand furniture so his rental apartment would pass muster with the social worker. And on and on.

I knew Danny would get back on his feet. I also knew when a couple is in love, things are never equal. One has to do more during tough times for the other. That person just has to bear the brunt for a while.

Still, I couldn't remember the last time Danny asked anything about my life. He knew very little about me. He didn't know I tracked down and confronted my father. I'd never told him about it. I felt uneasy making it part of our relationship, and I had to wonder why.

Our life together was all about making Danny feel safe and comfortable. He seemed to be just fine with the way things were going. Wasn't it time I put myself back in the picture, if even as a secondary character?

# CHAPTER 44

**DANNY**

There were days I wondered if the divorce would ever be finalized. Would I be living in its shadow for the rest of my life? Then the end finally came.

Nearly two years after Sally had filed, my lawyer received notification the paperwork had been completed. All Sally and I needed to do was sign. Neither of us was completely happy with the outcome, but at least we were free of each other. Our lives could go on.

I started to do a lot of reflecting, something that's best for me to avoid. Once the strife died down, I could recognize the good parts of our marriage. The family dinners at the McAllisters. Moving into our own house. And finally becoming parents and watching Charlie grow. Why couldn't I have settled for what I had?

If Sally were a car, she would be a white Chevy van. Dependable but not exhilarating. Once Charlie came along, we focused our attention on him. After we put him to bed, we would silently watch TV or retreat into our own spaces. I finally got tired of her religious homilies, and she got tired of my excuses. We lashed out at each other over small things. Then, we didn't even have the energy for that.

In contrast to Sally, Joanna was a Ferrari. We were passionate lovers. She made me feel alive in ways I had never experienced. She was vibrant, confident, and adventurous, willing to explore my deepest fantasies. Yet, as time went by, it started to become evident to me that we skirted painful issues rather than confronting them.

We had shared significant parts of our childhood, but we had trouble exploring those times further with each other. Neither of us did well with conflict resolution. If a conflict did come up, we'd try to sweep it under the rug. Her desire to keep things neat and orderly – both on the surface and deep within – differed from my own chaotic life. I was gradually growing aware Joanna wanted to snatch me out of my childhood and married years and move forward with the here-and-now Danny, without any of the messy past.

In that regard, she reminded me of Sally, who wanted to reinvent me. I wasn't totally convinced Joanna and I were the best fit, either.

Early in the relationship, right after we made love, Joanna wanted me to tell her what I liked most about her. "How into me you are," I answered unthinkingly.

I realized I'd hurt her feelings and quickly added, "Oh, and of course, your wicked mind and your beautiful body and the way we fit together."

In truth, my first answer was the real one. A good part of my attraction was I liked being the hero for Joanna. No one had ever worshipped me the way she had. When I was with her, I could do no wrong. I was the most powerful man in the world, high on a pedestal that never would crash down.

I turned out to be nobody's hero, certainly not Joanna's. She began to miss the life she had before me. The trendy restaurants, museum openings, hard-to-get theater tickets, and lavish get-togethers.

Those things never mattered to me. I didn't care about $500 artsy ceramic dishes that didn't look much different from the colorful dinner sets you could buy at Macy's. I couldn't tell a Jean-Michel Basquiat painting from one of Charlie's fingerpainting projects. And I didn't want to change to please Joanna. How would that end up playing out? In the meantime, as 1990 drew to a close, my divorce was finalized.

IN THE SUPERIOR COURT OF THE STATE OF NEW YORK FOR THE COUNTY OF WESTCHESTER

No. BC678901

SALLY MCALLISTER MONAHAN, Plaintiff, vs. DANIEL JAMES MONAHAN, Defendant

## DIVORCE DECREE

The Court, having considered the evidence and arguments presented by the parties, and being fully advised in the premises, hereby makes the following findings and orders:

1. The parties were married on June 3, 1973.
2. The parties have one child together, a son named Charles Francis, who was born on June 13, 1982.
3. The parties have been living separate and apart for more than one year.
4. Plaintiff has proven by clear and convincing evidence that Defendant committed adultery. Further allegations that Defendant had anger management issues were ruled inconclusive.
5. The Plaintiff is the innocent party in this divorce.

IT IS THEREFORE ORDERED, ADJUDGED, AND DECREED as follows:

6. The marriage of the parties is dissolved.
7. The Plaintiff shall have sole legal and physical custody of Charles. The Defendant shall have visitation rights with Charles as follows:

(a) The Defendant shall initially have supervised visitation with Charles every other weekend from Friday at 6:00 p.m. to Sunday at 6:00 p.m. (b) After six months, determined on the supervisor's report, Defendant may be awarded visitation with Charles on one weekday evening per week from 6:00 p.m. to 9:00 p.m. (c) Based on the report, it may be determined that the Defendant shall have visitation with Charles for two weeks during the summer, to be determined by the parties in the event of a dispute. The defendant shall pay child support to Plaintiff for $475 per month.

8. Plaintiff shall be awarded the marital home, located at 123 Albemarle Road, White Plains, New York.
9. The parties shall equally divide the marital assets, including all bank accounts, retirement accounts, and investments.
10. The parties shall equally divide the marital debts.
11. The Defendant shall pay the Plaintiff's attorney's $2,500 fees.

This Decree is entered on this 1st day of November 1990.
/s/ Judge of the Superior Court

# PART III

# CHAPTER 45

## REBA

Sometimes I ask myself, "What the hell was I thinking?" Marrying a rich guy and becoming his trophy wife. Why would I need to do *that*?

It seemed like a good idea at the time. I didn't grow up wealthy. My father worked as a door-to-door salesman for World Book Encyclopedia. My mother was a legal secretary. They had ambitions, though. They scrimped, saved, and even hit up relatives for a loan when necessary. They bought a house right off Ocean Parkway in Brooklyn and ensured my sister and I got into the best public school. They made me believe there was nothing in the world I couldn't do.

I had honey-blonde hair, long bangs, a petite nose, and widely spaced hazel eyes. My grandmother, who lived with us, said I had a "goyishe kop" because I always had my head in the clouds. She'd also pinch my cheek and call me "shayna maidel" – pretty girl. Lots of people made that particular comment to me. But I was determined I would be more than a pretty face.

When I attended college in the early 60s, women still gravitated toward three majors: teaching, nursing, or home economics. Not me. I earned a partial scholarship to Cornell and my classes were in business and the humanities. I graduated Summa Cum Laude without a clue about what would come next. All I knew was "=I was going to achieve something big.

My best friend Natalie and I drove down to South Miami Beach after graduation. We needed some relaxation after the last few hectic months of final exams. Towering palm trees and candy-colored hotels seemed just the thing. One of Natalie's friends had a small place there, and she let us crash for as long as we wanted. Mostly, we hung out at the pools and landed waitressing jobs at LIV Nightclub. It catered to names like Frank Sinatra, Elvis Presley, Tony Bennett, and a guy named Martin Knauss.

Okay, Martin wasn't as well-known as the others. He came from family money. To my innocent eyes, he was a gazillionaire. He had a cousin twice removed whose family spearheaded Revlon, one of the most famous cosmetics brands on the market.

Martin was indeed rich, though not as rich as I fantasized. He was 18 years older than me, divorced twice, and our romance was a whirlwind. He bought me dazzling necklaces, flew me around in a Cessna jet he co-owned, and gazed into my eyes with intense adoration. Who could resist?

So I married him. At age 22, I was propelled into a world with a spacious co-op on the Upper East Side of New York and an art deco home in South Beach. My new husband, who had known me all of six months, thought I was gutsy, classy, and beautiful. He encouraged me to go into acting or modeling, but I convinced him to teach me the business.

He thought I was oh-so-cute. But he didn't count on me being talented. I entered an intensive 24-month rotational program to find out more about the company. Then, I became one of the few women accepted into Columbia Business School, where I pursued my MBA.

At that point, Martin stopped thinking this was cute. He wanted arm candy, not an equal. But that was the last thing I wanted. I didn't see myself having his babies and attending his galas in the latest designer gown.

There would be no little Knausses if I had anything to do with it. One evening, I was studying for my exam in his huge den. He came home inebriated from some business gala and took me by force. The Pill had just been approved by the FDA in 1960 and not many women were on it yet. But I was. I had gone behind his back and gotten a prescription.

Still, for someone who considered herself savvy, I was incredibly naïve. Once I earned my MBA and showed I could survive in a man's world, I figured Martin would open all sorts of doors for me. No way. I had to look for jobs at other companies. Despite his best efforts to sabotage me, I was hired for a prestigious position. When Martin heard the news, he went through the roof.

Often, I wonder: why did it take so long for us to get divorced? I could have served papers on him for any number of dalliances. Some of them were highly publicized. But I had my own dalliances, too, and Martin could have gone after me. He was cheap, though. He knew he'd have to give up a large sum of money to get rid of me. And I would have demanded it. What else would you have expected from a girl who grew up humble in Brooklyn?

We made peace of sorts. I would give him the children he thought he wanted, and he would keep his affairs discreet. We had a son and a daughter. We promptly sent them off to boarding school – him to Phillips Academy Andover and her to the Brearley School. We would see them mostly on holidays and family vacations.

Our children grew up knowing their parents' marriage was a sham. I lived in a separate wing of the house. Martin and I saw each other as little as possible. Eventually, he fell out of favor with his cousin twice removed. As my husband aged, he became even less appealing. We could have drifted on like this forever, but there's nothing like facing 50 to make a woman face reality.

Focusing more and more on my career, I was pleased to be appointed to lead the skin and personal care division of Proctor & Gamble at their Midtown East location in New York. Martin was happy I was working late and not nagging him. One of my responsibilities was to interface with our advertising agency, Cooper, Masters & Young. I worked with Danny Monahan, their senior vice president of accounts.

I was quickly attracted to Danny's looks, his wit, and his intelligence – not that I would have ever acted upon that attraction. It was clear he was not someone to get romantically involved with. He was married with a young son at the time. I also heard from reliable sources he was having a lurid affair with some video production person in the industry.

Sure, I was tired of living a lie with a husband I had fallen out of love with decades ago. But I knew the rules for a woman in my position. I'm proud to say for the entire time Danny and I worked together, I resisted temptation.

That doesn't mean I didn't look forward to our working sessions. I enjoyed the flirtation. To be totally honest, I did fantasize about him from time to time. But I wasn't about to get involved with a man who was almost a decade younger than me and who had not just one, but two entanglements.

I'd have to be crazy to do that. And let me tell you, I'm very far from crazy.

# CHAPTER 46

**DANNY**

Certainly, I had been involved in team presentations to Reba before. But I never spent significant time with her – one-on-one – until I was promoted to Senior Director of Accounts. Before then, I was on standby when she and Evan met to go over campaign strategies. She didn't like Evan much. But I could tell she respected his insights.

Now I had her ear, and I was intimidated and awed. The lady reeked of self-assurance, and man, oh man, she was beautiful. The trade mags dubbed her as our industry's own Farrah Fawcett.

Reba was rich, a dynamo, and great looking. But she wasn't happy. I could sense it.

She was married then. Everyone knew her husband by name. This lady was out of my league, and the last thing I needed was to complicate my life further. Nor did I want to.

I was in love with Joanna. I needed to untangle myself from Sally. There was no way I needed more on my plate.

That was okay because Reba was professional in every way. A real workaholic. That's what got me wondering. If she had such a perfect life – and from the photos hanging in her office of her and her husband sailing, on safari, skiing in Aspen with some celebrities, she did – then why was she working those crazy hours in the office night after night?

Evan complained about it and now I could see first-hand: Reba was a demanding task-maker. She often summoned her agency partners to her office after 5 pm. The brain-storming sessions lasted into the late hours.

Sometimes she would abruptly call meetings a few times a week. She made it evident anyone who could not keep up with her would be summarily canned. Two other agencies were dropped.

Within a few months, I had the lion's share of the P&G account. My name began to show up often in Ad Age and Ad Week. I even got an appealing offer from one of our competitors to jump ship. I was golden.

Naturally, I was tempted. But the real reason I hung in there was that Reba and the P&G account presented a challenge – and an opportunity – I couldn't resist. It was a career-maker. And so, the meetings kept running later and later. Just when I thought we were about to finish, she would order some sandwiches and coffee and segue to another point. I was taking a lot of heat from Sally. Even Joanna was questioning the limited time I had now. My life was becoming very complicated.

Soon I began to suspect she had a thing for me. I'd consider it for a minute or two, and then I'd think, "Nah – not happening."

Still, she'd stand a little too close. Smile a little too often. Hang on to my words, and believe me, I know I can be witty, but I'm not all that fascinating. And she started veering the conversation into the personal as we were wrapping it up. Like, "I suppose your wife – you have a wife, right – can't be too thrilled with all the time we've been putting in here. Please thank her for me." That kind of thing.

I was flattered. Who wouldn't be? I was at a tipping point in my life – pretty sure I didn't want to spend another 30 or 40 years with Sally, yet afraid – yeah, I admit it – Joanna and I might not have what takes for a successful future together.

I had only been involved with Joanna for six months or so back then. I was crazy about her, and our times together were magical. But we hadn't spent more than one night together, which I was determined to rectify. I was grounded enough to know that sex, no matter how fantastic and lots of intense moments, didn't add up to a lasting partnership.

It wasn't as if I were clueless. I knew marriage meant loving someone at their worst as long as they're loving you back – whether they're acting out, lashing out, or in an old bathrobe with snot rolling down their face because they caught a cold. That's in the best of circumstances, of course. In reality? Not so much for Sally and me.

Joanna? She had this idealized vision of me, and in her eyes, I could do no wrong, even when I was being a cold son-of-a-bitch. I had to figure out if she'd love me once she saw me at my worst.

I was flailing, paralyzed about making any decision. Divorce Sally and lose custody? Too risky. Move forward with Joanna and risk being left alone when she figures out that I am not the perfect man she thought I was? Scary prospect.

Then, one of the most powerful women in the industry, who happens to be gorgeous, gives me some tantalizing signs. Yeah, I know, poor me. But I can't stress enough: it was a great little fantasy, but my emotions and energies were wrapped up in Joanna. Not Reba.

Why me? Beyond the obvious attraction, I suspect I had something she hadn't often encountered. First, I was unattainable – women love that shit. And maybe I was a sort of blank slate, not asking her to give too much of herself. But really, who knows? She was nine years older than me, and perhaps it was as simple as her need for a more virile younger man. Okay, that's a joke.

Anyway, I can't stress this enough. The entire time Reba and I were working together, nothing inappropriate happened. Not one thing. It all settled into what I considered an ideal working relationship between a client and her ad agency contact. We had a great deal of respect for each other.

Meanwhile, my feelings were deepening for Joanna. It scared the crap out of me. I was pretty sure that's why

I allowed myself to fantasize about Reba. It allowed me to build a little distance from the train, careening out of control.

When Joanna and I finally got away to Arizona for a week-long conference. I finally achieved my clarity. At that point I knew it was Joanna whom I wanted to be with. Period. But then Sally flew out to "surprise" me, and I no longer had the time or luxury to speculate, fantasize, or hold off. My marriage was over, and Joanna and I needed to make decisions fast.

I was being pulled in all directions. Reba still demanded 100% of me; Joanna gave me 100%. And Sally? She was determined to make me pay. I was worried about keeping my job and frantic about losing Charlie. Then, right at the wrong time, Reba recommended I spearhead the new business presentation for Old Spice Body Lotion. A few months before, I would have been thrilled. But I was existing on fumes, exhausted and anxious, knowing how much was at stake.

What happened? I fucked up. I got fired. I knew I had disappointed Reba and could only imagine what she was thinking about my "great performance." I couldn't dwell on it, though. It was all I could do to handle the mess my life had become. From a professional standpoint – and certainly from a personal one – Reba was no longer any part of it.

# CHAPTER 47

## REBA

During the Old Spice presentation, when Danny lost it, I recall thinking, "What the fuck happened?"

I had put my reputation on the line to get Danny in on the presentation. He deserved it. I viewed him as a buttoned-up guy, filled with great ideas and a compelling strategist with a visionary mind. I thought he'd be great at spearheading the business.

He arrived with his team, and right away, I knew something was terribly wrong. He looked haunted, spoke in a monotone, and constantly pulled at his tie. I knew college interns who could have done a better job. This was not the Danny I had worked with for all those months.

Watching him soldier on felt downright painful. Then he passed out. One of our junior team members called 911. My irritation with him switched into real concern. I feared he was having a heart attack. The presentation went on without him and careened into a train wreck. The next day, I called Jared at Cooper, Masters & Young to inquire about Danny and how he was doing.

Jared was friendly but curt. "Danny has been released. Turned out to be nothing serious."

"Thank you for the update," I said. "I was concerned."

"Reba, I want to apologize for the chaos," he said. "I realize this wasn't our finest moment. We can do better. We have done better. I do hope you keep that in mind."

"I think all of us at P&G know it was not the agency's fault. Or Danny's fault, for that matter. Please give him our best wishes."

By the end of the week, the grapevine was buzzing. The real story started coming out. Danny was going through a bitter divorce. His affair with Joanna was the cause of it. In fact, His wife had caught the two of them in the act.

I had conflicting feelings about what happened. Above all, I was disappointed. Danny had let his personal life get so out of control. He embarrassed himself and, by extension, me. I was the one who recommended him. Danny wasn't the consummate professional I thought he was. I knew a thing or two about messy personal lives. But I would never let my marital disaster impact how I functioned.

Later, I heard Jared had fired Danny. The agency sent over a newly hired woman with a sterling resume named Jeanette as his replacement. She didn't have Danny's star power but was organized, proficient, hard-working, and agreeable. I was happy to have someone to move us forward without messing things up.

# CHAPTER 48

**DANNY**

When I did think of Reba – rarely and uncomfortably – during the next hectic year, I winced. She reminded me of the mess I had made of my life.

With the avalanche of bills, I kept busy trying to land on my feet and staying solvent. And I was trying hard to navigate a real relationship with Joanna that consisted of more than hot, steamy sex whenever we could grab the chance.

By then, I had broken up with Sally. In my mind, I did not blindside her: I would have described our marriage as transactional for the past two years. We worked together as a well-oiled machine, carting Charlie to daycare, working on the household budget, and banning together to deal with unexpected issues, such as a broken furnace we had to replace.

We'd go out with other couples every so often. In fact, an outing with one of those couples was the spark that brought down the house. We agreed to a rare get-together with Evan and his latest girlfriend. During dinner, Evan kidded me about Joanna. Sally had a mind like an elephant and never forgot her name.

Our sex life? It had dwindled down to once every couple of weeks. I was always getting home late, and Sally was always exhausted. I deceived myself into thinking she would be a little relieved we were getting the issue into the open. Of course, I knew she'd feel betrayed. Knowing Sally, I also knew it would be humiliating for her to confess to her family and friends that I was leaving her. I hadn't counted on the extremity of Sally's anger and her desire for revenge.

I was unofficially living with Joanna. We were having a rockier time than I expected. Whenever we tried to talk it over, the words got in the way. I wanted it to work desperately. Looking back, she did as well. But how do two broken people create something pure and whole? Especially when each is scared of doing or saying anything that would ruin everything.

Somehow, we survived one year, followed by the next. Miraculously, the divorce came to an end and visitation was arranged with Charlie. I landed a new job. I began reaching out again to my few friends, Maureen being chief among them. Joanna was a little more distant, but she had been through a lot with me.

I began to form a few doubts. So did she. I thought we would eventually emerge on solid ground. Little did I know this was the beginning of yet another ending.

# CHAPTER 49

## JOANNA

One night Danny mentioned cavalierly—a little too cavalierly—that he might be getting home a little late Friday night.

"Remember I told you Maureen was interviewing for a new job?" he said. "Well, she got one. It's a good one."

"I'm happy to hear it. Where will she be working?"

"She'll be at a non-profit. It's a new foundation promoting healthy child development and positive parenting. She's passionate about child abuse and neglect, so it's right up her alley."

"She did mention she was looking," I said. "Her old job seemed to be getting to her. So you're taking her out to celebrate?"

"Yep. But I haven't even told you the good part. Talk about a small world. Seems the person who recruited her is someone I know. Do you remember my P&G client, Reba?"

"Yes, Reba. You hardly mention her anymore."

"Yes, we've been out of touch. Maureen tells me she had enough of P&G and the for-profit world. So she decided to make a big change. She took a salary cut and is now heading the start-up. It's called Stamp Out Child Abuse – SOCA."

"Well, that's nice."

"Anyway, Maureen suggested the three of us go out and catch up."

I looked Danny in the eye. "Think they'd mind if I came along?"

Danny looked skittish. "Well, here's the thing. It ended so badly for me at P&G. Falcon Elliott has been great to me, and I was thinking. If the situation presents itself, I could feel Reba out a little. See if there might be an opportunity for us to get in the door."

"Oh, I see."

"I'm not sure how she feels about letting me get involved. I may have blown any future chance there. But before that Old Spice situation, Reba thought highly of my work. So, yeah, I guess I have an ulterior motive with this dinner."

I was hoping Danny only had one ulterior motive. A distance was growing between us, partly due to me. But yeah, I remembered Reba alright. Specifically, the awe Danny used to have for her. He used to tell me how whip-smart and put-together she was, and I would feel uncomfortable.

Danny would never pull anything with Reba, after all we had been through. But then Sally had felt the same way, too. I decided to call Maureen in the guise of congratulating her. She answered on the first ring.

"Danny just told me the news about your job. Hey, congratulations! I hear he's meeting up with you and Reba this Friday."

Maureen wasn't a top-notch social worker for nothing. She picked up right away on the anxiety in my voice. "Oh Joanna, you don't think? Oh, for gosh sake, Reba is like a decade older than him and she's all business."

"Oh, I know. I was wondering, though."

"I'm crazy about the two of you. I would never have agreed to the dinner if I thought there was any ulterior motive."

I laughed along with her. After we hung up, I felt relieved for a minute before I realized Danny had lied to me. The dinner had been proposed by him, not by Maureen and Reba, as he told me. And Maureen had no idea how the last couple of months had been going between him and me.

# CHAPTER 50

## REBA

There truly is such a thing as six degrees of separation. Or actually, two degrees, in my case. I hired a new employee, Maureen Boyd, for the new not-for-profit I was spearheading: Stamp Out Child Abuse. Surprise: she knew Danny.

Hiring Maureen felt like a no-brainer. She was passionate about fighting child abuse, she had massive experience, and she had ideas. We hit it off like long-lost sisters.

During after-work drinks a few months later, I asked her why she chose fighting child abuse as a career.

"As a kid, a little boy lived next door to me. I witnessed first-hand what it was like to be in the crossfire of a toxic situation at home."

"What happened?"

"His father would beat up his mother on a regular basis. She would never report him to the police, though. The boy, Danny, was a few years younger than me. He would come over to my house to get away from the chaos. He didn't talk about what happened. Still, I felt like I was helping him just by being there. That I could make a difference."

"Did you ever find out what happened to him?" I asked.

"He grew up and he did just fine," Maureen said. "At least outwardly so. He ended up with some big job at this ad agency, Cooper, Masters & Young."

"Oh, Cooper, Masters & Young?"

"Yes, you know of it? He worked with their biggest client. He was married then. His controlling wife didn't want him to have much to do with me. So I don't know much about those years."

"What happened then?"

"Eventually he grew some balls and left her. He's with a really supportive woman now. We keep in touch whenever we can."

"Does he talk about those childhood experiences?"

"No, not at all. I'm not naïve. The damage done to him likely scarred him for good. But he's become adept at the masquerade. He's doing okay for himself. Sometimes, that's the best result we can hope for."

Throughout the conversation, I felt a growing sense of unease. "Maureen," I said haltingly. "By any chance, are you talking about *Danny Monahan*?"

"Why, yes." She looked shocked. "Do you know him?"

I smiled ruefully. "I was that big client," I said. "That is, Proctor & Gamble was. Danny and I worked together quite closely. I had no idea about his background. He seemed assured, confident and buttoned up to me. At least until his meltdown at a major presentation to my company. He got fired, and I haven't kept up with him since."

"Oh, my God," said Maureen. "That presentation. His wife had put the screws on him about picking up Charlie. His little boy. Charlie fell ill, and Danny got frantic. He called me hours to pick him up and stay with him until he finished."

"So that's why he blew it."

"Yes."

"I never did quite understand why he was so out of control," I said.

"Is it okay if I let Danny know we're working together?" Maureen asked.

"Of course. I wish him well. The three of us could have lunch and catch up at some point.

"I don't know how he'd feel about getting together. Might bring up uncomfortable memories of when he wasn't in control. He's guarded, you know. But at least I'll send him your best." Maureen said.

# CHAPTER 51

**DANNY**

When Maureen called and told me her boss was Reba, my first reaction was anxiety

I had never told Maureen much about my working life. She wasn't involved with advertising, so it wasn't interesting to her. She knew about the big presentation and how badly it went off. I don't recall mentioning Reba's name – why would I? – or even the division I was presenting to.

Maureen was great, but she could run off her mouth sometimes. I didn't want Reba to hear all about my fucked-up childhood. Nor did I want Reba to tell Maureen all the details about how I performed that day. I still thought of Maureen as a big sister and hated for her to realize I was still "Danny Boy from the 'hood."

I quizzed Maureen a little about how Reba found out we knew each other. She 'fessed up that she mentioned we had grown up as neighbors. That my dad was abusive. She swore

285

the conversation never got into too much depth and never went into the details of what I had been through.

"Why would I talk out of turn?" she said innocently. "Reba only has friendly remembrances of you."

An idea started forming. First, I rejected it of hand. But the more I thought about it, the more it made sense to meet up with Reba again. If I could bring in a small portion of the P&G business, I'd be golden. Promotion, raise, the works. It was worth a try. All I needed was a name to reach out to and her blessings.

I floated the idea past Maureen. She checked with Reba, and we decided to meet for a fast lunch at a local luncheonette downtown called The New Haig. It was right off Pine and Water Streets, around the corner from Chock Full o' Nuts. The women were a little early and snagged one of the few tables, so we didn't have to eat at the counter.

I greeted both of them warmly. If Reba knew more than Maureen was admitting to, she didn't show it. She asked what I was up to, and I gave her the basics. Divorced, living with Joanna, plugging away at work at Falcon Elliott. She updated me on her professional life and spoke enthusiastically about her plans for the foundation.

Maureen and I exchanged some childhood banter, which made Reba laugh. A line was forming at the door; before we knew it, it was time to part. I never did get a chance to make my pitch. Timing was everything, and the timing didn't feel right.

We all hugged, and I hailed a cab back to the office. Reba looked smashing. She was so kind and forgiving. I didn't want to start anything with her – that was for certain. But I did want to see her again. For old time's sake. And to get my chance to ask about the recommendation.

# CHAPTER 52

**REBA**

I would never have pegged Danny as a survivor of child abuse. In our former work meetings, he came across as self-assured, even a little exploitative and narcissistic. He seemed obsessed with getting ahead and being admired.

My view of him changed dramatically when Maureen filled me in on his past. His doomed presentation took on a whole new meaning. I now recognized Danny as traumatized and overwhelmed. Too many people had let him down. What I had taken to be Danny's narcissism was really a form of self-protectiveness.

Survivors like him are often chameleons. My new work at the foundation enlightened me about childhood trauma. I learned it could lead to shame, anxiety, overwhelming fears, and depression.

Danny had been through hard times. But the man who sat across from me in the restaurant with Maureen was different from the one I knew before. He wasn't trying to impress me. For the first time, I saw his authentic self.

Not long after that lunch, Danny called me.

"Hi, Reba, I wanted to ask you a favor. You can say no if you want to. But I thought I'd give it a try."

"What is it, Danny?"

"You still in touch with people at P&G?"

"I've kept some contacts."

"Is there, um, any chance I would be able to present Falcon Elliott to one of the P&G divisions?"

I couldn't help but laugh. "If you promise it won't be a variant of the Witch Witch Witch campaign. P&G is sensitive to demonizing women."

"Even witches need cold cream and dream of beautiful flowing hair."

"Ha! I don't know how it will go over. Falcon Elliott isn't an agency that would be top of mind at P&G. But I'm willing to discuss a few possibilities with you. Why don't you meet me for lunch next week, and we'll talk about it."

"Oh, that would be great. Thanks."

That's how it started. I'll admit I was attracted to Danny. But I wasn't about to mess up his relationship with Joanna. Maureen was very impressed with their chemistry, and he needed stability.

When we met, there wasn't any sort of flirtation. But something was in the air. I filled him in on the new culture at P&G, gave him a few names to contact, and told him he could use my name. Neither of us was willing to leave it there, though. Danny said he wanted to learn more about my new foundation. Would I be willing to meet up for another lunch?

Things moved forward from there. Very slowly. A few lunches later, Danny finally brought up the failed presentation. I was glad to clear the air.

"Admittedly, I was totally flabbergasted at what you did," I said. "You acted way out of character. I'm aware now of what you were going through. Your ex left you in a terrible predicament. In that situation, anyone might have reacted the same way."

"Thanks for the support," he said. "Yeah, it was a pretty awful moment. Sally really knew how to get at me."

Then, I went out on a limb. "You know, Maureen shared just a little about your childhood with me."

He winced and squeezed his eyes shut. When he opened them, they held a forced merriment. "Can't trust that girl with nothing," he said, affectionately shaking his head.

Guard up again.

It took a few more get-togethers for Danny to open up. And it was only after I shared some of the foundation's work and its success stories with survivors of abuse.

I ran through my elevator speech: the foundation's goal was to help survivors of child abuse and also prevent it from happening in the first place. We funded some promising interventions, such as NET, which is narrative exposure therapy. It focused on embedding trauma exposure into kind of a timeline, which is called an autobiographical context.

Sometimes people zone out at this point. Danny, however, was rapt.

He haltingly told me about his father's unpredictability and violence. He feared him. Drunk and hulking, he would belt out Danny's name. Danny had been beaten with a strap until he couldn't sit down. He had also been humiliated, forced into silence. Family dinners would escalate at a moment's notice into screaming savage attacks and hospitalizations. He would witness his mother on the floor, bleeding from her nose and mouth. Bones were broken, too.

Maureen knew most of the story, Danny confessed. Sally and later Joanna only heard parts of it. Now I knew it. He thought, based on my work at the foundation, I'd be able to understand without judgment.

Now that he had opened up, I needed to reciprocate with some of my own trauma. It wouldn't do for Danny to believe I was all-powerful and that he was damaged and reliant on my kindness.

I didn't have anything as monumental to tell him. But I did mention the rape early in my marriage and the marriage itself. A transactional arrangement with no love after the first few years.

He reached toward my hand but quickly withdrew. I knew he didn't want to screw things up with Joanna. But I wondered about that relationship. To me, Danny didn't seem like a man fully in love.

# CHAPTER 53

## JOANNA

It all came to a head over an offhand remark.

I had brought home some take-out dinner from Zabar's. Danny set the table. We exchanged some pleasantries about our day. A new client on the docket for him, a presentation on my end.

"Heard some industry gossip at a luncheon today," I said. "You know Bob Dougherty, who took Reba's place at P&G? Well, it seems like he flew the coop. He got an offer at Revlon, so now P&G has to start their search all over again."

"Actually, they decided to solve the issue internally. They're moving Susan Randall in from another division," Danny said. "That's the latest. Reba was just telling me today."

I froze. "I didn't know you met up with Reba today."

"Oh, didn't I mention it? We went to lunch. Catching up on what was going on at P&G. Reba came through for me big time. Turns out I will be getting a foot in the door after all." His expression was impassive.

"You and Reba have been lunching regularly?"

"A few times. It took me a little bit to broach the subject of Falcon Elliott to her. Didn't feel comfortable just springing it on her. No big deal."

"Up until now, I thought you had one lunch with her and Maureen and that was it."

Danny sighed. "Joanna, not this again. Do you think I'm having an affair with her? You must know I don't have any intention of destroying what's between us. Why would I? It's just lunch between two people who used to work together. Now can we put it to rest?"

I couldn't let it drop. Finding out about his cover-up with Reba brought forth all my festering doubts about our relationship.

"We've been together almost three years now," I said. "Three years. I knew we'd have a lot of obstacles to overcome. The divorce from Sally. Setting up visits with Charlie. But with all that behind us, I thought we'd be moving forward at last."

"Well, we are, I think," he said haltingly.

"No, we're not. You never ask me what I'd like out of this relationship. Does what I want matter to you? As it happens, I'd like to move to a larger apartment. Maybe a brownstone."

"You could have brought that up, Joanna. Am I supposed to read your mind?"

"Truth is, I'm getting into my mid-30s. Maybe I want to have a child. One thing occurred to me today. The divorce is final, but you're still renting the apartment in White Plains. Why is that?"

"That's for Charlie's visits."

"You're not required under the divorce decree to have that apartment. Charlie is older. It's high time you introduced me into his life. Why would you continue to spend hundreds of dollars on a place you use twice a month for his weekend visits?"

Suddenly, it dawned on me. "You're keeping it because you want a safe place. If things don't work out between us."

Danny paled. "Oh, come on, Joanna."

"No. How stupid could I be? That's where your head's been at all along. You need an out. I'm thinking about our future while you're thinking about how to save yourself."

"I'm trying to get to the bottom of my trust issues for us, for you," he said. "The way I grew up, it's hard to trust the future. I see Reba because she gives me insights into what I went through. Her foundation deals with childhood abuse."

"So now you're ready to admit it," I said. "You're a victim of abuse. You always pretended it was just your mother who was abused. Your father was tough with you, but somehow, you got through it just fine. I knew you had to have been affected, too."

"I'm just beginning to understand that."

"Yet instead of coming to me to talk about it, you go to Reba. And you don't even tell me about your meetups. It's a big secret."

"Joanna, listen, I know. You've been here for me in a big way. I couldn't have made it through without you. It's hard for me to talk about. I'm sorry if you feel I've shut you out."

"I wonder if that's what you did to Sally, too," I said.

"What? You know what Sally was like. Rigid, sanctimonious, and hard to live with. You're not like that."

"Okay, but did you ever try talking things out with her? Did you ever sit down and tell her how you were feeling? Did you shut her out, too, Danny?"

"Joanna, that's not fair. I'm not trying to shut you out."

"Whether you intend to or not, that's what you're doing. And it doesn't feel good."

Danny's face went blank. If he could have levitated out of his chair and flown out of the window, he would have done so.

"What do you want to do?" he said.

"You need to get your head on straight. You might not be having a physical affair with Reba right now, but I think you're definitely in emotional affair territory."

"I don't want to have any kind of affair with Reba. You're the one I love."

"That's what you say, but what do you feel? I think we should take a break from each other. You need to move into your White Plains apartment until you figure out what you want. You don't have to go this weekend. But I do want you to leave here until you have some clarity. Do you see a future with me? Getting older, getting closer, maybe even bringing a child into what we have together? Or do you feel incapable of ever doing that?"

He didn't say a word. He stared at me, sad and uncomprehending.

I couldn't believe I had uttered these words. While I still had the emotional strength, I continued.

"I need more than a lover, Danny. I need a partner. Much as I love you – and I DO love you, by the way – love is no longer enough. Not when it tears apart any self-love I have.

"I'm sorry, Danny, but I just can't anymore."

# CHAPTER 54

**DANNY**

Ask me if I love Joanna and I'll answer, "Sure. Of course." I'll mean it, too. But the thing is, I don't do love well. Maybe my shrink is right. I always want what I can't have and devalue what I do have.

When I'm thinking straight, I believe Joanna and I are good together. But the doubts keep seeping in. I would like her to see me as a flawed but loving man. Yet she's determined to see me as some sort of hero or savior. Then I'd go along with that. There's nothing so intoxicating as someone thinking you can do no wrong, even when you know you're fucking up.

I'm beginning to believe Joanna loves being in love with me more than she loves me. She wants me to talk to her about my past, but she doesn't realize that would shatter her illusions. That isn't substantially different from what Sally wanted.

During the divorce battle, I constantly felt I was failing Joanna. I became the anxious, shut-down, out-of-control Danny. She never knew what to do with that person. "Give me the strong, inscrutable Danny!"

I couldn't deliver. What happens when you're no longer in control of your own actions and choices? When something from the past torpedoes you? When an overpowering need to bolt comes over you. A need so strong it pulses through you like a current.

I have to figure this out. Should I go with my instincts or am I making the worst mistake of my life? I feel like hiding away. Then I wouldn't disappoint anyone.

# CHAPTER 55

**THREE YEARS LATER**

**JOANNA**

Dear Danny,

I don't know what's driving me to write this letter. I guess I'm doing it to work through some thoughts I've been wrestling with lately. I plan to destroy this once I'm done.

I ran into Maureen the other day. I hadn't seen her in a couple of years. Not since you and I ended things. She was behind me at the cosmetic counter in Macy's. She noticed me right away, but it took me a moment to recognize her. She's got a new shorter and curlier hairstyle, and she's slimmed down.

She knew, of course, that you and I were no longer in touch. I suggested we grab some lunch and fill her in on some of the changes in my life. I'm getting married in a couple of months. His name is Jordan Petrillo. It wasn't love at first sight, but my feelings quickly grew. I'm crazy about him, but in a different way than I was with you.

We don't banter like you and I did, but his intensity won me over. Jordan is handsome – thick black hair, a strong jaw, and hazel eyes – and he's kind by nature. He doesn't try to invade the parts of me I want to keep hidden. And he's a poet at heart. He reads me Pablo Neruda and some of his own poems, which are surprisingly good.

Maureen told me she didn't talk to you for a few months after we ended things. She said you're living with Reba now and enjoying the good life. I heard you're seeing Charlie more often, and he's in a difficult stage. I hope you hang in there. Even though I haven't had kids of my own yet, I know things get better.

Hearing about you left me feeling surprisingly unsettled. Maybe because my life is in transition. I'm about to move in with Jordan. You remember how hard it is for me to share my space. I keep worrying the essence of me is about to get lost. Jordan promises that won't happen.

It's not that I want to see you again. Absolutely not. We had our time together. For a while it was glorious. But we're in very different places now.

Where did we go off track? The first few months were sheer exhilaration. You were kind and funny, strong and vulnerable. I thought we were soulmates. You were married, but to be honest, I didn't care about how it affected your family. All I thought about was how much I wanted you. I realize now how selfish and short-sighted that was.

I should have known our kind of intimacy was false. You felt uncomfortable being close. You once told me that closeness made you feel exposed, with nowhere to hide. With parents like yours, is that any wonder?

Me, I wanted unconditional love. The kind I never got from my father. I didn't want the messy world to intervene. Having to argue about who got to work in the den, living through weeks of uncertainty. We each needed to have the full focus of the other. But life doesn't work that way.

I was never in denial. I knew almost half the time, relationships like ours end in another affair. But I also knew your heart. You married Sally to put your past behind you. But you were running scared. Like me, you'd sabotage anything that made you confront your feelings.

I realize now the time we had together was destined to fade away. We both had a childlike fantasy about what love was all about. We didn't understand love takes work. How could we have ever made it when neither of us wanted to be the grown-up?

I hope Reba can be that grown-up. Can she soothe the frightened child in you lurking right under the surface? I know Jordan is doing that for me, and it's what we both need.

Are you happier now, Danny? I like to think you are. I don't hate you. I have great memories of us. But memories belong in the past.

Yours,
Joanna

# CHAPTER 56

**DANNY**

Reba is the third relationship of my life. They say the third time is a charm, right?

Many times, Reba probed me about my relationships with two women before her – Sally and Joanna. She never acted threatened. Slowly, she helped me recognize truths.

There was a reason the first two women didn't work out. With my ex, Sally, the problem was pretty simple. I wanted her close-knit family life more than I wanted her. Before long, we began clashing on everything. We had opposite views of how the world works. She thought everything was God's plan; I knew differently. The healthier I got emotionally, the more I felt stifled by her.

My passion for Joanna, on the other hand, was very real but not meant to last. She and I were each damaged in our own way. While Sally wanted to change me, Joanna wanted to change herself. She imagined an idealized version of me: always strong, loving, and protective. Bigger than life. Except in reality, I wasn't that man.

Too often, I was lost and flailing and in need of help for myself. Joanna gave me that support in concrete ways, opening up her home and her heart. Yet when the real Danny emerged – who happened to be far less exciting and more mundane than the Danny she thought she fell in love with – cracks began appearing quickly in our relationship.

I shared my insights with my therapist, who liked Reba almost from the start. At that time, I felt despondent I would ever find a woman who could deal with me.

"I get it. It's hard for you to trust," Walt said. "You've been through the wringer. You need someone who is stable, an attentive listener, and can express her feelings in a healthy way. She has to be able to keep your confidences without making judgments. And she needs to treat you with kindness and compassion."

"Come on, Walt, there isn't a woman alive like that!"

"Yes, there is, and you've already met her."

"What? You mean Reba? She's got everything going for her. Why would she want to settle in long-term with me?"

"Have you ever thought she has everything except what she really wants? She has career recognition and a good life. What she doesn't have is a lasting connection, and it sounds like she has never experienced a real love."

Walt had a point. After reconnecting with her, I recognized Reba as mature, grounded, intelligent, witty, and not a game player. She wasn't looking for me to complete her. As a plus, she offered a passport to a grander life than I could ever have hoped for.

"Then you're saying I'm where I'm supposed to be," I said.

"It's not that easy," he responded. "Chances are, you'll try to sabotage your happiness because you believe you're not worthy. You'll be afraid of being hurt again."

"Anything I can do about that?

"We'll need to work together so you can develop strategies to cope with these negative feelings. Anytime unwarranted dark thoughts emerge you'll need to ask yourself, is there any evidence that what I'm thinking is true?"

Walt was right. I kept fighting off fears Reba would suddenly discover some aspect of my past and decide I wasn't good enough for her. I had to mindfully take it one day at a time. Tough task for someone like me, who avoids thinking too hard.

In the meantime, I tried to go with the flow. Reba had snapped up a co-op on the Upper East Side not long after our relationship took off. I moved in. The 1920s apartment exceeded my wildest expectations of a place I'd live in. With 10-foot-high ceilings, large windows with original stained glass, and parquet floors, it was certainly well beyond my means. Reba said not to worry. She regarded it as a well-earned prize from her divorce. She urged me to regard it that way, too.

From the start, she felt totally at home on the East Side. She visited the boutiques, antique and art galleries, and the Metropolitan Museum of Art and saw movies at the Ziegfeld

Theatre. I felt like an imposter, although I enjoyed my morning jogs in Central Park, only blocks away.

Despite having everything at our front door, we lived a quiet life. Although she loved elegant things, she was no longer compelled to purchase more. She already had plenty from her marriage. The designer clothes, the fancy jewelry, the ski gear for her Aspen home, the beach wear for regular getaways on Turks and Caicos.

Maybe she would have kept accumulating more, but something changed when she hit the magical five-o. She wanted a far less messy life, she wanted to give back, and most of all, she wanted me. And that boggled my mind.

I still wasn't quite sure what I wanted. I should have been thrilled but as Walt predicted, I didn't feel worthy. I wished I'd had a normal childhood, but you can't rewrite the past. I yearned for more time with my son, but my lawyer said I was lucky to get to see him as much as I did.

I was a work in progress, just learning how to accept what I was given. I thought I was out of the woods. Yeah, right. I've always been good at self-deception.

# CHAPTER 57

## JOANNA

My life took a wondrous turn after I met Jordan. The attraction felt powerful. It was not as powerful as I initially had with Danny, but it was enough to leave me exhilarated and hopeful.

I had learned a lot about myself between the time Danny left, and Jordan came into my life. I didn't regret the couple of years Danny and I were together. But it slowly dawned on me – a relationship couldn't be about drama or the other person. I had my needs as well. I needed a confident man who could take me as I am – flawed and sometimes confused – and accept me. Someone who wasn't afraid of revealing his inner self, who would share and grow with me.

Jordan was that man. I surprised myself by telling him early on about my father's desertion and about my failed relationships, including the one with Danny. Gently, he asked me questions, all the while reaffirming I was a worthy person, so deserving of love. When Jordan and I were apart, I found myself missing him enormously. He felt the same about me.

He had tried marriage before, not long after college, but it didn't work. He hadn't been ready. But he was ready now. He knew what he wanted, and that was me. Months after meeting, we began planning our wedding. I was determined to create the fairy-tale affair I always dreamed of. The venue would be Tavern on the Green. The plan was to dine al fresco in the Courtyard, where the bistro lights and spectacular views of the Manhattan skyline would dazzle our guests.

We kept the guest list small, confined to immediate family, our closest friends, and some people from work. The only thing missing would be my father walking me down the aisle. Jordan's father gladly accepted the role. That would have to do.

Meanwhile, Jordan and I applied for ownership in a co-op. We were approved and began the arduous and time-consuming process of moving in. We each had to discard many of our old possessions and buy new ones for our shared life. He and I trolled the markets each weekend for artwork, furniture, and rugs.

I knew I could never find anyone as right for me as Jordan. He had a world of patience. And yet I felt anxious. I had just celebrated my 37th birthday. My biological clock was ticking. I would become a married woman and quite possibly a mother soon after.

I would be joining the ranks of women who had to balance work with homelife. Is that what I wanted or was I trying to live up to society's expectations? Shouldn't I feel happier? Jordan understood my unfounded fears and reassured me. He did not feel threatened. I felt safe with him.

In the middle of all of this, my partners at work decided to send me to a large advertising conference in Las Vegas. It would be a good place to court new clients, and everyone agreed I would be the best person to do it.

The timing was inconvenient with the wedding only two months away. Being separated for several days wasn't optimal for either Jordan or me. But no one would feel too sorry for me. The conference would be held at the MGM Grand and I would have a room there, too.

With over 6,000 rooms, the MGM Grand took its place as the largest hotel and casino in the world since its opening in December 1993. The building resembled a giant Egyptian pyramid, and its roof was topped with a sphinx.

It boasted a number of celebrity-owned restaurants. Jordan made me promise to try the Pink Adobe, opened by owners of the like-named eatery in Santa Fe, New Mexico. I said this would be a working conference, and I'd have no time, but he told me he didn't buy that.

My work would be cut out for me. In addition to meeting up with potential clients, I would host the company booth in the Exhibit Hall for several hours each day. I didn't look forward to it.

With the three-hour time difference, I felt tired when the plane landed at 2:15 pm. I revived when I got onto the Las Vegas strip. The bright lights and crowds exhilarated me. I fought the urge to follow the people and duck into a casino or two. Tomorrow would be a grueling day, and I had to be sharp. I got to the hotel, checked in, and called Jordan from the room.

Hearing his warm voice over the wire, I felt an instant rush of comfort. I loved this man. It was the first time we would be separated for several days in months. But after I hung up the phone, unease started to set in. Would I end up disappointing him? Would he disappoint me? What made me think we could keep up the feelings we had together at this moment? Relationships tend to fail. Didn't they?

I needed to get away from these negative thoughts, so I walked around the property. The lobby had a soaring ceiling and a grand staircase. The casino was packed with slot machines, table games, restaurants, and shops. I noted a theme park, a bowling alley, and a concert arena. The Rolling Stones had played there weeks before.

I snapped some photos to develop and share with Jordan when I got home and share. I also abandoned my intention to go back to my room and order room service. I felt wide awake. Later, I learned MGM Grand, like many Las Vegas hotels, pumped in fresh oxygen to keep guests alert and euphoric. The strategy was working.

Before I had to switch over to work mode and meet with potential clients, why not see if I could get into the Pink Adobe? Treat myself to the famed Pink Adobe Chili and the Pink Adobe Margarita? Jordan would be thrilled and want to know all about it. It was still early. I could finish dinner by nine and still get a good night's sleep.

I made my way to Pink Adobe, hoping it would be easy to find. Turns out I couldn't have missed it. The pink exterior drew me right in. The maître de told me I was lucky – a table had just been canceled, and he could seat me immediately. I followed him to my seat, marveling at the Mexican folk art, colorful murals, and twinkling lights.

I told the waiter to bring me a margarita for starters. It came immediately, and I sipped it, gazing around the room. Then I did a double take. Just two tables down from me, I saw a man with reddish-blonde hair sitting by himself, drinking a Coke.

He gazed straight ahead and slowly turned his head toward me.

Danny.

# CHAPTER 57

**DANNY**

I never believed thinking of someone would instantly conjure that person up.

But here I was, sitting in the Pink Adobe restaurant at the MGM Grand, remembering the times when Joanna and I would run into each other during industry conferences. I looked up, and to my shock, Joanna was there, sitting a few tables down from me. I did a double-take. So did she. She looked startled to see me.

Before I could figure out if it were a good or bad thing, I rose from my chair.

"Joanna," I said as I approached. "I should have suspected you'd be exhibiting at this conference."

She smiled – a little sadly, I thought. "Danny. Of course, you'd be here."

I nodded at the empty chair across from her, and she shook her head up and down. Yes.

I didn't hesitate. Walt would have advised me not to. But he wasn't here, was he? I took my seat.

She looked fantastic. Her long gleaming auburn hair now reached her shoulders, and the effect was quite flattering. She had always been a great dresser. Her lime green suit looked made for her and clung to her in all the right places.

There it was – the familiar tug at my groin. And here I was, ignoring my better instincts. After all my time in therapy trying to figure things out. Walt would be mortified.

"You look great," I said sincerely. "It's so good to see you."

"You, too," she responded. "You haven't changed." She looked me over. Then, after a pause: "I hear you and Reba are a couple now. Congratulations."

I winced. "Yes, we are. I never thought...I mean, I never expected to..."

Joanna said, "Relax, Danny. It's all okay. I'm not sure you heard, but I'm getting married in two months myself. Jordan's a great guy, and I feel very lucky."

I felt my face reddening. Truth is, I hadn't heard. Now that I did, I found myself not liking the idea of Joanna getting married.

"I didn't know," I said. "Congratulations back. Jordan is a very lucky guy. Is he from the biz?"

"Thankfully not," she said. "He's an architect."

"How did you meet?"

"The old-fashioned way, Working out in the gym. It didn't take us long to know we were right for each other."

"Well, that's nice."

"He's rehabbing a gray stone for us in the upper West Side. He's predicting the area will be taking off soon. I'm slowly moving in, but it's like a construction zone with all the dust and chaos."

"Yeah, I know how you feel about mess and chaos," I said.

She looked for the expression on my face, then evidently decided I wasn't criticizing. She gave me a brief smile.

"I'm getting a crash course in organization," I said. "Reba's a neatnik. Everything has to be in its place."

"Poor Reba," she chuckled. We both did.

"Hey," I said, changing the subject. "I owe you a big thanks."

"What for?"

"For connecting me with Walt."

"Walt, Walt. Oh yeah, the therapist who's –"

"…in the wheelchair," I completed. "I think one of your partners at work suggested him."

"That's right."

"He's an incredible guy," I said. "He's helped me realize a lot about myself. I'm beginning to understand. I wasn't in a good place when you and I were together. The fact is, I hadn't been in a good place for many years."

Joanna didn't seem to want to go there. She took another sip of her margarita and looked down. I glanced around the room and saw a few men gazing at her longingly.

I said, "Right now, all these men in this restaurant are looking right at me."

"Why?" she said, not understanding at all.

"Come on...look at you. You're...beautiful. Your hair, that outfit you're wearing, your smile, your energy. I'm betting every one of them wishes he were in my place."

Now it was her turn to blush. "Unfortunately for them, I'll soon be off the market," she said. "At last."

We both ordered Pink Adobe's famous chili. When our food came, she made some joke about the farting scene in "Blazing Saddles." "I guess those men might not find me so appealing after I finish this."

I was caught off guard by her lightening the mood and laughed appreciatively.

"Tell me about Jordan," I said. "What's he like?"

"He knows what he wants and where he needs to go. He's humble. He's not so full of himself that he forgets to be kind. Everybody likes him."

"Sounds like quite a guy."

"Jordan's interested in everything. How things fit together and what makes them aesthetically pleasing. He manages all his projects well, including me. He knows I'm a work in progress, and he's okay with that."

"Do you love him?" I asked her. It flashed back to me that I had asked her the same question about Gregg in what felt like a lifetime ago.

Again, that smile. "I don't do well with love," I said. "So how should I answer? As much as I'm able, yes, I do love him. I may even be falling in love with him, which is another thing entirely. As you well know. How about you? How goes it with Reba?"

314

"Joanna, I just have to say again. When you and I were together there wasn't anything romantic going on between Reba and me."

"Oh, God, I'm not worrying about *that* anymore."

"You know, Maureen was mad at me for screwing things up with you. But I think she understands now that Reba is the balancing force I needed."

Did I detect a flash of hurt, or was it just my imagination? Probably the latter. For the next two hours, Joanna and I talked about everything. The diners around us were settling their bills, and we were still chatting away. We spoke about how we met, how we both felt that undefinable spark, and how we managed to screw everything up.

I admitted I was uncommunicative and selfish and that I was unable to view our relationship from any other perspective than my own. I was hurt and confused and scared. Now Joanna joined in. She told me she, too, had messed it up. She feared asking me pointed questions, frightened a little reality would break us apart.

"But honestly, I think a little reality is just what we needed," she said. "Even when we were living together, we existed in a bubble. Neither of us wanted to expose what we had to the outside world. We were lost in our masquerades."

"Wasn't that a song by George Benson?"

"And the Carpenters, too. Written by Leon Russell. You know the words? 'Are we really happy here, with this lonely game we play? Looking for words to say, searching but not finding understanding anywhere. We're lost in a masquerade.' "

"Do you know the second verse? 'Both afraid to say we're just too far away from being close together from the start. We tried to talk it over but the words got in the way. We're lost inside this lonely game we play.'"

We smiled shyly at each other.

"So sad. It might have described how we were back then," I said.

"Maybe. At this point in life, we might have had a chance of making it. But I don't know. Maybe we both had too much early damage done to us," she said. "Now here we are, like old friends. It worked out the way it should."

"Maybe."

"By the way, how's Charlie?"

"He's hard to be around right now. What can I say? He's nearly a teenager."

"Wow, he's a teenager! It seems not so long ago he was a little boy."

"Yes, he's grown up. He's different. I see him every so often, but mostly he's with Sally."

"And how's Sally? I guess you see her at the hand-offs."

"Just for a second. She pretty much hates me still. She never moved on. Likes to wear her martyrdom on her sleeve."

Joanna laughed. "That's so true. She can really ooze resentment, can't she?"

"Yeah. But it's Charlie who worries me. Now that he's older, I catch him looking at me in a curious way. Who knows how I damaged him?"

"Oh, Danny, I'm sorry," Joanna said. She seemed to mean it.

Our eyes met and I did what seemed natural. I reached across the table and took her hand. She didn't push it away.

"What time do you need to get to the Exhibit Hall tomorrow?" I asked.

"At least by seven. The place opens at 10," she said. "I've got an assistant helping out, but the hall will be packed."

"Then maybe we should get the check," I said, signaling for the waiter.

I glanced at her. She looked far away and lost.

# CHAPTER 59

**JOANNA**

Danny and I got into the elevator without exchanging a word.

I pushed the button for my floor. Floor 11. Danny entered his floor as well. Floor 14.

The elevator ascended silently and neither of us spoke. The door opened and I got out. Danny hesitated and then followed.

"Let me just walk you to your room," he said.

My room was at the end of the hall. I turned the key and the door opened to reveal an Art Deco room with a king-size bed, and an expansive sitting area with a sofa, armchairs, and a coffee table.

"Would you mind if I came in?" Danny asked, surprisingly formally. "I feel kind of wired up tonight. You can kick me out when you want me to go. I know we both have a big day tomorrow."

I gestured for him to follow me in. Every nerve ending in my body was on fire. This was crazy!

Danny's breathing was ragged and audible. I turned around and saw the longing in his eyes.

"Danny, we can't..." I started. His lips were on mine before I could get the next word out. His tongue was searching, exploring. Every ounce of me remembered. He was imprinted on me – his scent, his taste, the way our bodies locked together.

I drew him into me, the tempo of my own breath matching his. We tore at each other like two drowning people, clinging to each other to survive. There was no subtlety to what we were doing. We weren't making love; we were fighting for our very lives.

His body was even firmer than I remembered, and that reddish blonde hair I loved was illuminated by the moonlight streaking in from the oversized windows. I grabbed his face, kissing every inch of him as he entered me.

"Whatever you do, don't stop," I gasped.

"Not a chance," he said. Our rhythm grew more frantic, and I arched my back. My orgasm came in waves. I didn't recognize the high-pitched animal sounds I was making. He came moments later, closing his eyes and roaring with pleasure. He stayed inside me for minutes before he rolled over, covered with glistening sweat.

His eyes remained closed. My hand gently stroked his chest. We didn't speak.

"Joanna I..."

"Shhhhhh."

"I still think of you."

"No, Danny. Don't go there."

"Maybe we gave up too easily. Let's give it another try. I'm different now. You and I..."

"Oh, Danny." The magnitude of how cavalierly we had sex started to hit me. What had I done to Jordan and his trust in me? Why did I think betraying that kind, sweet man was all right?

"You and I," I said, picking up where he let off. "We both are composed of broken pieces. Except the broken pieces don't match up. They jab, hurt, and eventually tear away at us. But we're alike in one way. We sure know how to self-sabotage. We've each found someone who is good for us. Who keeps us in check and sane. Love us when we're unlovable.

"Right now, we're wading into unfamiliar waters. I'm getting married. You...you're living comfortably with someone who adores you. So alarm bells go off in us that scream, 'Danger ahead!' Naturally, we head for familiar shallow waters and try to keep ourselves safe."

Danny started to say something, but I shook my head.

"That may feel good for a moment...a night...a year. But it won't last forever. A few years ago, when we were together, I thought we could create a loving home. I didn't realize neither of us ever felt safe at home. Yours was filled with unpredictability and danger, and mine? It was filled with absence. We need someone to help us understand that home can be a safe place. We're not good for each other, Danny. Not in the long run."

There were tears in his eyes. Mine, too. I reached for him and this time, it wasn't a hug of passion. It was a gesture of goodbye.

"Reba sounds like a fine woman," I said. "Don't sabotage it. No need to tell her about what happened here. Why hurt her? As for me, I'm not going to say a word to Jordan. Before we mess up the best thing that ever happened to either of us, let's say goodnight. You need to go back to your room.

"You know, I have a feeling you'll be okay. Both of us will be. You may not think you're not worthy of all Reba is giving you, but I know differently. And maybe I can become worthy of what I have in my life, too."

Watching him walk out of my hotel room, turning back once, and then closing the door, felt like the worst kind of loss. I ached for him. Yet I knew what I was really aching for was the Joanna I used to be and would never be again.

I didn't yet realize that was a good thing. I glimpsed Danny from a distance the next morning at the conference, deep in talks with a client. I never saw him again.

# CHAPTER 60

## JOANNA

On our third anniversary. Jordan surprised me with an Agnolotti del Plin from the Piedmont tradition, stuffed with mixed meats and vegetables and seasoned with roast sauce.

"You're not lifting a finger today," he said. "I'm doing the cooking."

He's quite the cook. In fact, he excels at everything he does. Our little son, Rory, wanted to "help Daddy" and ended up spilling the butter sauce on the floor, and we both laughed. We were besotted with our adorable boy.

We had reached a satisfying point in our marriage. The first year hadn't been at all easy. Since I was already 37 when we finally tied the knot – and Jordan was pushing 40 – we decided I should go off the pill a couple of months before the wedding. Who knew how long it would take to conceive at my age? We figured it would take at least six months.

It didn't.

Weeks before our wedding, I began to feel a queasiness. I was tired, my breasts felt sore, and any strong smell had me running to the bathroom. I knew I was pregnant before my visit to the doctor.

I hoped to make it through the ceremony and reception. I almost did. The ceremony went on without a hitch, but I had to dash out quickly as the main course was being served. I retched in the toilet, wiped my mouth, reapplied my lipstick, and was back in a jiffy No one was the wiser.

Except of course, for Jordan. He knew, and he was beyond ecstatic. Gaining a wife and a son or daughter all in a matter of months? Life didn't get better. He got right to work, designing the baby's room, actually constructing a crib, and brushing up on Italian baby songs like "Pallocino Blu" and "Volevo un Gatto Nero". I couldn't have asked for a more involved partner for this baby.

Rory was born on a sunny day in May when flowers started blooming in New York. My labor took just eight hours. Out came a 7-pound, 5-ounce boy, and we instantly fell in love with him. He has cornflower blue eyes, wisps of pale hair, and sweet little cheeks. Jordan was so enchanted he could hardly tear himself away to go to work.

Our son is so beautiful that strangers stop me on the street and say he should be in commercials. They particularly love his hair. It is reddish-blonde, thick, and curly. He looks nothing like Jordan or his immediate family with their dark hair, olive skin, and liquid brown eyes. Jordan's parents love him to pieces and often speculate where Rory's coloring came from.

"My Uncle Mario from Sicily was blonde, and so are his girls," his father said. "That explains it."

"Maybe he gets his coloring from Joanna's side," Jordan's mother said. "Her auburn hair accounts for the red tones. But the blonde – now that's unique! Tell me, Joanna, do you have any blondes in your family?

"Oh yes," I said. "Rory's hair color is the spitting image of my father's."

"There we have it," Jordan's mother concluded.

I have my suspicions, and I keep them firmly to myself. Almost as soon as I returned from Las Vegas, I knew I was pregnant. A pregnancy test confirmed it. Jordan had no reason to doubt whether the baby was his. We had made love the night before I left for Vegas.

But I was well aware Rory could have been conceived on my Las Vegas trip. I didn't share that possibility with my husband. Setting aside Rory's biological origin, Jordan is his father in every other sense of the word.

Father and son are adorable together. They play with Rory's Legos, read the book "*Goodnight, Moon*," and cuddle with his stuffed dinosaur. Jordan is the dad my own father had never been. Never in a million years would Jordan desert his child.

Now we are preparing to welcome our second one in a couple of months. A little girl. This time, I'm betting our child will look like Jordan. I rarely think of Danny, and when I do, I hope he's happy. He is in my rearview mirror, getting smaller as my life expands.

# CHAPTER 61

**DANNY**

"It's good to see you again, Danny," Walt said. "I must say, something about you looks different."

He pantomimed stroking his chin, alluding to my beard. Since I had last seen Walt, I had shaved it off. My face was now bare.

Being back in Walt's office felt comforting. He still had the same cozy couch from the last time, nearly two years ago. The throw pillows were new, though. They had a red and gold Indian design, which added a note of intrigue.

The three-dimensional painting across the room was also new. Bold and oversized, it took up much of the wall. The solid gray background gave the appearance of being ripped open. A hand grasped a corner of the rip, and a face was emerging. The mouth was open in wonderment; the eyes were screwed shut.

Walt noted me staring at it. "Oh, yes, the picture!" he said, swiveling around. "I saw it and it immediately caught my fancy. Found it at a small gallery in Soho. What do you think?"

"I can see why you'd like it," I said. "It's got that psychological flair. Looks like a chick pecking its way out of an egg. Is that why you chose it?"

"Oh yes. I see the gray as a cozy blanket of denial. It's being torn away, and you see nakedness and vulnerability underneath. I view it as something positive. Any thoughts?"

"Well," I said, "We often put on a mask for others. But it backfires. Then, it becomes impossible for us to know who we are. In this painting, I'm guessing the guy has decided to break through and try to become who he really is."

"Great insights," Walt said. "You've come a long way since our first session."

"It hasn't been easy. It's definitely been a process."

"Tell me, have you managed to break free? Like the man in the painting?"

"That's the thing," I said. "I thought I was getting there, but I regressed. It happened a couple of years ago, after our last session. I had this conference in Las Vegas, and Joanna was there, too. We began talking, and it turned out we... slept together."

"I see." My confession didn't faze him. "Go on."

"Right at the moment, I wanted her, but I felt like shit afterward. You warned me about self-sabotaging, but I thought, no, I'll never do that again. Then I went and did it. So stupid and short-sighted of me, and I was furious you hadn't protected me from myself. Easier to throw the blame at you rather than at myself. I decided therapy wasn't working, so I quit."

"Therapy is like that, though," Walt said. "Two steps forward and one step backward."

"I've obviously had time to think," I said. "Now I believe I hooked up with Joanna because I wanted to distance myself from Reba. The emotional intimacy I had begun to build with her scared me to death. I didn't see how it would ever last. I figured she would find me out and stop loving me."

"Yes," Walt said. "That's why it might have seemed like a good thing at the moment. Going backward, to Joanna. When that kind of thing happens, we refer to it as the imposter syndrome. Feeling unworthy. Harboring lots of feelings of inadequacy and self-doubt. It becomes so easy to self-sabotage. By doing so, we can claim it wasn't our destiny rather than dealing with the uncomfortable feeling we will be rejected. Does what I'm saying make sense?"

I slowly nodded.

"It's a protective mechanism created by the psyche and happens to a lot of people. It has even happened to me."

"To you, too?" I asked. "With everything you know about how self-sabotaging works, how could you let it happen to yourself?"

"Because it's a powerful force," Walt said. "It's easy to give into it, even if we know we shouldn't. Our actions confirm the stories we tell about ourselves. Your story has always been that you're not worthy of love."

"Well, if you say so."

"No, Danny," he said. "I don't want this to be me telling you what to think. This is your life. You control the narrative. Now, about Joanna, I'm assuming you didn't see her again."

"That's right. Joanna was about to get married. To a guy I never met. From what she shared, I think he might be good for her. The wedding was two months away at the time, so I assume she's his wife now. By now, they might even have a kid. Before we broke up, she told me her biological clock was ticking."

"You went back to Reba after that?"

"Yes. I never told her what happened in Vegas. Since then, we've had our ups and downs, but things have been mostly good. More stable than with Sally or Joanna, that's for sure. I still have my moments where I don't think I'm enough. I'm gradually becoming better able to deal with those times."

"That's encouraging, "Walt said. "One question. Why did you decide to come back into therapy?"

"I've been thinking about the future," I said. "A lot has been going on. I think I told you before that Reba changed jobs. She got a lot of money out of her divorce and did great in her own right. She didn't need to earn a living anymore and wanted to give back. So now she's heading a foundation that helps abused children."

"A great cause."

"She wants me to co-direct it with her. She thinks my own experiences would be valuable. But I..."

Walt smiled, and it was a sad and knowing smile. "You're about to say you were never abused. At least that's what you always told me."

"Well, I...I don't like to talk about that."

"I think you're strong enough to talk about it now."

"You think so?" I cleared my throat. My heart began racing. I averted his eyes as the words began to spill out of my mouth.

"I must have been close to 14. One night, pretty late, about 11 o'clock or so, my father came home with a couple of his union buddies. They were pretty ruthless guys. You know, the kind who torture cats and pull wings off of flies. I could smell their stench all the way from my room. They were reeking of booze.

"He was calling out for my mother, but she'd fled. She must have figured it was so late, nothing good was going to happen that night. She left me all alone with them. Probably figured I'd be sleeping, and he'd leave me alone."

I fell silent. I needed to sit there for a moment and compose myself before I could continue.

"The old man, he flew into a rage. He pulled me out of my bed. Marched me into the kitchen. His friends were laughing. He asked me where the fuck my mother had gone. I told him I didn't know.

He glowered at me like I was some obstinate schoolkid who had willfully given him the wrong answer. "We'll see about that. I'm going out, and I'll find that damn bitch," he said. "I'll pull her back here by her hair. I swear I will. You morons! Watch my kid. Do something with him."

"Oh, they did something, all right. They were tough and cruel and stinking drunk. One of them had recently been released from prison. As soon as he closed the door, one of them held me down. The other pulled off my pajama bottoms, and he...and he..."

The memories I repressed came flooding back. I caught my breath. A tear started to roll down my cheek.

"It's okay, Danny," Walt said. "You're in a safe space."

I couldn't meet Walt's eyes. "I remember the first guy. His bad breath, his slobbering mouth on mine. He was so much bigger than me. Then came the pain. Red-hot, sharp. I felt like I was being split in two. I started yelling.

"Shut the fuck up,' the other guy said. He slapped me – hard – when I didn't. The first guy kept going and going. When I tried to push him off, the other one found my father's carving knife and held it to my chest to stop my hollering. I have a..." I motioned and pointed to my upper chest, to the nasty scar Joanna had seen long ago. "Every time I tried to push him off me, the other guy would prod me with the knife, deeper and deeper.

"Then suddenly, my father burst into the room without my mother. He saw me lying there, crying, snot pouring out of my nose, my ass and my chest covered with blood.

"Jeez," he said, taking in the scene and staring at me with repulsion. "What the fuck's going on here? Damn, what am I supposed to do now? If Rosalie finds out…"

He paused a minute, squinting his eyes and barely able to stand on his feet.

"The kid was asking for it," one of the guys said. "Pretty Boy like him. We did him a favor." The two doubled over with laughter.

"My old man glared at them before turning to me. "Okay, go take a shower, Danny, and then get to bed. I'll handle this. Don't tell your mother. I mean it; I'll kill you if you tell her."

"As I shuffled off, I could hear him yelling at his buddies. 'What the fuck got into you? That's my kid!' he screamed. He grabbed a broomstick and lunged at them. But he was too damn drunk and fell on his face. They just sniggered. He came at them again, this time grabbing one of his other carving knives. They easily sidestepped him. One of them mimicked his stumbling gait. They thought he was hilarious, and their laughter was now high-pitched.

"Laughing at me? Fuckers. Get the hell out of here,' he screamed. 'Now! There's going to be hell to pay!' They were still howling when they left. Like my old man would ever have the balls to beat up anyone who wasn't defenseless.

"When my mother finally arrived home in the early morning, he was snoring on the couch, and I was in my room, cowering. He never took me to a doctor. He could barely stand the sight of me after that. He never mentioned what happened. I didn't either. I put it all behind me and tried to make something of myself."

"Did your mother figure out what went on?" Walt asked.

"She didn't talk about it, but I think so. She came into my room unexpectedly when I had my shirt off and saw the knife wound. She asked me what happened. I made up a story. Me and a friend were playing Zorro at school, and I got stabbed. My mother wanted to take it up with the school. But the old man said that would make it worse for me. The other boys would call me a sissy. As usual, he prevailed."

"Then what happened?" Walt asked. "I think you said you were also 14 when your father went to prison."

"Yes, a few months later. His binges got worse. Since he couldn't beat up his friends, she was the surrogate. He beat her up badly. One time, she couldn't even lift herself off the floor. Someone called 911. The ambulance came to take her, and he went to the slammer.

"After that, things went straight downhill for me. The kids at school heard about my father in prison and I became a big joke. That's when I got into a fight, so I got expelled."

We sat in silence for a minute or two.

"I'm glad you had the courage to share this," Walt said "You were a defenseless child, and your father and his friends were sick people who abused you. The fact you had the strength to forge through this and survive speaks volumes."

Walt paused. "Have you told any of this to Reba?"

"No. I've tried very hard to push it out of my memory. I've never told a living soul. But like I said, I think she's guessed something happened. I wonder if she'd feel the same way about me if I told her that story. My father couldn't bear to look at me again. Maybe she wouldn't either."

"You know what?" Walt said. "I think you should tell her. I believe she loves you just the way you are. I think you need to hear those words directly from her."

"I don't know if I can," I said.

"Danny, there's nothing wrong with you. You're free to be the authentic person you are. The fact you're here today is an encouraging sign. You're a survivor, Danny."

"Well, I'm trying," I said.

"From everything you've told me, I think Reba is great for you. You've found a woman who is self-possessed and strong in her own right. She doesn't need anything from you. She just wants you to be yourself."

"Yes, but...I'm just figuring out what being myself really means."

"And you will, Danny. I have no doubt you will. We need to end our session here," Walt said. He smiled up at me from his wheelchair. "We have a lot more to talk about. I hope you'll be coming back."

I stood up and pulled out my checkbook to pay him. "Yes, I'll be back. Do you have some time next week?"

"Turns out I've got this slot open."

"Sounds good."

"Say, I didn't have a chance to ask about Charlie. How's he doing?"

"He's a teenager now," I said. "He lets me know how I ruined his life every chance he gets. Okay, I did make some mistakes. I wish I could try raising him all over again."

"The teenage years are rough," Walt said. "We can talk about Charlie in the next session." He paused. "You know, Danny, I think you have some good things ahead of you."

He reached out his hand, and I shook it. "See you next week."

I gathered my briefcase and walked outdoors to the bright sun. It was time to embrace the future.

# CHAPTER 62

**JOANNA**

The collage of colorful baby animals was whirling over-head and playing a peaceful children's tune. Even though he thought of himself as a "big boy," Rory still loved drifting off to sleep to the collage's sights and sounds.

I tucked my tired little boy into bed. The boy Danny and I created.

Jordan's son.

9 798822 943810